THE MAKING OF MARIGOLD MCGRATH

A Novel of London in the Second World War

CARRIE HAYES

HTPH PRESS
New York

ISBN: 979-8-9953239-0-7 (ebook)
ISBN: 979-8-9953239-1-4 (Paperback)

Cover Design: Spike Gragard
Cover Image: Arcangel Images
Book Production & Marketing: BookWhisperer.ink

For Gail

*"We do what we can—we give what we have. Our doubt is
our passion, and our passion is our task. The rest is the
madness of art."*

— Henry James

Part I

A Case of Poor Judgement

New York City
Winter, 1936

THE CINEMA WAS NEARLY DESERTED, AND THE TWO girls took the best seats in the house. They opened their bags of peanuts and chocolate covered raisins, silently munching until the movie got to their favorite part.

Marigold mouthed along with the woman on the screen who spoke first. "*Not because I love England, but because it will pay me better.*" She continued, "*The very brilliant agent of a certain foreign power on the point of obtaining a secret vital to your air defense.*"

Trude whispered, "*I tracked two of his men to that music hall. Unfortunately, they recognized me.*" The two girls took bites of their candy. Trude continued, "*That's why they're after me now.*"

Marigold smiled from ear to ear. She loved this part. "*You ever heard of a thing called persecution mania?*"

Trude's eyes grew wide. She said, "*You don't believe me?*"

As if from nowhere, the usher appeared and shushed them.

Marigold scowled at him then turned back to Trude. "*Frankly I don't.*"

THEY HAD BEEN DOING this for days now. Rather than go to math class, they skipped school instead. That nobody reported them was because they were the kind of girls who did well enough and their absences didn't seem to matter. So, for two weeks running, they faithfully bought tickets for the 2:55 show to watch *The 39 Steps* until they knew it cold.

Afterwards, they stood by the window outside the ladies' room, and Marigold watched the traffic below.

Trude pointed a finger, "*Go and look down into the street then.*" She always said this with a campy accent. Trude's father was Swiss and he spoke like that. Her late mother had been British and Marigold thought everything about Trude was glamorous in the most spectacular way.

Marigold pretended to be afraid. "*Are they there?*"

Trude looked terrified. "*Yes. I'd hoped I'd shaken them off. I'm going to tell you something which is not very healthy to know. But now that they have followed me here, you are in it as much as I am.*"

Then she grabbed Marigold's hand and they bolted down the stairs, out through the back door, gasping and chuckling on the walk to the pharmacy.

When they arrived, Trude stopped short. "Oh, *mein Gott!*"

"What is it?"

"It's Will Carrington!" Trude pointed to the counter.

"I love him." Marigold spoke with as much gravity as she could muster. It was part of their shtick. Whenever Trude saw a boy they knew, Marigold would simply say, "I love him."

These declarations of love always made Trude laugh, then respond by either sticking something up her nose, or putting her spectacles on sideways. Anything, anything to make Marigold laugh back and Trude look like a freak.

Silently, they went to the counter. "Oh hi, Will," Marigold said, in her most modest, simple style. Trude looked away.

Will was blonde, handsome, an athlete. He was in the boys' section at school, so they rarely saw him outside of class. "Hi." He leaned past Marigold. "Hi Trude," which didn't surprise Marigold. All the boys were in love with Trude, who was beautiful, smart, and kind.

Trude turned to face Will. She'd stuck a raisin into each nostril, so they hung out just the smallest amount. "Will, hi!"

Will stopped short of recoiling. He paid his tab and said, "See you." Then gestured to his own nose, discreetly, for Trude's benefit.

She continued to smile, oblivious. "See you tomorrow."

"Girls." Home was on Riverside Drive, where Marigold's mother stood in the foyer, surrounded by boxes. Some were on the floor, others stacked upon the table, which normally held only letters and an orchid. On top of the boxes were large oblong tickets indicating their contents. The tickets were stamped with round and dashed holes, like eyelet made of cardstock.

Marigold opened one of the boxes. "Ooh. What are these?"

There had to be thousands inside. She passed a dozen cards over to Trude, who fanned herself with them.

"These could be dollahs, thousands of dollahs, nicht so, Schatze," Trude said.

"Jahwohl, they could." Marigold held up a card to the chandelier, examining the tiny square holes in the light. She held it over the face of her friend and it created dashes and dots upon Trude's skin. She moved to look through the dashes at her mother. Cool and elegant in her grey silk dress, with her creamy colored pearls and her white, white skin.

"They're some sort of punch cards, darling," her mother said. "They're for your father."

"I love them," Marigold said.

Trude raised an eyebrow. "As much as Will Carrington?"

Marigold bit her lip to keep from laughing. Her mother didn't know about her silly crushes. "Yes, even more so." Marigold spread the cards out upon the table. They looked vast and impersonal, like in that film. What was it? *Metropolis.* Oh, yes, she thought, just like *Metropolis.* "Say, Moms, how about I take some pictures of you and Trude with these cards?"

"Aren't you girls supposed to be doing algebra or something?"

"Yes, but let me take your picture first, Moms, and you should wear that dress, you know, with the print just like these cards."

"Marigold." She loved the way her mother folded the R in the word Marigold. It was always under the tongue with a delicate precision used by those whose English is flawless albeit foreign.

"Come on, Momsy. You'll be the living embodiment of industry, and Trude will be the future. It'll be fun!"

Her mother chuckled and left the room, then reemerged wearing a dress with the printed dashes and circles just like the punch cards. In her hand was a large silk scarf printed with the same design.

Marigold moved the boxes into a pile, one on top of the other, "We'll stack them like this. Then Trude, lean on them here and look up at Momsy, like so."

Marigold opened her camera case. She looked through the lens and adjusted the aperture. Her models struck a pose.

The light in the foyer was bright, bright.

Her mother was cool, aristocratic, and Trude simply brimming with life. Both of them were beautiful. Marigold wound the film and pressed the button.

"Perfect," she said and wound the film again.

Suddenly, her mother waved an arm and the scarf fluttered outward, like a wing. Trude moved her own arms upward.

"Wonderful!" Marigold pressed the button. "Wonderful!"

She did it again, then her models adjusted their poses in varying degrees, leaning away and toward each other.

"Fabulous!"

"What are you doing? Put those down." Marigold's father stood in the doorway. "Don't touch those. Put the camera down." Suddenly, he roared, "I said put the camera down!"

"Sorry." Marigold looked down at the ground. There was a tense silence. It was the same silence which often occurred if Marigold's parents were in the same room.

Her mother said, "She was merely experimenting."

"Not with my cards, she's not. Stupid girl."

"*Ta gueule*, Arnold." Her mother had been from Dinant, in Belgium. But she rarely spoke French. "Don't talk to her so."

Marigold watched her mother go into the kitchen as Trude gathered her coat and slipped out of the apartment.

Make amends, Marigold warned herself. "Excuse me, Dad." She stacked the cards and returned them to their boxes. "I just thought—"

"Don't think. They're not for you."

"Sorry."

"They're for my German clients." He glanced at himself in the mirror, his reflection confirming his golden hair and hazel eyes were still handsome, still distinguished.

"Sorry," she said again. "What are they used for?"

"These cards store information. Who is doing what and how much of it they're doing. Like who's buying how many apples, or how much money is withdrawn from a bank. Who lives where in what part of town. It's the latest technology, Marigold. They revolutionize how records are kept. And they come from IBM. They're the future. Not props for a childish fashion show."

With a small nod, he took a lapel pin out of his pocket. "Help me with this." He held it out to her and Marigold obliged, fastening it behind the worsted wool as he added, "I'm going to present them at tonight's dinner."

She turned the pin. The black lines echoed themselves as they had when the symbol meant good fortune, in Asian religions, long, long before it was used by the German government. Marigold rotated the pin the other way, so the black lines inside the white circle with the red background appeared in a more upright position.

* * *

RUNNING THROUGH CENTRAL PARK, ice skates flopping on her shoulders, Marigold slowed to catch her breath. She studied the bridge and the frozen pond. Tall buildings framed the naked trees. Sunshine shone low behind them, casting deep shadows on the snow. She pulled at her left mitten with her teeth and unbuttoned her coat. Inside was her Brownie. It was one of the new ones, with a bellows that folded. She fumbled with its case, groaning at the other mitten hindering her efforts. At last, at last, she looked down into the lens. She moved the aperture slowly to the left and then dialed it back a fraction to the right.

The trees, the light, buildings and snow. She pressed the button and wound the film.

"Gotcha!" Pink mittens wrapped around her eyes.

Marigold staggered forward. "Trude!" She laughed and turned. "Say cheese."

Trude put her arm in the air, a teasing coquette bundled in scarves and a pompom hat tied under the chin. Marigold blew on her fingers and moved the aperture a fraction one way, then she moved it the other.

The light had changed, and Trude was in shadow. Marigold took the picture.

Then as quickly as she'd appeared, Trude ran over the bridge toward the pond. "Last one there's a rotten egg!"

A dozen other skaters moved across the ice. Girls and boys about their own age, mostly from the neighborhood. Marigold hopped on one foot and then the other. Her earmuffs just weren't doing the trick and inside the mittens her fingers felt frozen. Trude spread a small blanket onto the snow and patted the spot next to her. "Come on, Mari, you'll feel so much better when you're skating."

Marigold doubted that very much. Lacing up her skates felt like torture and she willed her knees to stop shaking. She watched Trude expertly wrap the laces around her own slim ankles then tie a knot, tucking the laces inside the socks peeping above her skates. Trude clambered onto her knees and stood to make her way to the pond. In what seemed a single move, she was gliding across the ice, and then crowed, "Haha!" Somehow Trude's fluid grace made everything seem effortless.

Marigold watched her turn a flawless figure eight as boys

skated around her and everything sparkled. "Come on, Mari!" Trude waved her over.

Marigold muttered under her breath, come on, come on, chiding herself not to be so awkward, then responded, "I'm coming!" She took a deep breath and imagined herself the world-renowned figure skating movie star Sonja Henie. She extended her arms as she stepped onto the ice. But her left leg slowly slid out from her while her right leg began to move forward. Marigold's top half suddenly felt heavy. She waved her arms, her skates stepping forward and backward, her ankles wobbling.

"You can do it," Trude pirouetted beside her.

"I know, I know I can do it," Marigold's heart began thumping. The other skaters danced along the ice.

Trude whispered, "Bend your knees."

But Marigold's knees collapsed, pulling her bottom as if by a magnet. "I'm falling though, I am."

"No, you're not." Trude held out her hand, waiting.

"I am, oh my goodness." It was difficult to breathe, and she was suddenly warm. Her hands met the ice and her feet surrendered.

Trude still waited. "Come on, I've got you." She pulled Marigold up and placed her arm around her waist, then said, "Oh look. There's Will Carrington with a swishy, dishy friend."

Marigold froze in horror. Why was she such a klutz?

The boys called from across the ice. "Hello, Fräuleins."

Trude smiled and called, "Morgen, Herr Carrington. Wie gehts? Why don't you introduce us to your friend?"

Eagerly the boys skated over. Will said, "This is Chip."

Chip stopped in front of her, the edge of his skates making a smooth spray of ice. He held his hand out to Marigold. "You can hang on to me if you want. I'll teach you to skate." He placed an arm round her waist. She leant against him and he led her across the pond. Perhaps she'd be Sonja Henie after all.

"What grade are you in, Marigold?" Chip's eyes were heavily fringed and he had a cleft in his chin.

"I'm a senior."

Smiling, he picked up speed. "Me, too. Is this your first time on the ice?"

"Kind of." She thought it best not to say that despite years of lessons, she was just a lousy skater. "Where do you go to school, Chip?"

"I'm at Lawrenceville. You know, in New Jersey. It's a good place, not as many..." He gestured to a couple arguing in Yiddish. "People like that. As in New York."

Marigold looked up at him again. She hoped he didn't have the same lapel pin as her dad. Well, she thought to herself, at least he was handsome. Soon the streetlamps were lit. It was time to go home.

"Let's go to my place," Will offered. He lived in a brownstone only a block away. Everyone agreed and they went to his house, dumping their coats and skates upon ancient Chinese chairs just inside the door.

The half dozen guests traipsed upstairs, and Will procured some cocoa and cups on a tray from the housekeeper.

"Where is everybody?" Trude asked, by which she meant Will's younger brothers.

"At the movies with Nanny." He smiled wickedly. "Come on, let's play a game."

Out came a box from under the bed, inside of which was a bottle of rum. Shouts of approval went around as he generously poured it into the cups of hot chocolate. Some of the boys skipped the hot chocolate and drank the booze neat, laughing as it burned their throats and rendered them speechless.

"Let's play records," Trude said. Will agreed and she chose the very latest from his collection. A trumpet opened the refrain, soulful and longing, echoed by the orchestra. A man began to sing,

I've flown around the world in a plane,
I've settled revolutions in Spain, and the North Pole I have charted,

Still, I can't get started with you . . .

Chip took Marigold's hand. "May I?"

She moved toward him. His shoulders were square and he swayed as he danced, brushing against her. Marigold stepped closer, sensing the rise of his chest, the flatness of his stomach. She forgot having been frozen and grew toasty from the rum and Chip's handsome touch. Resting her head upon his shoulder she saw a mouse scurry across the floor. She stifled a gasp. If there was a time not to mind the mice at Will's house, this was the time. But the mix of the rum, her desire, and the mouse made her woozy.

"'Scuse me!" She squirmed away and stumbled to the powder room. She ran the water and rubbed her face, then looked at herself in the mirror. There was a knock on the door.

"Can I come in?" It was Trude, who promptly lifted her skirt and sat on the toilet. "Did you see the mouse?"

Marigold shuddered. "You know I did."

Trude finished and joined her at the mirror. "That Chip seems to like you."

Marigold flicked some water at her friend. "How would you know?"

"Because I have eyes in the back of my head." Trude refreshed her lipstick and handed it to Marigold. "I'm a regular spy." She then dropped her voice, "You know, like Mata Hari."

Marigold studied her now vibrant mouth. "I can't believe you're leaving me."

"Oh, you'll be fine."

"I won't be able to go skating." The thought of days without Trude felt intolerable.

"Yes, you will." Trude gestured to Marigold's lower lip. "You need a bit more."

Obediently, Marigold reapplied it.

Trude said, "Ask Chip. It'll be the Ice Capades before you know it."

Marigold decided not to share what she thought about Chip, murmuring, "And my only model will be my mother."

"But's she's a wonderful model."

"It's not the same." Movies without Trude, skating without Trude, soda fountains without her. Marigold gave herself a little shake. The fresh lipstick would look terrible if she began to cry.

Trude took off her glasses and wiped them with a handkerchief. "You'll just have to come and visit." She gave Marigold a cheesy smile in the mirror and held out her hand. "Come on. Back to the party."

"I don't want to go out there." Marigold sighed. "I really hate mice."

1937

Spring

The McGraths had supper at the Sherry-Netherland on Wednesdays. That was the maid's night off and Evangeline McGrath could not abide cooking. Truth be told, Arnold McGrath did not like his wife's cooking either. Besides, the hotel's location was convenient for everyone. Evangeline would arrive by taxi following a matinee or stroll up Fifth Avenue after some treatment at Elizabeth Arden, while Marigold went directly from Trude's apartment, which was just a few blocks uptown. For Arnold, it was most convenient. He either walked from his office on Madison, or over from the St. Regis after a session with his mistress.

That evening Marigold was the last to arrive, breathless and pink-cheeked from the cold. Her parents studied their menus while she wrestled with the small whirlwind of chaos that came with her school bag, her handbag, her camera, her camera bag, her hat, her gloves, and her coat, piling them on the back of the chair rather than leaving them with the coat check.

"Marigold." Evangeline shook her head only once. "Please try to be the young lady that you are. You're not a ragamuffin. Really, Marigold."

"I couldn't check the camera, Moms. I'd hate to forget it for any reason." She glanced over at her father who was studying the menu. Since that day with the punch cards, the temperature between her parents had only grown colder.

Arnold took a sip from his martini, dry, straight-up with one olive. "Where were you?"

"Oh. I was at Trude's." Marigold was surprised he should ask her a straight question. Since the punch cards, her father rarely spoke to her, too.

"You're going to miss her, aren't you?" Evangeline leant forward as Arnold lit her cigarette.

Marigold nodded. She watched her mother clasp her father's hand. Lighting cigarettes was the only time they ever seemed to touch. Evangeline exhaled. "Is she going to stay in Zurich for college?"

"I don't know."

"What about you, Marigold? What would you like to do?"

Marigold studied Evangeline's flawless face and perfect hair, framed by the simple beige hat. Had coming to this country and being the mother of only one child, married to a remote and difficult man been on that list of things Evangeline wanted to do?

Marigold shrugged, wishing she could hide behind her Brownie. She studied her menu instead.

"You'll go to Marymount," Arnold said. "All girls, no boys. Two-year college, just across the park. You won't get into any trouble with the nuns."

Marigold put the menu down and looked around the room. The man at the table next to theirs was reading a paper. She could see the headline and asked, "Do you think that Hauptmann man really kidnapped the Lindbergh baby?"

"Marigold." Her mother repeated that single shake of the head. "Don't talk about such things at the table."

"Could be a communist plot." Her father lit a cigarette for himself. "If he's a Jew, I'd say the chances of his guilt are pretty good."

"What's being Jewish got to do with it?" Trude was Jewish. So was Mr. Ganz at the camera store.

Evangeline exhaled. "Don't discuss religion at the table. Particularly when it's a subject you know nothing about." Then whispered to Marigold's father, "But that man, Hauptmann. He's a German."

Arnold gave a short laugh, "That's hardly incriminating. In

fact, Americans would be wise to take a few cues from Herr Hitler's playbook."

At this Evangeline turned back to Marigold as if Arnold hadn't spoken. "And do stop slouching. It does nothing for your figure."

WEEKS LATER, Marigold could not stop obsessing. Had Evangeline asked about college, knowing she would leave her? Had her mother decided what would happen next? Marigold placed her hands over her eyes. Bewildered grief drowned out the doctor's voice.

Her father replied in a hushed tone as the house keeper's sobs could be heard from the kitchen.

"It's a tragic mishap," The doctor shook his head, "Mixing medicine with cocktails, a terrible pity." Time stopped and with it, at least for Marigold, any sense of wonder.

After the funeral, Trude held her hand. "Mothers who become angels still watch over their daughters," she explained. "Mine watches over me." They were in Trude's vast living room, the furniture and paintings under white sheets, ready for the movers.

"Bernt!" Trude called out for the butler. "Do you think we could watch a movie, just one more?"

The silent man stood in the doorway.

"Please, Bernt." She clasped her hands together in supplication. "We're leaving tomorrow."

He made a motion as if to say no but then reconsidered. The walls were now empty; there was no need for a screen. After some searching, he wheeled out the projector and the maid brought them the last of the ginger snaps and milk.

"Well, this is fitting," Bernt said. "What is cued up is your favorite."

"*Queen Cristina*?" Marigold loved that movie. She wondered if Trude and Bernt had planned it.

"Jawohl!" Trude chuckled. "Let's have some Garbo just to shake things up."

Thirty minutes in, Trude said in her husky Garbo voice, "*You come from a country that is close to my heart.*"

And Marigold answered, "*You know Spain?*"

"*Somewhat. I shall like news of your countrymen.*"

"*My countrymen?*"

"*Yes, I shall like news of Velázquez.*"

To which Marigold began to laugh through the tears she couldn't hold back. Trude always said the line lisping every z and s sound.

Marigold asked, "*Have you ever traveled? Have you ever been far from home? Have you ever been homesick?*" The pleasure of reciting these lines dimmed at the thought of a young Evangeline coming to New York, far from everything familiar, with only Arnold, her husband, to guide her.

"*I have never been out of Sweden.*"

"*Then you don't know what it is to be homesick.*" Her mother would gloss over the past, never complaining of homesickness. "*You don't know what it means to feel that sense of loss. The pain of nostalgia.*"

Trude looked at the screen and back at Marigold. "*One can feel nostalgia for places one has never seen.*"

Marigold could not keep the tears from her voice. "*Yes, that's quite true.*" Then both of them cried as if their hearts would break. Life without her mother, and now Trude leaving.

"I'm going to miss you so much!" Marigold wept.

"Shut up," Trude sobbed. "I'm going to miss you more!"

After the movie ended Trude brought a small box to her friend. "This is for you." Marigold unwrapped the package. It was a camera, a Leica, small and elegant. "I know you want one and it will be something new for you to work with."

Brilliant Trude, so industrious and forward thinking. "Thank you, Queen Cristina."

"Come to England," Trude said.

"England? I thought you were moving to Zurich."

"I've decided to go to Oxford."

"Oh Trude!" Marigold could barely keep the wail from her voice. She steadied her breath and gulped back her tears. "The camera is beautiful."

"You'll have to visit." Trude wiped her own tears from her face. "Say that you will, Marigold."

"I will." Marigold nodded. "I will. I'll visit soon."

Summer

Arnold hired a driver to bring his mother from Connecticut, insisting she be of service.

"I'm here to help you sort through her effects," Marigold's grandmother announced.

"What does that mean?" Marigold stood on the opposite side of what had been her parents' bed, across from the woman who had never hugged nor spoiled her, certainly not the way Evangeline had.

"Her effects," her grandmother sighed. The elderly Mrs. McGrath had never liked her daughter-in-law. Now that Evangeline was dead, the old woman liked her even less. "It means your mother's things."

"Why can't I keep them?" It took every ounce of Marigold's strength to keep her lower lip from wobbling. She struggled not to fling herself upon the bed and prevent anyone from moving Evangeline's stuff.

Her grandmother tried again. "Certainly, you shall have what you want. But only keep the things of value, dear." Stylish gloves and dresses were neatly laid out before them. Instinctively, Marigold took a scarf and placed it round her neck.

Apart from clothing and jewelry, Evangeline had only left some photo albums behind.

Marigold considered a snapshot of a young Arnold and Evangeline. It was in London just after the war. Apart from the clothes, Evangeline in the photo might have been Marigold, so closely did they resemble each other.

"I was a dancer, he was a poet," Evangeline had blithely explained. But she had said this when Marigold was little and believed everything she was told. She imagined her mother coming to New York, with no one, save for a husband who was emotionally distant more often than not. Had he always been like that?

Marigold knew better than to ask why it was that she was born just months after their wedding, or why it was that her parents had fallen out of love. How her father had stopped writing was never discussed. When Marigold had asked her mother about her own family, Evangeline had answered very softly, "When the Germans came, they passed through Dinant on the way to France." Then her face had grown still. "Everyone died, darling."

"Everyone?"

"In my family, yes. I'll explain it to you when you're older." Then she added, "And I was lucky, because- well, I escaped to London." When Marigold would ask her more, Evangeline would say, "The British were very kind to us Belgians and the war— many of us lost everything. And Marigold, no one, not a living soul, wants to watch a person grieve. So, always keep your feelings in check. Whatever sadness you feel, it's better not to think about it." Then Evangeline had smiled. "And we needn't worry. There will never be another war. You can be sure of that."

Marigold watched her grandmother sort through the hats and fold the silk scarves. There was one with small violets embroidered along the edges. Marigold reached for it. *Keep your feelings in check.* The scarf still smelled of Evangeline. She'd worn it when she'd taken Marigold to the theatre. The show had been *Tonight at 8.30*, by Noel Coward. At one point in the play, the man had said to the woman, "You must snatch every bit of happiness that you can." Then Evangeline had turned to her and whispered, "That's very true, you know. Make sure that you do that."

Had her mother snatched every bit of happiness? Marigold put the scarf back on the pile.

Softly, her grandmother asked, "What would you like to keep, dear?"

That Evangeline should die, the way that she had, could only have been because——

The anguish tumbled out in a frightening rage, "Why didn't you like her?" Then before her grandmother answered, she yelled, "And why are you here? You don't even like me!" Flooded by tears and snot, Marigold ran from the room, sobbing.

Muffled voices could be heard outside her bedroom door. "She has a hateful streak that girl." Said the elderly Mrs. McGrath. "I'm sure she didn't get it from her father."

Marigold heard the housekeeper offer Mrs. McGrath a glass of sherry whereupon the old woman added, "But I suppose the poor child is in shock."

EVENTUALLY, the sad business concluded. Evangeline McGrath's things were placed in the back of the cedar closet next to the maid's room. Marigold refused the offer of a stay in Connecticut and the housekeeper wept when her grandmother left. As for the whereabouts of Arnold McGrath, that was anybody's guess.

Truly, no one knew what to say. Without Evangeline, the apartment was empty.

"I'm going to the movies," Marigold told the housekeeper.

If it weren't for the movies, if it weren't for her camera, the loneliness would have killed her.

Autumn

Ganz Cameras was on the corner of Broadway and 80th Street next to the deli where it always smelled of coffee beans. In the camera shop's front window were photographs of mountains and the sea. There were also moody portraits of people, who, Mr. Ganz explained, had been actors at the beginning of the century. "That's Erich von Stroheim, and this is Willy Fritsch." There were photographs of Marlene Dietrich and Louise Brooks.

"I took these with a UR Leica," he explained. "The 1920 model. The shutter moves just so, and the speed is like this." He moved his hand with a small gesture. "Very good for set photography *in kino*." He shuffled to find Marigold some film he thought she should try. "But that was in Berlin. Long, long ago. We didn't even have sound then."

"Why don't you still do it? Why not be in Hollywood?"

"Ah, the world was different then. Now I have my shop." She followed him into the darkroom where he'd allowed her to print her own film. "Here in my shop, I come downstairs every morning. Get my coffee from Eli next door. My universe is here. The greatest city in the world." His smile was tender and kind. "Ain't that right?"

He took her prints down from where they were hanging on a line. Central Park, with its naked trees nearly black and the snow so very white. The skaters were in a small group in the foreground on the left-hand side.

Marigold imagined Mr. Ganz leaving his home under cover, in

fear of being spied upon. He shuffled over to her. "Yeah, these are very good, Marigold. You have a keen eye."

What if Mr. Ganz had been a spy? What if he had to leave because the kaiser had been on his tail?

The old man continued, "At every opportunity you must take your camera with. You never know when that moment will be ready for you to capture it." He pointed to a photograph he'd taken of a crowded street, where a fruit vendor's wares had tipped over onto the sidewalk. The passersby moved on, oblivious, yet a boy had bent over to offer the vendor an apple. "Like so." He nodded, "I had my camera. Like so."

When she told Mr. Ganz about her mother, he listened silently, then asked, "Do you have a photo you love of her?"

Marigold did the inventory in her mind. There were quite a few from when Evangeline had modeled, but then she thought of one she'd seen that was less formal. It was of Evangeline in London, smiling, with a group of people. The women's dresses went to their ankles, and their hair was long. None of them wore makeup.

"It was before I knew your father," Evangeline had told her. "We were refugees and England took us in. There were so many of us Belgians."

When Marigold asked who had taken the picture, Evangeline had said, "It was taken by a dear, dear friend. He's now a great photographer."

Marigold told Mr. Ganz about the photograph. "Bring it in," he said. "We'll reproduce it, then you can have it with you. Always."

MARYMOUNT MANHATTAN COLLEGE was directly across the park on 85th Street. Walking to class, she'd pass nannies with prams and butlers with dogs. Marigold imagined herself as Ginger Rogers walking a snazzy Pomeranian, or perhaps a snooty poodle across the deck of an ocean liner, while Fred Astaire walked in the other direction with a common beagle on a leash. Then she imagined him walking past again, this time upgraded with a spaniel, until finally he catches Ginger's attention by walking a Great Dane. She thought about the two Great Danes Greta Garbo had in *Queen Cristina.* Those dogs made Marigold chuckle every single time. If only her mother were there, they could laugh about it together. Or Trude. If Trude were still there, they would laugh about it too.

AT MARYMOUNT, Marigold's two elective classes were conversational German and introduction to photography.

The German teacher was an elderly man who'd emigrated to America twenty years earlier. "When you've seen countless wars move a border back and forth, back and forth, it makes a city like New York refreshingly different," he said. "There are no geographical lines here. Merely this island wherein we invent ourselves and are only limited by our ambitions. Remember girls, you'll be told to be modest, but I would challenge you to be daring."

In photography, a young nun announced, "Ladies, I am Sister Elsbeth. Today we're going to discuss the work of two pioneering photographers from the last century, Clementina Hawarden and Julia Margaret Cameron. Their work was mostly portraiture, but I think were you to emulate their approach to their subjects, you will do very well indeed."

Marigold imagined going to Switzerland and wowing Trude with her newly acquired German while taking glamorous photographs of Trude's house, or college in Oxford. But there was no one in New York to talk about this with. Then again, studying her Leica, Marigold knew that wasn't entirely true. Sometimes, there was Mr. Ganz.

LIGHTING, film speed, drapery, and posing. Afternoons spent at the movies were now replaced with photography. When the students weren't photographing each other, they were on assignment, moving through the city, photographing the same buildings as the greats.

"You must photograph the Flatiron Building," instructed Sister Elspeth, "and then compare your efforts with Edward Steichen's." The exercise was repeated at the arch in Washington Square. The work filled Marigold's time and muffled her grief. Looking at the world through a lens helped push the gnawing sadness away. And always, she shared her assignments with Mr. Ganz at the camera shop.

Studying her pictures, he nodded approvingly. "We are only steps from some of the greatest works of art in the world," by which he meant the Metropolitan Museum of Art. They were in the darkroom, as he supervised her developing her homework. They watched the photo come into view. "Marigold, you must capture how sculptors describe movement in stone, what is essentially a static immovable mass, no? Photographs, even ones of people, are really not so different, I think."

"What do you mean? A person isn't frozen like a sculpture."

"Ah, but the picture—the piece of paper we print it on—is." He chuckled. "You remind me of my granddaughter. She is the same age as you. Also, a photographer. I want her to come together with her parents here. I tell them to come, but they say they are not ready. That it is not so urgent." He sighed. "It's a terrible business, Marigold. Terrible."

Wednesday night suppers were still at the Sherry-Netherland. Marigold and her father usually ate in silence, both of them too consumed with their own troubles to know what to say to the other.

Sometimes, Arnold would ask, "How's school?"

"Meine Klasse auf Deutsch ist schön." She didn't say, *but I miss Trude so much I could scream.*

"Good," he nodded approvingly. "And?"

"Photography is wonderful." She took a sip of her water then added, "Wunderbar."

All while thinking, *I wish you took an interest in my pictures.*

"What about your economics class?"

She was afraid to tell him that she found it so tedious she barely stayed awake during the lectures. "It's fine," Marigold said. "Economics is fine. Es ist gut auch."

ECONOMICS CLASS WAS HELD in what had once been the ballroom of a mansion. The professor was a retired colonel with a sweet manner and a profound limp. Halfway through term he announced, "Young ladies, may I introduce my teaching assistant, Mr. Miller? He will lead this afternoon's lecture. He is also the unfortunate soul tasked with marking your midterm exams."

Mr. Miller's eyes were deep and chocolaty. His thick hair was black and curly. He had a square chin and was clearly athletic. He looked to be not much older than the students.

"I just want to melt!" one girl said to another as they made their way to lunch. Watching Mr. Miller clean the chalkboard, Marigold agreed. She also wanted to melt. She wrote to Trude (who was now at Oxford) about it, filling her letters with silly phrases about swimming pools and going to the post office and other sentences one masters in foreign language instruction.

"He looks like Laurence Olivier in *As You Like It*," the girl sitting next to her whispered in class the next day. Marigold noticed the girl's hands. She wondered how they would look if they were photographed in a position of prayer like a saint. "I think he's better looking than Laurence Olivier," Marigold answered.

They were in the front row and Mr. Miller wrote an equation on the chalkboard. She imagined the muscles of his back expanding and contracting as he wrote across the board. How one captures the movement of something essentially static. She imagined his hands around her waist, his mouth upon hers—

"Miss McGrath."

Marigold opened her eyes and sat upright.

Just then, a mouse run across the floor behind him. Marigold's throat opened and she screamed, joined by the others in less than a second. Within moments, chaos erupted. Some girls fled the room, some of them jumped upon chairs.

"I guess you're afraid of mice," he said afterwards. The classroom was empty now.

Marigold was still in her seat, holding her head with her hands, struggling to steady her heart. "Yes, I am." Marigold nodded. "I am very sorry."

"I've never seen a place empty like that."

"I'm . . . I'm sorry," she said again.

"How are you doing in this class?"

Marigold waited a moment before answering. "All right, I guess."

"Do you want to grab a beer?"

A beer. She had never gone somewhere and "grabbed a beer." She'd had sherry with her parents and wine occasionally, but she'd never gone to a place and "grabbed a beer."

"Uh, yes. Yes, I would." A small buzz of anticipation began to run through her.

Silently, she followed Mr. Miller out of the building, keeping enough distance between them so no one should mistake them for a couple. Inside Marigold's mind, Gershwin's musical interlude from *Shall We Dance* accompanied her steps. If Mr. Miller had a dog, and if Marigold walked in the opposite direction... She realized she would need to have a dog, too. But the only dog on the street was doing its business in a flower bed. Marigold sighed. She continued following Mr. Miller. It was not like that movie in the slightest.

They crossed three blocks east over to Lexington where there was a bar outside the downtown subway stop. He held the door open, and she noticed his hand on the small of her back when he followed her inside.

THE LIGHTS WERE dim and the floor was sticky. The bar was empty and a smell of wet ashtrays hung in the air. Mr. Miller gestured for Marigold to choose a table.

"So." He brought over the beers. "How long have you had this hang-up with rodents?"

She took a small sip from her glass. It was cold and vaguely foul, but it was delicious, too. Since she'd begun taking pictures across the city, Marigold found much of life now felt this way. Cold and foul, but exciting and desirable at the same time. She carefully licked the foam off her upper lip. "I've always had it. Don't you have something you're afraid of?"

"Not that I can think of." He leant back and lit a cigarette, studying her. Then he shrugged, "Nazis, maybe."

"Nazis?"

He nodded. "Well, I'm a Jew. We hear rumors from cousins and news reports. I think about what I would do if I were in Europe."

"What would you do?"

"I ask myself that question a lot. Would I have the guts to take out those Nazi scum bastards? I don't know."

Marigold liked this feeling of his warm eyes assessing her, in their own private world. His handsome face and dark hair against the smoky darkness of the bar. She wondered if he would let her take his picture.

She cleared her throat, "Well, you don't need to be afraid here, Mr. Miller. We don't have any Nazi's in New York."

He smiled. "You're an innocent, but you're a good kid, Miss McGrath. Don't let the Bund catch you taking that position, even if you are an innocent."

HIS NAME WAS ALAN. He came from Boston and was finishing his PhD at Columbia. He taught on Wednesdays and Thursdays. The visits to the tavern soon became routine. Leaving Marymount's building alone, Marigold would hum her movie music until she'd meet him on the corner of 84th street, and head over to Lexington to "their place."

Despite expounding upon a myriad of subjects, Alan asked Marigold little about herself. It went without saying that he seemed to know how dazzled she was to be alone with him in a grown-up, albeit lackluster place. Afterwards, he'd take the subway, and she'd wander south to catch the cross-town bus.

There had been several such visits when she passed him in the hallway and he said, "Miss McGrath, follow me please."

No one else was there. She thought the door he held open led to a classroom or office. But it was in fact a cleaning closet. Alan closed the door, submerging them in darkness. Her adrenalin fluttered, sensing he was only an inch away from her.

"It's raining out, did you notice?"

"No, I didn't," she whispered, and then his mouth was upon hers. His lips were full. The feeling of his tongue upon hers sent a charge of desire through her torso. Her arms went up around his neck and he pressed himself against her. His hair was impossibly soft. It felt nothing like it had with boys in high school.

Alan slowly pushed her backwards where there was a table or a counter behind her. His hands hoisted her upon it. He stepped closer. The kissing continued, more urgently now as he leant against her and she wrapped her legs around his waist. His fingers were on the edge of her underpants. She thought of their surroundings. Tins of powdered bleach and old filthy rags, various wrenches and screwdrivers took pride of place while his fingers traced the edge of her thigh where her pubic hair began. No one – not for lack of trying- had done this to her. The thrill of it terrified her.

A moan escaped from her throat. Alan took a step back. "Don't tell me you see a mouse."

Embarrassed, Marigold pulled down her skirt. "No." She straightened her belt. "But I will need extra help with the homework assignment."

Afterward, they sat in the bar. He discussed politics and the masses, and the deportation of Jews while she sipped tepid beer, knowing he had little interest in the comments she'd contribute. She marveled how her heart had raced even as time slowed in that closet, reeking of dirty mops, motor oil and floor wax.

Finally, she said, "I think you should let me take your picture."

He smiled at this. "Why would I do that?"

"Because you're beautiful and I know how to take a good picture."

To which he laughed, and said, "You're a crazy girl, you know that?"

THE VISITS to the broom closet were soon formalized with military precision. Three fifteen became the time for Marigold's rush of desire to flood everything away. Strained suppers with her father, her loneliness for Trude, even her mother's death, felt less important. Heart pounding, she'd eagerly assist Alan unbuttoning her blouse, joining in whichever way he moved against her. Then he'd ferociously shudder and wipe himself off with a handkerchief as she trembled, rearranging her bra to button herself back up.

Alan rented a room from a family in Turtle Bay, so he wasn't in a position to invite her to visit. Marigold wondered if he'd come over to Riverside Drive.

He shook his head smiling, "Don't you like the broom closet?"

It became impossible to think about anything else. Rather than concentrate on her schoolwork, Marigold now spent afternoons daydreaming about how they might be in bed, properly together. She managed to take his picture and demurred politely from identifying him to Mr. Ganz.

Before the end of term finals, she and Alan met in the broom closet at the appointed time. Marigold said, "I just want to say…"

"Shh. It's always better to say nothing." He kissed her neck, then added, "Think about nothing." He slid the opening of her panties aside and said, "This is going to hurt, Marigold." She winced as he thrust his finger inside her. "You're going to bleed, too."

"But what about—"

"Don't worry," he chuckled, "I brought this." He held out the packet and slipped on the condom. "There."

It did hurt, yet there was something else, too. It was something else much more than hurt.

"Yeah," he groaned. "Oh yeah, right there."

Somewhere, tucked very deep inside of Marigold, she wondered where 'right there' actually was, really. Then she'd remind herself not to be so silly, because whatever they were doing in that closet wasn't half bad. It wasn't half bad at all.

A SIGNIFICANT CHANGE occurred in the weekly meals at the Sherry-Netherland. The week after Thanksgiving, Marigold and her father were joined by Mrs. Fenton, who had been widowed in much the same way as Arnold McGrath.

Often, Marigold watched Mrs. Fenton laugh uproariously at something her father had said. Mrs. Fenton's head always tilted back, her elegant throat punctuated by a triple strand of pearls. "Of course you must bring it up with Fritz Kuhn, he'll love that idea." Mrs. Fenton smiled and glanced over at Marigold to include her in the conversation. "Really, anything we can do to promote the cause of the Reich will only bring our countries closer together, don't you think?"

Then Mrs. Fenton's smile would widen. "Oh Marigold, your father's such a wit, isn't he?"

1938

Winter

"Did you do the assignment?" Alan always asked. Then he'd take her in his arms before she could answer. But she would be ready, longing for his kiss. It never occurred to her to ask why he didn't enquire how she was faring in her other classes, nor where she imagined herself after she finished college. Instead, there were his chocolate eyes, in which she was happy to melt as he hiked up her skirt, shoving her panties aside, knowing she was as eager as he, because she never resisted. She always moved as instructed, glad to be lost, yet somehow, never totally so, even as he moaned and then pulled away.

Afterwards there was the tavern, which they always left before five. That way, he assured her, they wouldn't run into other professors or students. Marigold, in her innocence, never disputed any of this, it was enough just to be with him. When he left marks on her skin, she wore her mother's scarf around her neck to hide them, recalling his heavily fringed eyes, fluttering as he came. Which was what Alan was doing when the custodian found them in the broom closet.

Marigold was mistaken in believing the custodian would say nothing because that wasn't the case. Staring at the books behind the dean of students, she saw volumes by her professor, the one for whom Alan was the assistant.

The dean was still speaking about standards and conduct, morality and scandal. "Your grades, Miss McGrath, would indicate you're not really cut out for a life of academe, are you?"

"No, ma'am," Marigold agreed. Embarrassed, she had no idea whether Alan would be fired or not. Humiliated, she willed her tears back inside, keeping her mouth still, her jaw indifferent to the ensuing disaster.

"So, Miss McGrath, while what happened between you and Mr. Miller is entirely your affair, I'll remind you that the college's property is not the place for you to conduct it. If we made allowances for every time a student stumbles in this regard, Marymount's carefully won reputation would suffer, much more than you can possibly imagine."

"I'm sorry," Marigold said.

"So am I. You seem to be a nice girl. And what a shame that you show such little respect not only for higher learning, but such little respect for yourself as well."

Sitting in the bar, Marigold didn't tell Alan about her meeting with the dean. Instead, she handed him a copy of the photograph she'd taken of him. He admired it and then put his hand over hers. "Say, that's a pretty good picture."

Marigold blushed with pleasure, despite her earlier appointment with the Dean. "Well, the camera likes you. I mean, it really likes you!"

"Hey, I don't think we should worry about earlier." By which he meant the closet. "You know, this is my field work through Columbia. I'm not an employee or on the faculty or anything. Professor Preston will have to write up an incident report, and I'll sit through an official warning. It isn't a big deal." He removed his hand to light a cigarette. "I mean, let's call a spade a spade."

She noted the warmth she still felt from his fingertips. She wished he would kiss her. Just softly, on the mouth. Marigold realized Alan was still speaking. She watched his beautiful lips moving, "It's not like anybody got hurt. And I could see, it's what you've wanted, right? And, hey, it's not as though your dance card is full."

She still didn't follow. "What does that mean?" There weren't any boys at Marymount. How could her dance card be full?

Alan continued, "And you can't find fault with my extracurricular instruction." He smiled at her, as if this was the wittiest utterance of the day. "It's why I chose you. I could tell you wanted it. And knowing you're a virgin, you're not about to give me anything. I mean, Jesus Christ, imagine having to explain that to my fiancée!"

"Your fiancée?"

"Yeah, she's at Barnard."

A lump of shame lodged in Marigold's throat.

Alan said, "The way I see it, I'm doing you a favor, Marigold."

But she failed to hear this because she saw something scurry along the front of the bar. She grabbed her purse and camera and dashed out. It was too big to be a mouse. It had to be a rat.

OUTSIDE IT WAS RAINING. She couldn't bring herself to go home. Passing the cinema, she bought a ticket and ducked inside. The theatre was nearly empty. Onscreen, Cary Grant and Katharine Hepburn bickered endlessly about something. Marigold sat down, waiting for the tears, which had now caught up with the rain on her face, to subside.

She noticed a movement at the end of the aisle. It was a man, watching her as he thrust his arm back and forth. He gestured to his crotch with the other hand. She swiftly stood up and ran out of the theatre.

SHE COULDN'T IMAGINE what she'd say to her father. By the time she reached the Sherry-Netherland she was soaked through and through.

When she sat down, Arnold said, "I spoke with the dean of students."

"Why don't you take a moment in the powder room?" Mrs. Fenton suggested. "Here's my comb and some lipstick."

"Thank you," Marigold mumbled, and glanced at her father. He was studying his menu although he ate the same dish every single week. Emerging from the ladies' room she heard the violin's rendition of "Beautiful Dreamer" and braced herself for whatever punishment she was sure he'd eke out.

Arnold looked up and said, "I've told Mrs. Fenton about your predicament."

Marigold handed Mrs. Fenton the comb and lipstick.

"Feel better?" Mrs. Fenton smiled and put her comb and lipstick back in her purse.

"Yes, thank you."

"I suggested to your father that you might want to broaden your horizons."

"You did? Oh. Yes."

When he excused himself at dessert, Mrs. Fenton leant over and said, "I trust you won't need a D&C. Will you?"

"What's that?" She had no idea what that meant.

"Dusting and cleaning, dear." Mrs. Fenton patted Marigold's hand. "I'll take you to my doctor. Don't worry about a thing."

"I'm not worried. I'm going to England." Up until the moment she said it, Marigold hadn't realized that's what she would do, but there it was. She'd go to England.

"Lovely!" Mrs. Fenton beamed. "What a good idea. Perhaps you can retrace your mother's footsteps. But not too much! Anyway, you needn't worry, we all know there isn't going to be a war. After all, it's America for the Americans, just like it's Germany for the Germans, isn't it?"

Marigold wondered if Mrs. Fenton mightn't marry Arnold as soon as could be arranged.

"What is your first name, Mrs. Fenton?"

"It's Mamie, dear. Why don't you call me Mamie, from now on? And when you get to London, if you move with the right people, who knows? You might even run into those handsome Kennedy boys."

* * *

THE DOCTOR SAID, "I'm not going to hurt you, but you will find the speculum alarmingly cold."

Staring at the ceiling, it was impossible to keep her knees from knocking as the doctor peered out of view saying, "Scooch down. That's a good girl."

Afterwards he said, "Everything is right as rain. But you're going to have to watch yourself." He gestured to a small plastic case on his desk. It was the size of a compact. "Take this with you and learn to use it. I don't want you coming back for the wrong set of reasons."

WHEN MARIGOLD TOLD Mr. Ganz she was leaving, he said, "You have a gift. But you must nurture it for it to grow. And you must always be looking, to begin to understand what is happening. There is much going on that we don't want to see here, but it is happening. You will need to record it. For posterity, for yourself and for the record. Yeah." He placed a large box of film in her arms. "Good luck to you, Marigold McGrath."

Part II

Every Scrap of Happiness

London
1938

"THIS YOUR FIRST TRIP TO LONDON, MISS?"

"That's right."

"I'll give you a bit of history then, if I may." The taxi circled the statue of Lord Nelson. "This is Trafalgar Square, named in honor of Horatio, Lord Nelson, who defeated the French at the battle of Trafalgar. Now, here we have...." The taxi drove down Piccadilly over to Knightsbridge; veering left onto Brompton Road and then another left onto Sloane Street where Knightsbridge underground marked the turn. ". . . Sloane Street. Off Sloane Street are the homes of Sir Charles Laughton, his lovely wife, Miss Elsa Lanchester, of course, and then here we have the former home of Lillie Langtry next to the Cadogan Hotel."

"Golly!" In spite of herself, Marigold was starstruck.

The driver glanced at her in the rear mirror and laughed. "Now, down the King's Road we have what is more commonly known as the small village that is actually Chelsea. Here we have the home of Thomas Carlyle and just a few doors down is the Chelsea Town Hall."

The Chelsea Town Hall was where her parents had married.

"I was a dancer and he was a poet," Evangeline had said. This phrase, this phrase. Marigold shook her head and read the signs on the storefronts. Picture frame maker, tobacconist, baker, tailor, confectioner, fishmonger, butcher, draper, grocer.

The taxi slowed. "This is it. 275 King's Road."

It was a black painted door with a brass kickplate, next to an antiques shop on a corner. The cabbie got out and whistled at some boys playing down the street. "Oy! Give us a hand."

One of them skipped over. He didn't reach Marigold's shoulder. She wondered how old he was. "Where to, gov'nor?"

"Young lady's going across the street."

"Rightio. This way, miss." Although it was winter, the boy was in shorts and a sweater. His knees looked as though it would take more than a bath to get them clean.

She paid the driver and went to the door. The boy smiled at her, and she handed him a shilling. "Is this all right?"

"Ta!" His face lit up. "Thanks very much, miss." They both waited for the other to speak. He squinted for a moment, "You American then?"

"That's right. Straight off the boat."

"Are you from Hollywood?"

"No," she laughed, "I'm from New York."

"I'll go to America one day. Will that be all, miss?"

"Yes."

"Right then." The boy gave her a winning smile.

She wondered if a shilling had been the right amount. "Thanks for your help."

"Cheerio!" He tipped his cap and skipped off to join the other boys.

THE DOOR OPENED. Mrs. Falaise Cooper was small and apple shaped in tweeds and a cardigan. "My dear." She wrapped Marigold in her arms. "You look so much like your mother. Let's get you situated." Evangeline had lodged with Falaise twenty years before, during the war. "When your father cabled me, I thought of course, you must come."

They'd never met, but seeing Falaise, who'd known her mother in a previous life, allowed Marigold's grief to finally unwind. She wondered whether Falaise knew what really happened. Should she say that she thought Evangeline decided to take those pills on purpose? The effort of keeping the heartache in check, the humiliation from Alan and just missing her mother so much felt so overwhelming that——

Falaise held up her hand. "Wait one moment, dear," she said, and pulled a small white horn out of her pocket. She held it up to her ear. "I can hear you now, dear. What is it you wanted to say?"

Marigold's eyes filled with tears.

"Now, now, there's no need for that, dear," Falaise took her hand and squeezed it.

Marigold smiled and gave herself a little shake. "I just wanted to say thank you for welcoming me."

A FEW HOURS LATER, Falaise said, "When the weather's fine, I always toddle down to the Arts Club. I've been doing it for more years than I can count. Let's get your brolly and head over, shall we?"

They crossed King's Road over to Old Church Street. The air was heavy with wet and time, then the skies cleared. Sunshine seeped between the buildings, striping the pavement. The light was different than in New York, cooler yet more vivid against the brick, broken by old buildings and higgledy houses that had seen more history than anything she'd imagined.

Falaise closed her umbrella. "Now, your father cabled me about your poor mother. But we should have a G and T first, so you can tell me yourself what happened and why you've decided to come to England. Hmm?"

Sitting in the lounge, Marigold had a sense of déjà vu, then realized her mother must have been in this place. Perhaps she'd seen photos of her here. Finally, she said, "Well you see, Falaise," then paused for Falaise to pick up her ear trumpet. Marigold spoke a little louder now. "I seem to have a case of poor judgement."

"What's that, dear?"

"Poor judgement. I have poor judgement."

"Oh, my dear. I'm sure you don't." Falaise patted her knee.

"Whatever's transpired, let's just trust that it's innocence, shall we?"

* * *

"I've invited Marek and Zosia Dagger for our Sunday roast. Darling Zosia is how I met your mother, really."

The doorbell rang and Marigold heard them chattering as they let themselves in. They were tall and stylish. They were also the same age that Evangeline would have been.

"Darling!" Zosia kissed Falaise and handed her a bottle of champagne.

"Zosia, it's my favorite. How kind." Falaise handed the champagne to Marigold. "And Marek, little Marigold here has told me she's a photographer."

"Well, I take pictures." Marigold blushed.

"Then you must come and use the darkroom, anytime at all." He was handsome and dark and made her think of Clark Gable.

"Thank you." She felt herself blushing even harder.

"I loved your mother."

"We all did," Zosia added.

He continued as if she hadn't spoken. "Anything I can do to help you settle in is my pleasure."

They moved to the dining room. It was painted salmon and covered in watercolors and photographs. Marek said, "Falaise, you saucy minx, have you hidden the corkscrew?"

"No, no, it's where I always leave it." The small table was laden with food, all of which was hot and steaming, albeit strange to Marigold. They poured wine then ate and drank with gusto. It was the kind of meal Marigold thought only existed in movies.

"It's like *Private Lives* or *Design for Living*."

"What is, dear?" Zosia asked.

"This!" Marigold realized she was a little bit drunk. "Perhaps more like *Tonight at 8.30*."

Falaise asked, "Did you see that show?"

"My mom took me." She thought of the moment when the actor said, 'You must grab every scrap of happiness that you can," and Evangeline had whispered into Marigold's ear. "Don't forget that, Marigold, not for one second."

Marek began clearing their plates. "Yes, well, let's have pudding, shall we?"

It was something they referred to as a spotted dick, at which Marigold was confused.

Marek laughed. "I like to eat mine drowning in custard."

Zosia explained, "It became popular in the war, and Falaise is just masterful with it, aren't you, Falaise?"

"What's that? Did you say something important, dear?"

Zosia shouted, "About the pudding!"

"I do think Noël Coward's acting is sometimes wooden."

"No, the pudding." Marek said.

"Oh yes, it's been around for ages. Long before the war. It's Victorian, you know. Something from my childhood, yes. Marek, darling, are you going to make us the coffee? And Zosia, dear, describe to Marigold what you mentioned to me."

"Ah yes. Marigold, there seems to be some question about how best to fill your time, and well, your mother and I met during the war when we were both—" Zosia paused for a moment and then said, "Well, we were refugees, actually."

"Are you Belgian, too?" Evangeline had never described herself as a refugee.

"No, Marek and I were Hungarian, and then we were Austrian. Now we're British. The people I work with, they're also refugees. I'm part of a charity. It's similar to the one which helped your mother and me."

"So, would that interest you?" Marek returned with the coffee.

"Tell me what I can do."

Woburn House was located in Bloomsbury and had once been a mansion for an earl. A woman bent over a typewriter at a desk in the lobby. Behind her was a large portrait of the new king, with his wife and daughters. The woman looked up and squinted at Marigold.

"It's going to be a wait I'm afraid." She pointed at a line of women sitting on a bench along the wall.

"Oh no, I— I'm here to help. Zosia Dagger sent me."

"Ah, well in that case . . ."

She directed Marigold to an office on the second floor. Two women worked at small desks; the third desk along the back wall was empty. Adjacent to the wall facing the windows was another office, whose door was kept closed.

"That belongs to Colonel Mayhew," the older woman, Mrs. Krumbull, explained. "We report to him." She continued, "This team places domestics. Most of the people who write to us are theatrical artists who, for whatever reason, need to leave Germany."

"Why do they need to leave Germany?"

The younger one, Miss Breen, gave her a funny look. "You don't know?"

Marigold shook her head. She wondered if it was too soon to find the restroom.

Mrs. Krumbull frowned. "How did you come here?"

"Zosia Dagger sent me." Marigold's face began to redden.

"Did she?" The women were silent for a few moments. Mrs. Krumbull then cleared her throat. "If you don't mind my asking, how old are you?"

"I'm eighteen."

"I see." Mrs. Krumbull gave her a considered look. "You're American, aren't you?"

Marigold nodded.

"Well, I don't know what they're telling you in America, but here, all of these people"—She gestured to the piles upon piles of applications— "need to leave because they're Jews. Or, if they're not Jewish, they probably have a life that their government does not approve of."

She brought Marigold to a desk covered in stacks of papers with photographs attached. "At the moment, we only have house-maid positions. So, we can place the women, but to find the men a chauffeuring position or something, has proven to be far more challenging. Do you speak German?"

Several hours later, Marigold thought her bladder might explode. The other two women had taken a break but not invited her to do so. When they returned, they continued working in silence, and she'd sorted through two boxes of applications, those with domestic experience and those without. Those who spoke English and those who did not. Those who were married and those who were single.

She looked at her wristwatch. It was just after four. "Uh, excuse me. Mrs. Krumbull?" Marigold stood up. "Where is the powder room?"

The older woman's face was blank like stone. Then after a few seconds, her eyes lit up. "Oh, you mean the toilet, is that right?"

Each day continued much like the one before. But the quantity of boxes began to increase exponentially. Applications of women were sorted into "For review" piles. Men making application without wives or families were placed into a discard pile. Marigold wondered what they were fleeing, why they would leave their occupations (some of them she was sure she recognized) to work as somebody's servant. What Mr. Ganz described, what Alan had alluded to— none of it had interested her before. But now, sorting through their letters, placing single men into the "no" pile, reports on the radio and in the papers took on a new urgency.

MAREK DAGGER'S studio was a short walk from Falaise, just behind Lots Road. One entered Lark Mews through an archway, where a small row of houses perched on a cobblestone street.

Marigold noticed the yellow daffodils on the corner of every stoop. She found the house number and timidly knocked.

"Come!"

His studio was bright, bright and a fire roared in its small fireplace. Her eyes adjusted to the white painted walls and white painted floors. Marek and another man stood on either side of the mantel, an orange cat sleeping on a patch of kilim rug between them.

"This is Stefan, Marigold. If you're going to take pictures, his magazines are where you'll publish."

"That's right," Stefan said, and shook her hand. "Not just *Vogue*."

"Well, uh— Marvelous!" Her cheeks were scarlet. She wished she knew what to say when meeting people. She felt such a dummy.

Marek said, "Take a look around and I'll get us some tea."

On one wall there were photographs and prints of every shape and description. She heard Marek and Stefan hold forth in German, then in English, then in another language she didn't recognize. On the other wall, hung four large photographs, each of a figure moving, caught in a dance, a scarf floating around the body. Marek came and stood beside her, looking up at the wall with a hundred pictures. Amongst them were several formal portraits, the sitters dressed in finery from the previous century.

"Is that you and Zosia?" Marigold pointed to the boy and girl in the pictures.

"Yes. That was in Hungary." He smiled. "Before we became Austrian."

"When did you come here?"

"The spring of '14. Almost twenty-five years ago." Evangeline arrived in 1916.

"Did your parents come, too?"

"No. They moved to the South of France." He cleared his throat. "They died in the flu epidemic. Just after the war."

"Oh. I— Um."

Marek said, "Marigold"—He held her gaze for a moment— "we were broken up to learn about Evangeline."

Marigold looked away first. Her eyes moved along the wall and there it was. Her mother laughing, just as a girl, with long hair in a long dress. Bangles on her wrists and a fringed scarf upon her shoulders. A young Zosia was beside her. There was a willow tree to the right of them. "You took this?"

"Yes, at the Chelsea Arts Club. We'll sit by this very tree when it warms up."

Marigold could hear the memory's smile in his voice.

"Here's another one." He pointed up and across the other end of the wall. The photo, somewhat larger than the other snapshots, was of Evangeline. She was radiant and holding a camera. She looked out at the viewer, the same age as Marigold was now, seeing her mother across time. "I truly loved your mother, Marigold."

But when Marigold turned to face Marek, his back was to her, and he was pouring the tea.

* * *

There was a letter for her on the landing. Trude. Trude was at Oxford.

> *Rest assured, my lodging is very quiet. My landlady is strict and has imposed every kind of curfew. We're not allowed gentlemen callers of any kind. Really, there's no mischief that we might make, whatsoever. My father was sure of that before leaving me here at Oxford last term.*

Marigold looked at Falaise, who put down her ear horn and said, "You should go. It will do you a world of good to be with people your own age. And say what one will, Zosia's work has a rather melancholy aspect, does it not?"

Marigold threw her arms around the old woman. "I'll see you Sunday evening."

TRUDE MET her at the door. "Welcome to Somerville!" A piano played in the room above them, competing with a victrola blasting jazz while girls raced up and down the stairs in various forms of fancy dress.

That Trude's letter had been patently false made Marigold smile from ear to ear.

"This way," Trude led her to a small room at the top of the stairs. "These are my digs. I call it the garret." The walls were papered a soft blue. Beautiful drapes framed the small dormer. Marigold gave a little gasp. "It looks just like Park Avenue."

"Ha! It does, doesn't it? Daddy called the same decorator we had there." Trude chuckled. "Having a doting pater has its advantages, after all."

On the bed were some leotards, tights, and a strange sort of cape made of netting. Trude handed her a leotard. "Time to get your kit on."

"What's this for?"

"The Skoliasts at Balliol are throwing a carnival bash."

"What are the Skoliasts? What's Balliol?" The two girls climbed into their costumes.

"Skoliasts are those who study classics, you know, Greek, Latin, that kind of thing. Balliol is a college here. And carnival— Mardi Gras?" Trude put her hands on her hips.

"I know what carnival is!" They studied themselves in the full-length mirror. They were the same height, the same slender build, but Marigold's hair was chestnut, while Trude's was a very light blonde. "Trude, we look liked crazed escapees from a dance troupe or something."

"Good! That was exactly what I was hoping for." Trude fastened the cape to her costume. "We're going as wood sprites of course."

"What are these for?" There were two enormous masks on the bed, at least three times larger than life. They were made of papier-mâché with round rosy cheeks and deranged looking smiles.

"A heightened sense of theatricality of course." Trude handed one to Marigold. "It goes over your shoulders. They'll be very striking."

"Aren't we from a fairy tale though?"

"Yes of course. We're a Brothers Grimm thingamajig. Wood nymphs show up everywhere, don't they? We can be elves that worked for the cobbler, or some kind of magical force for children lost in the forest, you know."

"Just your typical New York City wood nymph, hunh?" Marigold placed the mask over her head. She could see through two small holes.

"You better believe it."

"What? I can't hear you in here!" But that didn't matter really. It was crazy and it was fun to be together again, whether they were in a library failing not to laugh, or in these insane carnival costumes. Just being with Trude was grand.

"I said, you better believe it!" Trude put on her own mask and continued, shouting, "Carnival is about the reversal of societal norms and a brief ceasing of acceptable behaviors! To do that successfully, we must be completely disguised."

"You know you're completely crazy!" Marigold shouted. She took a deep breath and moved forward. It was quite difficult to see. It had been a year since they'd last been together. Trude held out her hand and Marigold took it. To her mind, Trude was even more spectacular than before.

Hundreds of revelers surrounded the venue. Inside, an orchestra played *Jumpin' at the Woodside*. The girls began moving. They loved this piece, and its rhythmic jazz, hopping, jumping. The music and dancing became faster, then paused. Everyone in the room shouted, "Hey!"

Then the band resumed playing. The dancers formed a conga line, as the music sped up, wilder and more raucous. The person dancing in front of Marigold was a good head taller than she. He was dressed as an indiscriminate forest type, too. His enormous head bobbed and weaved, and she held on to his waist. The music stopped.

"Hey! Hey!"

The band started back up, and they resumed moving, kicking one foot out and then the other. Finally, the band slowed down. People paused and applauded, but the man in front of her still danced with Marigold in tow until they were a conga line of only two. Then he stopped, and shouted, "Hey!"

And she responded, "Hey! Hey!"

He turned around and she faced him. He gestured, "Hey!"

And she gestured back, "Hey! Hey! Hey!"

It was hot and impossible to keep the mask on. She held up her hand and gestured she had to remove her mask. The tall voice said, "Can I help you to do it?"

She nodded. Gingerly, the large hands removed her mask and handed it to her. Her hair was pasted to her skin and she wiped it away.

"Will you help me with mine?" he asked.

"Yes."

Slowly, he bent his knees and placed his hands upon them, bowing his head so she might reach his mask. It was a small struggle, but eventually she took it off. His blonde hair was thinning. He looked up and smiled at her. "Thank you." His eyes were clear and blue. His face was kind. "I am Joop."

Marigold couldn't hear him. "What?"

He spelled out, "J-O-O-P!"

"Jupe?" She thought he spelled out the French word for skirt.

"No, Joop. It's Dutch. Short for Joseph. I'm Dutch. We say Joop like you say rope. Or hope." Joop was handsome. He continued to stand near her. "And your name?"

"I'm Marigold."

"Goudsbloem."

"Is that Marigold in Dutch?"

He nodded, smiling. "You are at Somerville with Trude?" He gestured to the crowd at the bar. Marigold looked over to see Trude wave at them both. The crowd spilled out into the night, and the two girls flanked him, making their way to a pub to resume their festivities.

Joop fetched them all beers and said, "Goudsbloem, Marigoude. It's like the cheese."

"No, it's not, Joop. It's a flower." Trude was very stern. "Just because you keep repeating a thing doesn't make it so."

"I thought I would give it my best, do you say, shot?" He put on a pair of spectacles, which Marigold thought only made him more handsome.

"What kind of cheese is howda?" she asked Trude.

"He means Gouda. They say Gouda like how-da."

"Really?"

Trude nodded and turned back to a boy on her right. They began debating politics.

"Yes." Joop reached for a handkerchief to wipe the rain from his brow. "It's quite delicious. I love it." After a moment, he said, "What do you study?"

"Oh no, I am staying in London. Not studying. Working."

"What kind of working?"

"I help at a Jewish relief agency."

His smile lightened, "Are you Jewish?"

She shrugged. "No. Are you?"

"No. Have you helped many people?"

"There are more people than there is help that we can give. What do you study?"

"Ah. Logic and mathematics," he said. "I love it. It's like music. Do you want to dance?"

"But there isn't anything playing."

"There isn't?" He began to sway. "You don't hear anything?"

Until that moment, she'd always thought she was the only one who heard music when there was none. That it was better to keep that to herself. "No, I don't." It was too good to be true. Marigold smiled at this handsome stranger.

"Does that mean you're saying, *I won't dance don't ask me, I won't dance don't ask me?*"

Which brought her laugh right out and sing, "*I won't dance monsieur with you,*" and they moved, singing and dancing, "*My heart won't let my feet do things that they should do.*"

When the last call sounded, Joop asked, "Do you have a card?"

"I live on King's Road in Chelsea. Number 275."

"May I write to you?"

Marigold sipped her beer, wiping the foam from her lip. Unlike the beer in New York, it was cold and delicious. There was nothing vaguely foul about it.

She smiled and then nodded, "Yes, you may."

THE NEXT DAY, Trude walked her to the station.

Marigold stole a glance at her friend and felt suddenly shy. "Are you keen on Joop?"

Trude shrugged. "He's very clever. He's kind, too."

"So, you like him?"

"Oh, I don't know. I mean, what's not to like?" Marigold wondered if she was teasing her. "All the boys here are brainy."

Oh god, Marigold thought, just tell me, Trude. "Is Joop keen on you?"

Trude pretended to look serious. "If he is, he hasn't said anything. I wouldn't be surprised, though."

"All boys are keen on you, Trude."

Trude chuckled. "It must be my animal magnetism." Then she raised just one eyebrow, adding, "After all, what man can resist a spy?" She then dropped her voice and said in her best Greta Garbo, "You know, like Mata Hari."

"What if I have a crush on him?"

"Ah, now that didn't take very long." Trude folded her arms across her chest. "Don't tell me, you love him."

"Would that be a problem?"

"Well, Joop is a genius," Trude said, as if that were the determining factor.

"Really?"

Trude nodded. "But there's quite a lot of them here. It's a refreshing change, really. I mean the boys still act like idiots, but a lot of them are surprisingly brilliant, too."

"So, what does that mean?"

The conductor shouted, "All aboard!"

Marigold entered the compartment. She lowered the window and leaned out, "Do you love him, Trude?"

To which Trude laughed but didn't answer as the train pulled out of the station.

* * *

"Where did you learn to take pictures?" Marek studied her prints with a magnifying glass. He examined one, and then another.

"Oh, I had a Brownie forever. My dad says that with a Brownie, anyone can be a photographer."

Marek said, "That may be so, but you didn't take these with a Brownie. The clarity and the precision of the light. What did you use?"

Shyly she said, "My friend Trude gave me a Leica."

He studied a picture she'd taken of the local flower seller, whose nose was deep in a bouquet of roses. There was one of a man watching a woman leave a phone box. Marek murmured, "I can only imagine what he's thinking." Then there were several of Falaise with her cat, clearly devoted, sitting together as kindred spirits.

Marek nodded. "Very nice. Very nice work, indeed, Marigold.

You have a great eye and clearly, a point of view. You take a good picture."

At this, she looked down. He was so kind.

The next day he watched her in the darkroom as she placed film into the enlarger.

"You know your way around."

"The man I bought film from has shown me a lot."

"Where's that?"

"In New York."

"As I said yesterday, you take a good picture. Now let's teach you to take great ones."

* * *

"Darling, there's not going to be a war." Hushed voices, enormous chandeliers, and windows looking out at Piccadilly. Marigold glanced at Zosia and then at the handsome Englishman sitting across from them. His name was Alex Reilly. "Versailles guaranteed that." He finished the last of his savory tart.

The day before, Zosia had insisted Marigold join them. "It'll be tea at the Ritz. It's really a must. You need to get out more." Now they sat in the magnificent room at a table covered with savories and cakes, but Zosia's expression was impossible to read.

"Alex"—Zosia leaned toward him— "the annexation of Austria is in direct violation, is it not? And now"—her voice trembled slightly— "I pale at the thought—"

"From all reports both Austrians and Germans are ecstatic at becoming one country. Economically, it can only help them."

Marigold opened her mouth to ask a question, but after the look on Zosia's face, thought better of it.

Afterward, Alex hailed them a cab outside the hotel. "I'm off to my club," he announced, and kissed Marigold on the cheek. "Lovely to meet you." He smiled at her. He really was very good looking. Then he kissed Zosia on the lips. "Tomorrow at seven?" And Zosia nodded, Marigold thought somewhat wistfully.

The taxi crept forward a thousand feet. The park was on their left. "He's very eligible," Zosia said. "His wife died last year. He has a little girl, Emily. She's rather sweet, you would like her."

"Oh?" Marigold didn't know many younger children.

Zosia continued, "His family, they're printers. They work with the Bank of England. They're quite rich. Well, at least they used to be."

"Zosia?"

"Yes, darling."

"When everyone's talking about politics, I don't quite—"

"Sometimes, it's best to remain silent, I'm afraid."

"I don't understand why all these people have to leave their home."

"It's because they're being declared enemies of the state."

"By who?"

"By the authorities, Marigold. The government. If people say or do things which are perceived as not sufficiently adulatory, then the next thing that happens is they lose their position, or they're arrested, or told they can no longer travel. Then they're harassed, until things become so impossible that they have no choice but to get out. And it's not just political agitators to whom this is happening. It's people like my brother, who are artists, or who are perceived as not Aryan."

"Aryan?"

"By which I mean white. Sadly, some people don't decide to leave until after the authorities have stolen everything that belonged to them in the first place."

"I don't understand."

"People who want to leave must pay a tax to get permission. But because the government's already stolen their assets, these people don't have enough funds to get out. It's just appalling."

"But why do their governments treat them that way?" She thought about her father and the glowing comments he'd make about Germany.

Zosia answered, "Because Adolf Hitler and Benito Mussolini

are fascists. They believe that you are either with or against them. If you are against them, they will make life a living hell for you. And I don't believe for one second that all of Austria is celebrating being annexed. That's absurd."

"Zosia—"

"Marigold. I am so glad that you are helping at Woburn House. This work is incredibly important. It's vital that those who can, leave."

"Zosia, you know, there are some people, some men for example, who aren't even considered by the Aid Society. If they manage to get here, they're sent directly to internment camps."

Zosia looked away for a moment. "I know. They're resident aliens and if we go to war, they'll be enemies of the state. It's dreadful."

The taxi inched forward. Rows of daffodils in the seemingly endless park beckoned to them and Marigold wished she had her camera. It was time to start taking pictures again.

"Let's walk," Marigold said.

Zosia smiled and swung her high-heeled shoe a fraction of inch. "No, let's not."

So, they stayed in the cab, going nowhere quickly.

* * *

"Good morning, Miss McGrath." The door to the elusive Colonel Mayhew's office was open, ready for his morning cup of tea.

"Morning!" Marigold glanced at the stacks of applications on her desk. They'd grown taller as the days progressed. But she was more consumed with the letters she'd exchanged with Joop than she was with those struggling to flee Germany. He was coming to London and had asked her to dinner and to see a movie. She wondered if Trude had been straight with her on whether she wanted Joop for herself.

"I don't have time for affairs of the heart, Mari," Trude had said. "I'm going to be a legal genius instead."

Marigold brought the colonel his tea and biscuits and he asked, "What do you have for us this morning, Miss McGrath?"

"Several vacancies. The best one is a request from Lord and Lady Soames, for an assistant housekeeper at their house in Somerset."

"How a cabaret singer would fit that bill is beyond me," muttered Mrs. Krumbull.

"Now, now, Mrs. Krumbull"—Colonel Mayhew smiled—"I'm sure many a singer would make a fine servant."

Marigold read the posting. "She must be able to liase with the house manager and butler, coordinate deliveries, and supervise the kitchen staff."

"Candidates?"

"There are three very good ones." She handed the Colonel applications from a torch singer, a ballet dancer, and a poet. "None of them have young families, so for them to travel without their husbands should not present any problems."

"Good! Very good. Put forth the poet and the dancer. I'm afraid the singer is somewhat known and will suffer from such a diminished status in a way the others might not."

Only briefly did Marigold imagine women saying goodbye to lives they were leaving behind. She gave the colonel a little smile, her mind on the night ahead of her.

THE UNDERGROUND WAS the quickest way back to Sloane Square, and from there she hopped onto the first bus going down the King's Road. Her navy dress with the lace collar was a good choice. Trude had given her some wonderful red lipstick, and her recent haircut had turned out very well. Trude flashed across her mind again. If she'd been interested in Joop, surely she would have said so.

"Mooi." Joop smiled when she met him at the door.

"What does that mean?"

"Beautiful." Which made Marigold's heart do a little leap.

"Well, hello to you, too." Marigold pulled the door shut behind them. The bus seemed to appear magically as if on cue. They jumped onto the back and climbed up the stairs to sit in the front where the curves were the tightest and the ride the most thrilling.

"Do you like Fred Astaire?" Joop was far better looking than she remembered.

"Oh my gosh, do I ever." Particularly without his papier-mâché carnival mask.

"Well then, tonight is *Carefree*. It's playing in Leicester Square. But first—" He pulled the bell. "Spaghetti."

It was a humble restaurant where the waiter brought them mountains of pasta rising above sauce and topped with several meatballs. When he offered them cheese, Joop said, "Yes please."

"Like so?"

"A little more." The waiter obliged and Joop gestured with his hand. "Yes, please, just a bit more, please."

The waiter left them and Joop filled Marigold's glass. She watched him relish every mouthful, even as he inhaled his food at the same time, as if he hadn't eaten in days. Then he paused for a moment and said, "Fred Astaire movies are so"—He looked for the word— "witty and . . . and . . ."

"Sophisticated?"

"Yeah!" Joop pressed his lips together and sucked in the last strand of spaghetti. "I think if that is life in New York or in America, then wow! That is really something."

"Well, New York is a little bit different than that." She took a sip of her wine. What had happened with Alan, and his having a fiancée the entire time they'd been in that broom closet. What if Joop was involved with Trude? She couldn't hurt Trude.

"Marigold?"

"Yes?"

He gestured gently toward her chin.

"Oh!" She dabbed her napkin against her face. "Did I get it?"

He gestured again. "Almost."

She moved the napkin.

"Nearly."

She moved it again.

"That's nearly it!"

Then she realized Joop was teasing. She flicked the napkin at him. "I guess I'm not very sophisticated, am I?"

He said, "You are to me."

As THE CINEMA lights went down, the British Pathé newsreel began.

"GERMAN TROOPS MARCH INTO AUSTRIA!
Since the Treaty of Versailles was signed in 1919, there have been only a few really momentous days in the history of Europe..."

A procession of troops, motorcycles, and armed vehicles was shown rolling into Vienna while throngs of people saluted, shouting "Heil Hitler!"

Massive banners emblazoned with swastikas unfurled from balconies and windows onto the street below. Her father's lapel pin, and Mamie Fenton's euphoric chirping about the Reich flashed in Marigold's mind. She thought of her late mother and shivered convulsively. Joop put his arm around her shoulder. She glanced up at him. His jaw was clenched, and he looked unspeakably sad.

Leaving the theater, he said, "I'm sorry about the newsreel."

"Do you think there'll be a war?"

"I don't know. The Netherlands . . . we were neutral in the last one. But my father, he was at Oxford, too. He joined the RFC."

"Was he an airman?"

"Briefly. He was injured then went home."

"Are you sure you don't have a girlfriend?"

"Sure, there are lots of girls I think are my friends."

"You know that's not what I mean, Joop."

"Are you asking if I have a sweetheart?"

"Do you?"

"It depends." They approached Piccadilly Circus. The traffic sped around the statue of Eros and the neon lights lit up the sky. "You know, Marigold, I am interested in category theory. And using category theory you could argue that girlfriends or a sweetheart could be defined by how we classify them or categorize them. If someone goes from a friend to a girlfriend to a sweetheart, we would have to examine which functors would transform this person from one category to the next."

"What is a functor?"

"Ha! It would be the function of this group of women, or sweethearts or what have you."

"This sounds to me like you're avoiding the question."

"No!" He looked at her very closely. The brightness of the signs overhead made it possible to see each other as if it were daylight. "I am just a little bit shy."

"Trude said you're a genius."

"Oh, you American girls will say anything won't you?"

"But why did she say that? What is it you study?"

"Category theory is a kind of maths."

"Oh."

"Don't you like numbers?"

"Well, I've had some bad experiences."

"But numbers are beautiful. You find them in nature, you find them in money, in music, everything. You take pictures, no? When you set up the viewfinder, surely your perspective is impacted by how you interpret the numbers. Being close, being far, it's the same thing. For me, what I love are statistics. But Oxford doesn't have the specific . . . well, the professor it turns out I should like to work with now isn't here."

"In Piccadilly?"

"Ha! No. No, he's in Leiden. It's where the ideas for this discipline are. At least for what I am studying. So, let's take a hypothesis, say, the amount of meatballs needed per night according to the dishes offered, times the number of guests, then the nights of the week, compounded by the price of sausage for the meatballs and you have an idea—"

"My father works at IBM."

"Really? Is he a scientist?"

"He works with, um, it's called, uh, data processing. With punch cards and such."

"Yes, it all comes back to numbers and how we tame them, how we wrestle an idea and express it so it becomes useful information. It's beautiful, no? Like what happens to music with dancing."

Joop gestured to the Eros statue, and to the brightly lit signs all around them. He said, "You know what is a lumen?"

"Yes, I do." She smiled, pleased to show she was not without a few technical chops of her own. "It's how much light comes from a lightbulb."

"Yes, so imagine, that for each of these bulbs together, casting millions of lumens into the night sky, what would happen if," He snapped his fingers, "if we turn the switch, everything is gone."

"But it wouldn't be gone."

"No, it would be just, shrouded in darkness. As if it were gone. Or like tonight, in the approaching fog. It's incredible, no?"

He took her hand, "I think about these things, and it makes me feel. . . feel like . . . Fred Astaire. This girl I would like to be my sweetheart will show that she is so when . . ." He looked up at the neon lights all around them. "Imagine, so many lights and so many people. We can divide the number of people by the number of lights and multiply it by those who are a little bit shy."

"Joop! What does this girl becoming your sweetheart depend on?"

"On whether you'd like to dance, Mademoiselle Marigoude

Goudesbloem!" Still holding her hand, they raced across the circle, dodging the cars that honked in annoyance. "Sydney Kyte and his orchestra are at the Piccadilly Hotel. Let's go be sophisticated!"

Her heart was pounding. He thought of her as his sweetheart. "I'm not really dressed for it."

"Then we will dance here." He led her around to the service side of the building. A window was open and the music poured through it. Someone from the kitchen sat on the stoop smoking a cigarette. Joop held out his arms and began swaying. She stepped forward. She wasn't hurting Trude.

"Joop." Marigold looked up at him.

He looked down at her. "Gouda."

"Joop!" He was no Fred Astaire, and standing there in the alley with his gaze smoldering such intensity she thought she'd keel over laughing.

The music became quicker and Joop's gracefulness surprised her. Pedestrians cut through the alley and stepped around them while he spun her about as if they were floating. His smile and their floating filled her with joy. The events abroad were miles away. Politics had nothing to do with them. Nothing to do with them at all.

Spring

U.S. Department Of State

FOR THE PRESS -MARCH 24, 1938

This Government has become so impressed with the urgency of the problem of political refugees that it has inquired of a number of Governments in Europe and in this hemisphere whether they would be willing to cooperate in setting up a special committee for the purpose of facilitating the emigration from Austria and presumably from Germany of political refugees. Our idea is that whereas such representatives would be designated by the Governments concerned, any financing of the emergency emigration referred to would be undertaken by private organizations within the respective countries. Furthermore, it should be understood that no country would be expected or asked to receive a greater number of emigrants than is permitted by its existing legislation. In making this proposal the Government of the United States has emphasized that it in no sense intends to discourage or interfere with such work as is already being done on the refugee problem by any existing international agency. It has been prompted to make its proposal because of the urgency of the problem with which the world is faced and the necessity of speedy cooperative effort under government supervision if widespread human suffering is to be averted.

* * *

"WHY DON'T YOU TRY THIS?" MAREK HANDED Marigold a small box. "Think of it as a step up."

A gasp of pleasure escaped her lips. It was the Rolleicord camera.

"It's not quite the same as mine, but close. You'll be able to master the basic techniques. I think you'll like it."

"I know I will! Oh thank you, Marek." They loaded film into each of their cameras and he showed her the basics to get started.

"Find something you want to capture. Have fun."

As Mr. Ganz and now Marek both instructed, her camera was always at the ready. She photographed Trude in Oxford wearing a cap and gown, her chin resting in her hand, her gaze off to the left, both skeptical and beautiful. Joop punting on the river in Oxford, Marigold's scarf hanging from the long pole, fluttering like a flag, everything reflected back in the water.

Trude in a hat, the brim down at a jaunty angle.

Joop on a bicycle, his arms straight up in the air.

The changing of the guard in their beefeater hats, one of them smiling in spite of himself.

Learning the Rolleicord wasn't impossible. She could manage it.

MEETING IN FRANCE ON REFUGEES URGED
Paris Accepts U.S. Suggestion for July Session at Evian

The United States Government has suggested that the first meeting of the intergovernmental committee to facilitate the migration of political refugees from Germany and Austria be held on July 6 at Evian, France, the State Department announced tonight. The French Government it was declared, has welcomed the suggestion. More than thirty governments have agreed to cooperate in the movement, and the United States has been consulting with them for some time. The State Department said the suggestion of the July 6 date at Evian was put forward "in order that the committee may meet with as little delay as possible."

— New York Times, May 12, 1938

Summer

Then Joop left for summer.

It had been only days but soon felt as though it had been months if not years since she'd seen him. The applications at Woburn House increased by the hundreds, and as Marigold continued typing in triplicate or sorting the boxes, Joop's playfulness filled her mind. More of the applications were placed into boxes labeled "No" than the ones labeled "Yes" and she imagined his statistical analysis of the trend. She thought of the smell of his soap and the way his collars were starched.

In the darkroom at Lark Mews, she studied the contact sheets. Every picture but one was cut off at the top. Damnit, she groaned, then wailed, "What am I doing wrong?"

"Steady on, steady on old thing." Marek looked at the contact sheet. "You've been using the top lens as the aperture instead of the other way around."

"I'm just not good at this."

"I beg your pardon."

"I seem to only get so far and then everything falls apart."

"Now why is that?"

"Because my boyfriend's gone!" She picked up the cat and buried her face in its neck.

Marek sighed. "Come on. Let's get a cocktail. And bring your camera. You're going to master this thing, Marigold. No wilting flowers here, my dear."

Obediently, she followed him to the Arts Club. Marigold stood beside a rosebush. Somehow, she couldn't help but sigh.

"Consider the water." Marek pointed to where its petals were still wet from rain earlier in the day. "Move a bit closer. Now, the top lens is how you'll focus the photo, and the bottom is where you adjust the aperture. Have you got it?"

"I think so." She pressed the shutter and advanced the film.

"Marigold," Marek said.

She turned toward him. He was watching her, a cigarette between his fingers, the other hand on his waist. She looked down at the viewfinder. "Yes, Marek." With the smallest of smiles in spite of herself.

His smile echoed hers. They were almost the same. She pressed the button. She advanced the film then turned and photographed Falaise who had joined them.

Falaise said, "Are you sad because that young man has left for summer?"

Wordlessly Marigold nodded. She looked at Falaise through the view finder.

"Well, there are many, many fish in the sea, dear."

"Listen to Falaise, Marigold." Marek said, "She's very wise."

Falaise held up her hand and placed her pocketbook behind her feet. "There dear, now go ahead."

Marigold adjusted the aperture. She wound the film and pressed the button.

* * *

MARIGOLD FOLLOWED Mrs. Krumbull into the colonel's office. Her back tingled, sensing Colonel Mayhew watch how she carried the tea and biscuits. He said, "We should have an attractive contingent, Mrs. Krumbull, do you not agree?"

"Colonel," Mrs. Krumbull passed him several forms for his signature. "I had rather thought our commitment to those we assist would be the determining factor."

"But, yes, England. Coming on the heels of Chamberlain, we can appear so . . . dreary really. We'll be in France, Miss Breen. It's important we give our allies something they can enjoy, what."

"Colonel Mayhew!"

"We should convey an air of optimism, at the very least. To that end, let's bring Miss McGrath in addition to Miss Breen. At least while papers are being presented. Her president is the one organizing this thing. We should offer someone easy on the eyes, to indicate we like their way of thinking, what."

"Will that be all, Colonel?" Marigold asked. It was impossible to keep from smiling.

"Yes, thank you, Miss McGrath."

WHEN MARIGOLD TOLD her about the conference in Evian, Trude said, "I know, let's meet in Lausanne. There's a snazzy jazz club there. You'll love it."

"How on earth will I get to Lausanne?"

"You just take a ferry, silly. It's as easy as pie." She spooned some sugar into her tea. Marigold admired how the tissue in Trude's shopping bag peeked upward, much like the ribbon on Trude's hat. "Then after the conference, you could spend the rest of the summer with me if you like. Marigold, why don't you?"

"I can't. My work is . . . apparently, it seems to matter."

Trude was thoughtful for a moment. "Yes, it does, actually. It does matter, Marigold."

* * *

AT KING'S ROAD, Falaise called to her up the stairs, "Marigold dear! We've a new lodger. Come and meet dear Norbert."

"Please, call me Buddy." He loomed over them but had the face of a young boy. "My friends call me Buddy." Buddy was thin as a rail. His clothes were ill fitting, but he was handsome enough. Yet he sounded like a fool, with his comical accent. Like something out of *Li'l Abner*.

"Buddy then," Falaise beamed, "This is darling Marigold.

She's been here a few months. She'll show you the ropes, dear, won't you Marigold?"

Marigold shrugged. "Charmed, I'm sure."

Buddy's room was in the attic, directly above Marigold's. "What brings you here, Norbert?" At the top of the landing, she watched him bring up his record player. In another box was a wireless radio. She saw him lug that up next.

"Buddy, please."

"Buddy, then."

"I've landed a job with Ed Murrow," he said.

"Who's that?" Lastly, he brought up his small, beat-up suitcase.

He stopped on the stairs. "You don't know?"

Marigold shook her head. "Should I?"

"He heads the news division of CBS."

"Oh. Hmm. Well, it was nice meeting you." She went into her room and collapsed on the bed. She missed Joop so much she thought she might choke.

THE NEXT MORNING, Falaise called up to the top of the stairs. "Buddy dear, join us for breakfast, won't you?"

He ate enough for a half-dozen men. "I'll finish this. I'll eat that." He said, "These eggs are delicious, Falaise."

She asked him questions and then promptly raised her ear horn when he started to speak. "How fascinating!" Falaise exclaimed. "Isn't Buddy a marvel?"

Marigold buttered her toast and said, "A marvel, I'm sure."

"Are all girls from New York as friendly as you?" he asked as they walked to the bus.

"Not by half."

"Well then, I'll just have to hope for the best. Do you know how I get to Portland Place?"

"What's at Portland Place?"

"The BBC Broadcasting House. I can't believe you don't

know this stuff! Someone said something about a number 22 bus?"

"You're going to need an A to Zed, Buddy."

"What's that?"

"It's a map showing every single street everywhere in this city. The cab drivers know them by heart. That's how they get their cabbie license."

"Is that a fact?"

"Yes, Buddy. It's a fact," She gave him a considered look. He had to be putting her on. "Are you always this—"

"Yes?"

"This, gosh shucks, well, gee whiz? Or is that an act?"

"Marigold, I'm just trying the best I can to get by. I'm in an incredible city on an amazing adventure. Aren't you?"

"Well—"

"If I don't have the suave sophistication of, of . . ."

"Yes?"

"William Powell."

"I don't like William Powell."

"Well, then, Cary Grant. There's not much I can do about that. I'll just have to ask you to bear with me now."

"What are you doing at the BBC?"

"I told you. I'm working for Ed Murrow."

"Who's that?"

"He's a reporter for CBS."

"Oh. I don't really follow the news."

"In a few months, I reckon you'll be following it all the time."

"I doubt that." Marigold thought he was terribly naïve.

He laughed. "Suit yourself." A series of buses pulled up just ahead. "Say, is that my bus?"

"Yes, quick! The next one isn't for a while."

She watched his legs pick up speed as he raced toward the bus. The conductor rang the bell. Buddy leapt on the back as it pulled away from the corner. He cupped his hand to his mouth, and called out, "You'll be listening to the news all the time!"

* * *

"Oh, Buddy, you are a darling, aren't you?" Falaise fawning on him was so annoying. But then Marigold thought guiltily, why shouldn't Falaise fawn on him? He was kind, good-looking, and he could move furniture that was too heavy for the two women to do alone.

"Bye, Miz F. You have a nice day now." He grabbed some toast and raced out the door. He left early and returned late. And he was so irritating! It irked her that everything about him was so likeable and nothing about him reminded her of Joop. Sometimes Marigold heard him finding the jazz station on his wireless upstairs. Then he'd start singing. It was just too much.

Whenever he spoke, Marigold could barely keep from roaring with laughter at Buddy's backwater style. Falaise had invited Zosia to join them for drinks on the terrace off the kitchen. The geraniums were in full bloom, and the fretworked walls of the building covered in ivy. The afternoon light off the Thames lit the scene in a way Marigold knew she should fetch her camera.

"I should take a picture."

"By jiminy, I reckon you should." Buddy was perched in a deck chair, his long legs folded like a cricket.

Marigold began to chuckle.

"What's so funny?" he asked with a simple smile.

Marigold shook her head. "Come on Buddy, nobody says 'by jiminy' like that."

Falaise put down her ear trumpet and gave Marigold a considered look. Zosia raised her eyebrows and stirred sugar in her tea.

"At least nobody here." Which she immediately regretted, realizing she'd been out of line, if not simply rude. What was it? Was she jealous of how everyone took to him?

Buddy's smile widened. "Well, maybe I'll start a trend. I mean, dang gun it, by jiminy, who knows? Anything's possible."

Zosia nodded approvingly. "That's right. Anything's possible, isn't it Marigold, darling?"

After he left, Zosia admonished her, "Don't get in trouble with that boy." Not knowing that Marigold was already in love with somebody else.

And she'd kept her own counsel, because that somebody else was truly the most marvelous person she had ever known.

"How exciting!" Falaise crowed at the Arts Club. "An international conference. My heavens."

"Well, I'm only one of six."

"And what will be your job, dear?"

"I'm to take notes and distribute copies of the colonel's presentation."

"Splendid! Splendid. Let's go to Peter Jones. There's a darling trouser suit which will be perfect on you."

Paris to Evian-les-Bains was a night train in a Pullman car. In addition to their own luggage, Marigold and Miss Breen had abstracts, handouts, letterhead, and a typewriter. Once in Paris they'd have to change stations, which involved tipping porters, hailing a cab, and cooperating with each other. Finally, at the station bistro of the Gare de Lyon, they sat down to order lunch.

Marigold took in the gilded ceilings, the frescoes, and the shiny brass lamps. "Wow. We don't have anything like this at the stations in New York." She wondered how Mr. Ganz in New York would recommend she photograph it.

When the waiter brought their food to the table, Miss Breen eyed the plat du jour with suspicion. "How is it?"

Marigold sighed and finished chewing. "It's delicious."

"I can't abide saucy French muck." Miss Breen studied the mushrooms on her fork. "Just a lamb chop suits me best."

Marigold said nothing and continued to stare at the vaulted ceiling.

When they boarded the train, and the porter set up their beds, Miss Breen crossed her arms. "I suppose you'll want the lower bunk."

"It doesn't matter to me, Miss Breen. Truly, it's your pick." To which Miss Breen remained silent. Marigold said, "I'll choose on the way back. Please. You decide for the way down."

Miss Breen placed her purse on the lower bunk. "Well then. I'll sleep here."

Marigold climbed onto the upper one and could hear Miss Breen's sighs as she prepared to sleep below. Marigold carefully removed the letter from her handbag.

"Evian is quite a distance from Amsterdam. Why don't we meet in Paris? We'll dance together at the Bastille, and we can do so on Bastille Day, no less! Please wire me when you get to Evian, Gouda. I want to know you are safe and to know you are coming to Paris. JOOP.

Marigold smiled and closed her eyes. Joop. Paris. Kissing. All of it was too wonderful to imagine.

* * *

Situated on the shore of Lake Geneva, Evian les Bains was beautiful, and the weather sublime. Every hotel was booked to capacity. There were dignitaries from thirty-two countries, each with their own entourage as well as two hundred members of the press corps in attendance. For civil servants who'd known each other, or wanted to know each other, amongst the philanthropists, philosophers, and other people of interest, the conference at Evian was the pinnacle event of the summer.

Mornings were spent at the Hôtel Royal with various meetings and symposia followed by meals and drinks and more meetings. Pretty girls such as Marigold and her ambitious male counterparts fought for pride of place behind the delegates, running messages and sending out wires for the governments at home.

A telegram from Trude arrived the first night. There was nothing from Joop.

Marigold told Miss Breen about the invitation. They were sharing a room to keep down expenses. The jazz club across the lake was just a twenty-minute ride on the ferry.

"Why don't you come with me?" Marigold said. "We can go after the supper."

"It sounds ill advised," Miss Breen declared.

"Miss Breen, it might be really fun."

Miss Breen's hair was in curlers and she tied a hairnet up over them. "And what time would we leave? What time would we come back?"

"We'll take the 8:10 and return on the 12:05. We'll be sound asleep before two. Do you like jazz?"

Miss Breen's usual scowl vanished and a pair of dimples appeared, "I do actually. I like it very much." It occurred to Marigold that Miss Breen wasn't much older than herself and that when she smiled, she was quite lovely.

THE FERRY WAS PACKED and the water surprisingly rough, but the club could be seen from the pier.

A burly man in a dinner jacket was stationed at the door. "Down the stairs, ladies."

Music and smoking, women in gowns, and everyone dancing. Trude was at a table in the front row. She was with a pair of soldiers. Instinctively, the girls took a step back.

Trude saw them. "Don't worry! They're Swiss." She smiled. "This is Eduard and this is Pierre." Both of the men stood and gave a small bow. They were very attractive.

"Trude, this is Elizabeth," she said of Miss Breen.

"Charmed!" said Miss Breen.

"What can I get you ladies?" the waiter asked.

"We're drinking Gin Daisies," Trude suggested.

"That's sounds splendid," said Miss Breen.

"Make it two," said Marigold.

The band was extraordinary, and within moments Miss Breen was swaying to the music. Marigold wondered if she was tipsy.

"So why are you lads in uniform?" Miss Breen asked. "I thought your country is neutral."

"Indeed, we are," said Pierre. "But we still have armed forces. One has to have security."

"Yes, I suppose that's true. But how are you at dancing?"

Pierre stood and offered her his hand. "Care to find out?"

Marigold and Trude watched as the pair began to dance like world winning champions. There was no stopping Elizabeth Breen. She laughed and swooped and spun and laughed some more.

At the break, she tottered over to them. "My heavens, I need to take my specs off. They're making me sweat something dreadful. Could you order another one of those cocktails, dearie?"

It was getting close to midnight. "We have to go, Miss Breen."

"More's the pity. I did have the time of my life."

"Thank you very much, Miss Breen." Pierre took her hand and bowed deeply over it. "With that conference across the lake, we thought the only girls here would be some of those yid sluts. And instead, we meet you lovely ladies."

The three girls froze.

Trude straightened her back. "Ah, what a pity." Her smile was glacial. "Because I am Jewish. You had it right the first time. Good night."

Outside the club Trude's chauffeur waited by the door.

Sitting on the ferry Marigold watched the approaching shoreline and the lights reflected in the water. There was nothing to say. That the night's companions turned out to be so hateful made the silence even worse.

She imagined Trude's car ride to wherever it was Trude was staying. They never discussed who was Jewish and who was not. Neither girl was religious. It simply wasn't a topic of discussion.

"A cable for mademoiselle," the night clerk handed Marigold a slip of paper with the room key. Marigold said nothing, her heart hammering in her chest.

Inside their room, Miss Breen's mouth had resumed its usual straight line. "We shan't be doing that again."

"No." Marigold walked to the bathroom, her toothbrush and telegram in the same hand.

Miss Breen rubbed her face with cold cream. "We'd be well advised to say nothing more about it." She placed her hair in curlers and tied a kerchief around them. "Would you not agree?"

"Understood," Marigold said. "Good night."

Miss Breen pulled a sleep mask over her eyes. Marigold closed the bathroom door. Next to Miss Breen's toothbrush, alongside a pair of earrings, was a slim golden chain. Hanging from the chain was a delicate Star of David.

* * *

See you under clock tower at Gare de Lyon on Bastille Day. Tell me what time you can make it STOP

I will be there grosses bises. JOOP

AFTER SIX DAYS, the participants at the conference were agreed. Heartbreaking plight of the refugees or no, none of the countries in the international community could propose a meaningful solution. Only the Dominican Republic offered a sizable number of visas. They would take in 100,000 refugees. When asked, their officials explained that their government wanted to "lighten" the skin of the Dominican population.

REFUGEE TASK LOOMING AS ENORMOUS PROBLEM

Evian Conference Finds Plethora of Good Intentions: but Scarcity of Material Collaboration

Where can a million persecuted Jews and others go now from countries which seek to get rid of them? And where can perhaps another million find refuge from lands which in the future may try to get rid of them? That is the grave question before the Evian Inter-Governmental Conference, meeting on the banks of Lake Leman, across the water from Geneva.

— – NY TIMES, July 10, 1938

Miss Breen looked up from her typewriter. "What's the matter with you?"

"I received a cable from a dear friend of my late mother's. Tante Sophie."

Miss Breen kept typing, then handed the copy to Marigold.

Marigold added the paper to the handouts for the delegates. "Tante Sophie lives in Paris, but she's taken ill. I had told her that we're here at least till next Friday, but now I'm afraid I might be too late."

"Too late for what?"

"Tante Sophie is very ill."

Miss Breen said nothing.

"She's at the American Hospital."

Miss Breen raised an eyebrow and handed Marigold another form. "Yes, I'm sure she is."

Marigold bowed her head over papers to be collated.

Finally, Miss Breen said, "Suit yourself, but I can't imagine what Colonel Mayhew is going to say." They were packing up the boxes and papers to go back to London.

"Why should he mind?" Marigold labeled the different countries' speeches. "He's already given his presentation and tomorrow is merely a summation of meetings which have already occurred."

"We're supposed to journey back on Friday's train." The horizontal line in place of Miss Breen's smile had emphatically returned. The time in France had only widened the gulf between them.

"I'll meet you at the ferry," Marigold said. "It's Friday at two, isn't it?"

Miss Breen shrugged again. "Suit yourself."

HER HEART THUMPING, blood singing, Marigold found a seat by the window on the Thursday morning five a.m. to Paris. She opened her camera case and fooled with the lens. Delegates and journalists had piled into the compartment and chatted back and forth, settling in for the journey home. Marigold pointed her camera out at the station platform through the window.

"How do you find that?" the man across from her asked. He gestured toward her Rolleicord.

"Er, I've only had it a few months. But so far so good. Do you have one?"

"I use UR Leica myself." He rolled his R's like a Scot, but had another accent as well.

"That's a beautiful camera."

The train pulled into a station. The Alps were on her right and the station was on her left. "I'll take your photo," the man said.

"Oh! Uh, thanks."

"You can send it to your parents. You're American, right?" His funny accent made her think of home, and all the different sounds she always heard in New York.

"Yes, I am." Then she realized London was like that, too. It was like home. But would her father even care about a photo taken by this stranger on a train? Marigold thought not. Falaise might like the photo though.

She handed him the camera then gave her hat a little tug, so it was angled forward over an eye.

"Very dapper," he said. "What'd you think of the conference?"

"Well . . ." How could she say she hadn't thought much of it at all? That she'd thought about dancing and the lake, those wretched rude soldiers, of her lost rapport with Miss Breen, and how she could not wait, could not wait to see Joop in a matter of hours. "It's very concerning."

"I thought it was outrageous. I have a sister and parents in Prague."

"Are you Czech?"

"I was. I'm British now. Married a Scottish girl. We have two kids, live in Dundee. I've booked my parents passage to leave, but—" he shook his head. "The whole thing is outrageous."

In PARIS, the train platform was mobbed. The line at the baggage check seemed endless so Marigold dragged her suitcase outside the station.

It had been raining, but the sky began to clear. She moved to step into the street.

"Ooopla!" A gentleman shielded her from the curb as a taxi splashed, barreling around the corner. "Faites attention, mademoiselle."

"Oui, merci." Her heart was so full, everyone seemed kindness itself. She turned back to face the station and saw the clock. Tentatively she made her way across the square and there he was, his blonde hair nearly white in the sunshine.

He trotted toward her. "Bonjour, mademoiselle!" He bent down and kissed her three times. He took her suitcase. "What shall we do with this? Would you like me to check it?"

"Yes, please." They had only a day, and she didn't want to drag it to and fro.

The receipt safely tucked inside her purse, Joop asked, "What shall we do?"

"I want to see everything." It was her first time in Paris. "Shall we just walk?"

"Not coffee with croissant first?" His accent made the word croissant comical in a loveable way.

"All right, coffee first." She worried she'd burst from smiling so much.

They sat at a café on the corner. There were trees and an adjacent street named for a mathematician. Watching his croissant crumbs fall into the plate whenever he took a bite, and then rest upon the corner of his lips, made Marigold want to watch him eat croissant every morning for the rest of her life. Pigeons shamelessly inched closer to their feet. Everyone wore sunglasses and the women had stylish scarves. Baguettes and flowers peeped from shopping baskets. Paris felt like heaven.

"Marigold, you are only here until dark?"

"Well—"

"When is your last train?" Truthfully, she hadn't decided quite yet. All she knew was that she would be here, and then she'd return to London. Also, the little plastic case from the doctor was tucked in that suitcase at the baggage claim. But it embarrassed her to admit such a thing.

"Oh, not for ages."

He kissed her hand and then asked, "Have you been to the Eiffel Tower?"

She shook her head. "I told you this is my first time here."

"Then let's go to the top!"

The streets continued to fill and someone began to play the accordion. "Ah," Joop said, "but first, we dance."

Afterwards, when she thought of that afternoon, she couldn't recall how he managed it or how he did it, but somehow, they were dancing more often than not, and the people around them seemed to dance, too. There were parades, flags, and well-wishers. There was sunshine and rosé wine. At the Eiffel Tower, they climbed the endless stairs, and it began to rain, causing the steps to become slick underfoot. At the top, the skies cleared. Marigold took out her camera.

"Excusez-moi," Marigold said to a pair of girls standing next to them.

"Bitte?" said one of them.

"Entshuldigen, Sie." Marigold blushed at their speaking German after a week of meetings about German villainy. It was odd to chat with people who came from the land that was tormenting and persecuting hundreds of thousands of Jews. But who could know what their position was?

"I'm Swiss!" Trude always shouted. Maybe these girls were refugees themselves.

Smoothly, in German, Joop asked them to take their picture. The girls smiled at him.

"Ja, naturlich," said one of the girls. She took Marigold's camera and said, "Oh I have this at home. I love it."

Joop placed his arm around Marigold's shoulder. The girl deftly took their photo. Then he placed his arm around Marigold's waist. And the girl took another.

Joop said, "Ich werde sie küssen. Ist das in Ordnung? (I'm going to kiss her, is that ok?)"

And the girls giggled, "Schon!"

"Gouda, please stand beside me. I'm going to lift you now."

"So long as you don't throw me off."

Joop placed his arm around Marigold's waist again. "Put your arm round my waist and lean against me." This time he lifted her, and her feet left the ground, both of their hands extended into the air. They turned their faces to each other.

Marigold said, "It's like the kissing Olympics."

And Joop gave her a long deep kiss.

The girl said, "Bravo! I got it."

Joop whispered to Marigold, "You're just a little bit heavy," and she thumped him gently on the arm. He laughed and said, "Just the right amount heavy."

Going back down, Marigold said, "Your German is beautiful, Joop."

At this he shrugged. "My mother's from Germany. We speak it a lot at home."

Marigold wondered how she hadn't known that.

Below the Eiffel Tower, they sat on the grass and he asked her about Evian.

"No one will take them, Joop. No one wants to do anything."

"Hmm."

"I went to meet Trude with a colleague."

"Oh yeah."

"It was wonderful, until . . ."

"What?"

"These soldiers said something . . . ugh."

"Don't think about that, Marigold. Let's think instead about this moment. Here at the Eiffel Tower, together. The Eiffel Tower, our posing like the Olympics and everything together. It's the spiritual expression of Leibniz's monad."

"What? What is that?"

"It's a math thing. One day I will explain it. Maybe today you need chocolat chaud instead."

They walked and walked along the Seine and studied the books for sale on the sidewalk. They crossed the river and walked through the Tuileries to a tearoom on the Rue de Rivoli. Joop said, "Deux chocolat chaud, s'il vous plait."

They sat at a small table surrounded by elegant Parisians and drank hot chocolate, which was so delicious Marigold thought she might weep. It was as if current events weren't happening, as if diplomats and statesmen weren't scurrying back and forth. "How do you know about this place?"

"My mother brought us when we were little. For the Dutch, the only thing as important as cheese is chocolate."

She made a face. "Joop."

"Is there anyone for whom you need a gift?" Joop's elbow was on the table and he gazed at her, smiling, his chin in his hand.

"For whom I need a gift ..." It only then occurred to her that she hadn't thought about anyone else. At all. She'd been so consumed with her trip, her experience, her happiness. She wondered when she'd become so thoughtless.

Wordlessly, she nodded.

"Who?"

"Something for Falaise. She's been just the best. Maybe Zosia, too."

Back on the street, it started to rain like in London, but then it stopped, because they were in Paris.

When the sun began to set, Joop asked, "When is your train?"

Marigold decided it wouldn't matter if she were late to the office. "I don't want to leave." If she missed unpacking Saturday, she would just make up for it Sunday. Besides, what was she supposed to do? Forgo being in Paris? She shrugged. "I want to stay a bit longer."

"Then I will show you something more, and something splendid too."

They walked to Montmartre where painters were hawking their wares. Then they walked down several hills and down flights of stairs until they were back on the Seine. A few benches were scattered here and there, facing the river.

They collapsed on a bench leaning against each other until Joop stood up. "I know this is wrong, but for some reason I cannot help it." He went around to the back of the bench. Marigold leaned over to watch him. There were names and initials carved into the wood. Joop discreetly removed a pen knife.

Marigold watched him carve J.K. + M.McG. 14.7.38 and then a small heart. "Have you done this before?"

"No." He shrugged and smiled. "Us boys just know about these things. In case when we're old, if the bench is still here, we can show our children."

She squeezed his hand and they kissed until the fireworks began. They leaned against each other again, no longer tentative, but longing for the moment to stay as it was, just like that, forever.

Eventually, Marigold asked, "What will you do if there's a war?"

"You mean when there's a war."

She could barely say the words. "Yes, when there's a war."

"We were neutral in the last one." He kissed her and then pushed her hair away from her face. "We'll be neutral again. The world cannot survive without Gouda cheese."

It was nearly midnight. They had walked and danced so much that Marigold's legs were like jelly. She said, "I can't walk another step, but I don't want to leave."

In response he said, "Let's try this," and he bent down, scooping her up so she sat on his shoulders. "Oopla!"

He staggered forward until he had his balance and shouted, "You're not so heavy, Marigoude!"

"Well merci beaucoup to you too!"

They came to a bridge. The streetlamps reflected the wet pavement and water below. Slowly, he let her down and they studied mermaids and dolphins carved from the bridge, frolicking on the river's side of the railing, larger than life, ready to jump into the Seine. Marigold took out her camera.

"I think my film's speed is ok." She looked at the bridge. She looked at him. She looked at the streetlights.

Paris was shrouded in romance. She pressed the button and advanced the film.

Joop said, "Gouda, you have surely missed every train to the ferry."

Marigold sighed. "Yes, I suppose so." Suddenly it began to rain again.

He kissed her and smiled. "We will need a place to stay."

"What do you suggest?" She wished she hadn't left that little box in her case.

"Let's go down there." Joop pointed further down the quai, where houseboats were tied along the edge.

"What are we going to do now?"

In response he grabbed her hand and led her to a small houseboat tethered to the dock. There was a padlock on the door. Joop said, "I know I shouldn't do this …" And he fiddled with the padlock.

She looked around to see if they were being observed. "Are you going to break it?" No one else was there. The city had gone to sleep.

The padlock sprang open. "I dabbled in very bad behavior growing up."

"Really? Do you still dabble in bad behavior?"

He placed his hand upon her cheek and said, "Only when I'm with American girls who are named after flowers." With his kind face, so full of gentle laughter, all doubt fell away, yet Marigold took a step away from him.

"Gouda, what is it?"

She whispered, "Everything is just really perfect."

Joop moved forward. He held her hands to his chest, then swayed the smallest bit, *"Isn't this a lovely night to be caught in the rain?"*

"The lyric is lovely day, Joop. Lovely day, not night."

"You were going on your way, now you've got to remain …" He sang and helped her step into the houseboat. The light from a streetlamp poured in through a hatch. Looking around, she took in the easels, the paints, the canvases and turpentine. And then she realized he was helping her off with her wet jacket and had carefully placed her hat on a table. A musty blanket was strewn across a chair.

Joop smoothed it onto the floor. "We can just wait out the rain," he murmured. "Do you mind, Marigoude?"

Which filled her with such desire she was afraid the péniche would ignite, but she shook her head the smallest amount, reminding her of her mother's tiny shake, just once to the left and then to the right.

"No, I don't mind," she whispered.

Joop took off his jacket and then his shirt. He glanced about for somewhere to drape them.

"There's a hook." Marigold pointed to one next to the door. He hung their things up, and then offered her his hand, which she placed on her breast. She helped him to unbutton her blouse, accidentally pulling off the button parallel to her bra. "Oh, well."

She smiled as he handed her the button. "I'll sew it back on for you, Marigold."

The answer to which was an endless kiss and Marigold was suddenly aligned with the world inside his tender hands. Awkwardly, they stumbled to the blanket on the floor, peeling off their wet trousers, their legs entangled with each other. Moving and slowly shuddering with love was the moment she had longed for.

AFTERWARD, Joop said, "I would like to take your picture."

"Why?" Marigold put on his spectacles with a serious expression.

"I think you know! We need to preserve this perfect moment."

"Oh Joop."

"I will take yours and then you can take mine. You don't have a flash, but do you think it's possible to take your picture now?"

"I don't know. We can try it."

There was a large lamp next to the mirror propped against a corner. The room filled with light. She pushed the glasses up to hold back her hair and leaned over Rolleicord. Joop placed an arm around her shoulder and kissed her cheek, and he looked, smiling, into the mirror as she pressed the button.

Then he placed the camera on the stool in front of the easel. "Beautiful Goudsbloem."

"Yes, Meneer Kasander."

"Say you are lekker." His smile was so tender. "Say, I am a lekker American girl."

WHEN THE SKY began to fade, Marigold remembered she was expected back in London before the end of the day. "I have to go."

Joop groaned, "Oh Gouda." He pulled her toward him. "What time is your train?"

They dressed and he expertly snapped the padlock back in position. They hurried across the gangplank, then Marigold stopped. "Joop. We forgot to put the blanket away."

"Then he'll know we were there. He'll have to invest in a better lock."

On the quai, they passed a man with a baguette. "Bonjour."

"Bonjour, monsieur," Marigold said. "Est ce que vous nous pourriez une grand faveur, s'il vous plait?" Marigold handed the man her camera, and he took pictures of them standing in front of the Seine.

"Merci! Merci!" they cried and ran toward the station, none of them knowing that it was he who had provided the lovers' shelter only hours before.

At the station, Joop said, "I promised my father I'd be at work today."

"I'm supposed to be at work, too."

He took her baggage claim ticket and stood in line, where the wait was an eternity. Joop asked, "What time is the ferry?"

"I don't know." Marigold really didn't know. At last, at last they were heading to the platform.

He walked her to the door of a compartment. "Gouda, will you be all right?"

"Yes of course. I'll write you."

"Marigold."

"Yes?"

"Ik houd van je."

"What?"

"I love you."

From Paris to Calais, the words 'I love you' rocked her to sleep. Then the train stopped. Marigold opened her eyes and checked her watch. They were in a field, surrounded by bright yellow crops. Calais was probably twenty minutes away.

She stood in the corridor until a conductor came by and apologized for the delay.

Eventually, the sunlight shifted and the shadow of the train rendered the fields a musky darker color. When they reached the port, it was nightfall.

"Ah no, Mademoiselle. We're expecting a storm. This evening's ferry has been cancelled."

"But—" She was expected in the office to unpack everything from Evian.

"Come back tomorrow," The man said and closed the blind of the ticket window.

Marigold sat on a bench against the far wall. There was no one else in the building. She felt suddenly small and rather stupid.

"Stop it, Marigold," she muttered and rolled her jacket into a pillow to lean against her suitcase. She imagined the headlines in the next day's paper. "American girl ravaged at the port of Calais!" She punched her jacket until it was more to her liking. "Smart girls from New York don't get ravaged." She said to the empty room. "At least they don't in Calais!"

It was Sunday night by the time the ferry resumed its schedule. The weather was terrible. Marigold lay down on a bench on deck, then sat up, wrestling seasickness, preferring to vomit over the rail, and not in the disgusting lavatories. She tried not to think about what to say to the Colonel and Mrs. Krumbull, because it was already Monday when the ferry arrived in Dover.

The train to London was filled with smokers, none of whom opened the windows. Still, the sunshine was glorious, and Marigold made her way directly to Woburn House.

MRS. KRUMBULL LOOKED up from her typewriter. "My goodness, but you're a fright." She stood up and pointed toward the lavatory. "Do something with your hair. Have you not slept?"

Marigold rinsed her face and pulled a comb through her hair. When she reemerged to sit at her desk, Mrs. Krumbull had already gone into the next office. Marigold looked at her inbox. It was overflowing with applications, some of which had photos of children. What was going to happen to them? Some of the faces looked to be very, very young. With her head throbbing, she stared at them, until she realized that the phone she heard ringing was the one on her desk.

She picked it up and mumbled, "Yes, may I help you?"

It was Colonel Mayhew. "Miss McGrath, please come into my office."

The colonel looked at her sadly. "I'm afraid you know what I'm going to say."

She fought back the urge to cry. "I made a mistake with the train schedule—"

"Miss McGrath."

"And then there was a storm on the channel and the ferry was delayed."

"Ah yes. That is regrettable. I'm afraid it's Mrs. Krumbull who runs the ship here, despite what you might think."

He waited a moment and then added, with a gentle smile, "If every girl like yourself should disappear upon a whim, whilst these children are losing their families, and their worlds are falling apart, we wouldn't be much help to them, would we? I'm very sorry, Marigold." He sighed, "It's time to go back to America, my dear."

She was too exhausted to cry. She cleaned her desk, attempting to not make a sound rather than face the humiliation of speaking with anyone. Mrs. Krumbull watched her take her things from the desk, while Miss Breen poured, as usual, over a typewriter.

On the bus, she ignored the other passengers who might be

wondering why she did indeed look so dreadful. Her hair was a mess, her makeup smeared, her clothes crushed.

The bus left her fifty paces from King's Road. Marigold knew her breath was horrible. It felt at least a lifetime since she'd slept. She'd lost her job, she'd misplaced her comb, and her button was missing from her blouse.

"Oh dear," Falaise said when Marigold entered the house. "I was afraid you'd been kidnapped."

"No," Marigold sighed, "but they did fire me at work."

"Are you all right? You look a fright, Marigold."

Marigold's lower lip trembled. "I . . . I'm fine. I just need to run an errand."

Inside her room, she threw down her bags then grabbed her UR Leica, running back down the stairs two at a time.

"Dear, you have some—"

Marigold said over her shoulder, "I won't be long!"

She found the boy who'd helped her on that first day. He was with his friends playing at World's End racing back and forth, kicking a ball, shouting and laughing.

Marigold called to him, "Hey, what's your name?"

"Well, I'm Kit, aren't I?"

She laughed, then looked through the lens and checked the light. "If you say so. I'm Marigold."

He saluted her. "Marigold, all right then."

She checked the speed.

It is the story you want to tell Mr. Ganz had said. *That will determine your point of view. Then everything else must become part of that story.*

"Marigold!" Kit shouted and waved to her. "Watch this!" He kicked the ball for her benefit. She pressed the button and advanced the film.

She shouted back. "Ignore me, I'm just trying something out."

How could she capture a boy's legs racing, his knees scraped, a sock dangling down to his ankle yet striving to connect with the ball? She moved closer and pushed the button. But was it his legs, or the whole person she wanted to catch? She wound the film and took the shot.

The sunlight moved and the shadows were longer, making the group of boys seem mythic in their play. The sunlight shifted again, and she continued to shoot the film. Their legs raced forward, crashing together, kicking the ball. Marigold loaded and reloaded the camera as the game moved into the darkness of a building obscuring the sun.

She squinted and took the shot.

Finally, exhausted, sweaty, and laughing, the boys called it a day. Keeping a good distance behind them, she photographed them as they walked back to the estate, holding the ball between them. A little girl in a blue cardigan passed from the other direction and, seeing the boys, wrinkled her nose with distaste. The boys continued, oblivious, until quite by chance Kit glanced over his shoulder at the girl, and then at Marigold, giving her the cheekiest of smiles.

Marigold pressed the button.

* * *

THE TELEGRAM and package were on the end of her bed. The telegram wasn't more than a few hours old. The package had been postmarked three weeks earlier. Marigold unwrapped the package. Inside was a letter and two boxes.

My dear Marigold,

> *Now that travel has become so difficult, I thought*
> *I should send you these items in case you decide to stay in*
> *London longer than originally planned.*

She opened one of the boxes. She recognized the pearls, a brooch, a watch, and a bracelet. Marigold put the watch on next to the one she was wearing and continued reading.

These aren't your mother's best pieces, but I'm sure you'll enjoy them, and we won't have to worry should they get lost in the mail.

Marigold imagined Mamie rifling through her mother's things, deciding which pieces to cull without anyone the wiser.

Now, I don't think you'll be surprised, but your father and I married in a quiet ceremony last weekend at the home of friends from the Bund. I've enclosed a couple of pictures to go along with some other photographs I know you'll treasure as well. When you do decide to come home, your father will join me in welcoming you back with open arms. Let bygones be bygones, Marigold!

Much love, Mamie.

Marigold glanced at the photos of their wedding. She held up a magnifying glass she kept for prints that she liked. All of the men wore lapel pins. The pins were swastikas. Marigold tossed the photographs into the wastebasket. "Bygones be bygones indeed."

She read the telegram. It was from her father.

YOU ARE TO COME HOME. STOP. IMMEDI-ATELY. STOP.

She crumpled the telegram and threw that in the wastebasket, too. Not once, not on any single occasion had he ever asked for or after Marigold. She was expected to obey or remain silent. She opened the box with the photographs. They were snapshots she'd never seen, from before the war, the exposures starting to fade and yellow with time. Her mother and Zosia were teenagers, with a younger Marek and some others. Was that Falaise? It must have been. She looked for her father amongst the faces. There he was but not standing next to her mother. Marigold leant against the wall, studying the pictures.

"Marigold dear," Falaise called, "it's Zosia for you." She hadn't heard the phone ring. Going back down the stairs, Falaise said, "She seems quite chastened. Yes, I'm sure Evie would want her to begin packing her bags." With a tight smile, she handed the phone to Marigold.

Her heart thumping in shame, Marigold stammered, "Hhhullo."

"Now listen, you stupid girl. I know everything."

"I—"

Zosia continued as if she hadn't spoken. "It's going to be very warm this week and you shouldn't stay in town for the hottest days of the year. Come to the house. While you make the necessary adjustments to learn how to think of someone other than yourself, we can take a dip and then you'll tell me all about it. I'm sure there's some element to all of this that you've conveniently omitted. Eh?"

When she hung up, Falaise handed her a towel. "You really do need a bath, dear."

Then Buddy made his appearance on the terrace where Marigold was drying her hair in the last of the day's sunshine. "Well, well, well . . ."—he gave a soft chuckle— "you've caused quite the scandal, Mac."

"Listen Buddy, I'm not going home." Her lower lip started trembling again. God, she wished it would stop.

"I heard a ticket is being arranged."

"I'm not going." She stomped her foot. "I'm not going to leave here with my tail between my legs."

"So, what do you propose?"

She wanted to sound tough, but wailed instead, "I've made a mistake and now I need to make it right!" What she didn't say was that she'd had the best day and night of her life, and she couldn't bear the idea of placing the Atlantic Ocean between herself and the possibility of having such a wonderful time again.

"How're you gonna do that?"

"Well," —her voice was trembling again— "I'll get a job. And"— goddamnit, now she was crying— "and I'll keep the job!"

"But what about college?" Buddy sat down and handed her his handkerchief.

"Thank you."

Buddy wasn't so bad, really.

"It didn't work out so well the last time." She began crying again. "I don't want to leave!"

"Why not?" When she didn't answer he added very softly, "There's gonna be a war, you know."

She knew he was right. "But I love it here." Then she whispered, "And, and the people at home are on the wrong side." That she abhorred everything her father supported was beyond awkward.

"What does that mean?"

"I can't get into it, Buddy."

"Are you a spy?" He gave her a hard look, "Are you a Nazi?"

"No." She met his gaze and refused to blink. "Are you?"

To which he laughed and said, "That's pretty funny." He lit a cigarette and thought for a moment. "So, Mac, what is it that you think you can do then? I mean, besides stay out late and miss your train home?"

"I can type a little. I can run errands."

"You mean, be a girl Friday, something like that."

"Yeah, I can be a girl Friday! I'm also handy with a camera."

"I'm talking about radio, Marigold, not newsprint."

"Well..." *Think fast,* she warned herself. He's trying to help you. "I could do the reconnoiter, take pictures of a place, and then the uh, reporting team will be able to quickly describe the scene at hand, because it's already been presented to them."

"Say, that's a thought. Hmm."

"Buddy. I really want to stay. I . . . I feel like I belong here, which I didn't feel at home. I do."

"You mean, besides amor?"

In spite of herself, she blushed furiously. "Yes, Buddy. Besides amor."

"Where can we get something to really eat around here?"

"Don't you like liver and bacon?"

He shrugged. "I like it fine. I'd like just a steak even better."

* * *

MAREK'S CAR turned the corner from King's Road on to Old Church Street. "Hop in." He reached over and opened the car door. "Time to whisk you away from the temptations of London town!"

Leaving the city, the car roared at an unimaginable speed. Marigold wondered when, indeed if, she'd see Joop again. The way he hummed Gershwin's "Promenade." The way he undid the padlock of the peniche, then spread the blanket before her. The way their lips met.

Eventually the buildings thinned out and the afternoon light cast long shadows across the countryside. The roads became single lanes masked by tall hedges around whose corners it was impossible to say.

The door of the Oust House was open, the summer air pouring into the kitchen across flagstones, the sunlight illuminating Zosia's elegant bare feet as she sliced tomatoes and then tossed a beautiful salad. Light and shadow. The coolness of the floor, the heat of the evening sun.

To Marigold, Zosia and Marek's life was perfect, brother and sister existing in peaceful rhythm, seeming to want for little, having already found the place that complemented themselves and each other.

Zosia looked up from her work. "Take a swim before supper.

The water is divine." She gave Marigold a mischievous smile. "And then you're going to tell me all about him."

The three of them sat beside the pool as the evening sky dimmed.

Marek murmured something in Hungarian and Marigold asked, "Why did you come to England when you did?"

He smiled at her and said, "Zosia, why did we come to England?"

"There was an issue with the Austrians in our village. They're not very friendly to Jews."

"Falaise said that Marek is a count or something."

"Our father was. If we had stayed, Marek might have been too. But if we had stayed, Marek would now be a dead count, that much is certain." The lamp flickered, bathing the night in that strange romance that was always there. Zosia whispered, "If we were there today, we'd just be dead Jews."

"What do you mean?"

"Marigold, open your eyes. Read the paper and listen to the radio. My God. Why do you think they hired you at Woburn House? It isn't a game, you know. The people who stay are losing everything they have. Eventually, they're going to be killed. It's what happened in the pogroms before. It's going to happen again."

There was a rustling against an outbuilding and Marek said, "I think there's a rat."

"Ugh." Marigold shuddered.

To which he shrugged and lit a cigarette. "Don't worry, I'll set a trap."

The next morning at breakfast, he said, "Get your camera, let's take a drive." They sped down the lane between hedges shading the car into darkness, until the road opened up and a stone tower was visible near the coast. They removed the cameras from their cases and got out of the car.

Marigold looked through the viewfinder. "Is that a castle?"

"No, it's the abbey. A girls' school actually. Very elite, diplomatic core and whatnot." He turned to Marigold. "Listen to Zosia, but not too much. She's still in mourning."

"What do you mean?"

"There are some things, Marigold, which you never get over. The events playing out now are distressingly familiar. It brings back the days we knew your mother, and before, when we all lived with Falaise." He snapped and then rewound his camera. "But the important thing, now remember this, is not to look away. You must see it for what it is and then decide."

"What should I decide?"

"What part you're going to play when it starts to roll out." He turned his camera toward her, and she raised hers to see him in the frame, on a late summer's day, effortlessly handsome, her own matinee idol. He pressed the button, which made her laugh, and she pressed hers too.

"My gosh, Marek. How's it going to roll out?" It was impossible to think the conflict wouldn't remain far from their lives, that nothing for them would really change.

"I don't know." Marek placed the cap on the lens and hopped back in his car. "Come on. It isn't too early for a cocktail."

Alex Reilly had brought Falaise who was helping prepare sandwiches in the kitchen upon their return. Marek raised an eyebrow to Marigold and said, "Falaise, would you be a darling and concoct one of those gin fizzes you do so well?"

"What's that?"

"Gin fizz!" he shouted.

"Oh darling, what a good idea. Why don't I make us some?" She tottered over to the bar cart.

During lunch, Alex said, "Oswald Mosley makes a very good point,"

"Oh no," Marek groaned. "Don't turn out to be fascist, for God's sake, Reilly. That you're walking across this field from your house to court my sister is all very well, but please. For the love of everything British . . ."

The phone rang that night, and it was Buddy on the line.

"Marigold, get your ass back here. Murrow has something for you. And remember to bring your gas mask. He's a real stickler about that."

BROADCASTING HOUSE WAS a new and glamorous building, located on Portland Place, only a simple bus ride on the 22, which brought one to the West End. Three different clerks at three different desks examined her credentials. One woman looked to see whether Marigold had brought her gas mask.

"Good, good." The woman nodded approvingly. "We've strict instructions. No visitors admitted without the appropriate protective gear. You'll find the Americans on the second floor."

The words Columbia Broadcasting System were painted on glass panels alongside a pair of doors. Marigold let herself in and thick cigarette smoke billowed out into the hall. The clack-clack-clacking of typewriters was deafening. Marigold looked around. There was only one other female at a desk.

"Hey there." Buddy emerged as if from nowhere. "Your idea, the advance team, with you taking pictures. He liked that. Come on, I'll introduce you."

Buddy knocked on an office door.

"Come!"

"Mr. Murrow, sir. This is Marigold."

Edward R. Murrow looked up from his desk. He was dark with a smoldering intensity. "Buddy says you take pictures."

She stammered, "Yes, yes, I do." No one had ever asked about her pictures before.

"Did you bring something for me to look at?"

Er . . . She couldn't believe that hadn't occurred to her. What was she thinking?

Suddenly, Murrow's face creased into a smile. "You're just a kid, aren't you?"

"I'm eighteen, Mr. Murrow."

"Well, let's try this. Did you bring a camera?"

"Yes, yes I did."

"Buddy has a list of the stories we're compiling. Go to three locations and take as many photos of them as you can. We don't need anything fancy or over the top. I'm looking for the common man. The guy who runs the newsagent, the greengrocer, the bobby on the corner. We're going to describe everyday life here in London, so that Americans can imagine what it's like for their English counterparts."

"Yes sir."

"And Marigold."

"Yes, Mr. Murrow?"

"None of our broadcasts are recorded in advance. Everything is done live. So, try to capture every single detail of what I might describe to an audience. What do the buildings look like? Is the street busy? Are there flowers, or some litter? Is the publican old or young? Is it his daughter or his wife behind the bar?"

"Yes sir."

"And Buddy."

"Mr. Murrow?"

"Make sure she has some press credentials. Write something up on letterhead. I don't want her picked up for spying."

"Yes, Mr. Murrow."

"And Buddy—"

"Yes sir?"

"Show her where to find the lab. Marigold, as soon as you're done, take the film to Mr. Platt. He'll develop it right away."

"Yes sir." Marigold felt her heart begin soaring. Thank you very much, sir!"

IN THE DARKROOM at Lark Mews, she could barely wait to tell Marek. "It's so exciting!"

But Marek shook his head. "Now how are you going to assist me if you're over at the BBC mucking about with Americans for CBS?"

"Um. Working with you weekends?"

He smiled. "I see. When I'm in Sussex?"

"No, no, but um, how about every other waking moment, because—"

"Because?" At her squirming, his smile was even wider.

"Because I'm staying out of trouble?"

"Good girl. First thing you can do is give Tony some kippers. Then over to Mr. Alwyn's, please. Two packs of Player's Navy Cut. Also, a fifth of single malt, he knows the one, and a copy of the afternoon's *Times*. Get to it, girl Friday, chop-chop!"

Autumn

It was Saturday and Trude and Joop had come down from Oxford. The cinema on King's Road was less than a block from Falaise's house on the other side of Old Church Street. It was packed but they found four seats in the second row. They had to crane their necks back, Joop and Buddy on either side of Marigold and Trude.

PEACE! FOUR POWER CONFERENCE

The Pathé newsreel appeared on the screen. Prime Minister Chamberlain disembarked from a plane, waving a document toward a crowd who stood cheering. The male voice overhead said,

Down the bright straight road, a new understanding in Europe. And so, at Hitler's Munich headquarters, the agreement that has made the biggest headlines since the Armistice, let no man say that too high a price has been paid for the peace of the world...

"What a disaster." Trude shook her head.

Marigold offered her a sweet. "Why? We don't want to go to war."

"Shh." Someone in the front row turned around.

"Because he's a liar. Hitler is a liar, Marigold."

"But Chamberlain is a hero, isn't he? It's peace, at all costs."

"Oh God. I'll explain it to you later."

"Shh! Shh!" The woman in the front gave them a frown.

"Sorry," Buddy said.

"I should hope so." The woman turned back around.

The music began, a riff on "I Can't Give You Anything but Love, Baby." Katharine Hepburn and Cary Grant in *Bringing Up Baby*!

"This will be sophisticated, no?" Joop whispered.

Marigold poked him in the ribs.

"Cary Grant's way too sophisticated for me." Buddy shrugged.

Joop reached round to pat Buddy's shoulder. "I think you look very sophisticated."

"Shh!" Both Marigold and Trude hissed.

Afterward, in the pub, Buddy said, "Munich is a boon for us, Mac." He lit a cigarette.

"Who do you mean by 'us'?" Trude asked. "Hitler's been handed the Czechs on a plate."

"I mean the press." Buddy leaned forward. "He's got the Sudetenland and we've at least one hundred plus stories to cover."

"That's very cynical, Buddy," Trude said. "You clearly don't know what you're talking about."

He clapped his hands together. "This is it. Conflict. News. Europe. It's where it's happening, baby!"

Trude said, "I think it's disgusting. They're just going to bully their way back, using the terms of Versailles to justify this outrageous behavior in building up their troops. Jeez."

Joop turned away from them and whispered to Marigold, "Did you like this movie?"

Marigold thought for a moment before answering, "Well, it's a little bit slapstick."

Joop frowned. "What is slapstick?"

"I'm sure you know what slapstick is."

"Tell me." She couldn't tell if he was putting her on or not.

"It's sort of silly and confused, like you."

"Ahh."

"But, still very clever. Also like you."

"Yes, well, this is the part about sophistication I just don't understand."

WORKING with Ed Murrow's advance team was simple because taking pictures was something Marigold excelled at. In the mornings, they received a list of locations for that evening's stories and would then scope them out, looking for the best areas to sample ambient sound and where Mr. Murrow should record. Marigold's ease with her Leica allowed her to make quick work of documenting a scene, so Murrow could use the photos to prepare his script when describing it. They'd return to BBC House by noon whereupon she'd send her work to the lab, and Mr. Platt would hand her the prints before the end of the day with an encouraging nod and a thumbs up.

The pace of the news, and the urgency of a nightly report gave her a sense of purpose and with it, the confidence that comes from being effective using her intellect and skill with her camera.

But in the early evenings, in one busy place or riding the bus home, she'd see parents with children and think about those applications at the Woburn House. She noticed the man sitting beside her reading the small ads in the back of the newspaper. Several were seeking homes for Jewish Viennese children. She wondered who had replaced her. Hateful Mrs. Krumbull, the wasted connection with Miss Breen, and the preoccupied Colonel Mayhew. She thought about those job vacancies for domestics. Singers, poets, and dancers who must *liase with a butler, coordinate deliveries, and supervise the staff.* There'd been many situations vacant. But there were hundreds of thousands of people who desperately needed those jobs.

Marigold brushed the pesky thoughts away. But then Marek and Zosia's words about their own situation came back. That if they hadn't escaped to England, they might have been killed.

THE ONLY FEMALE broadcaster on Ed Murrow's team was named Marvin Breckinridge. When asked, Marvin explained she didn't need to be judged as a woman, so she'd taken a man's name instead. Marvin had once been a photographer and was brilliant and tough, and Marigold loved working with her. She showed Marvin the pictures of Kit. His impish grin, the little girl in the cardigan looking at Kit with distaste.

"These are really lovely." Marvin said, "They're spirited, you know?"

That evening, at the Mews house, after feeding the cat and placing the *Times* where Marek instructed, Marigold came across a box of pictures. They were from the same collection as the ones Mamie had sent from New York. Small and yellowed from time, of people in the countryside, at a picnic. When Marigold held up a magnifying glass to inspect them, she found her mother instantly. She looked elated, happy in a way that Marigold rarely remembered seeing her. But Marigold recognized her own smiling features from the pictures with Joop in Paris. Capturing the moment when a subject was spirited, that was the key to a great photo. A sorrowful tenderness washed over Marigold. Marek had said he loved Evangeline. If those photographs were anything to go by, then he very clearly did.

MOVIETONE NEWS: AMERICA CONDEMNS NAZI TERRORISM!

They were in the middle of the cinema this time. The *Movietone News* theme music began, and the lights went down.

"Excuse me, excuse me." Joop climbed over one seat, then another, then another.

On the screen, President Roosevelt was at his desk with a grave expression. The announcer said,

"President Roosevelt in a statement without precedence speaks out against the persecution of minorities in

Germany. He says he could scarcely believe such things could occur..."

"Sit down!" said a man.

"Shhh!" said another.

Joop sat down beside Marigold. She leaned against him. "You're late."

...opinion as expressed by an ex-President and two former candidates for the presidency. The only living ex-President stresses the official attitude that Nazi violence is both anti-semitic and anti-Christian.

"Shh," someone said again.

Joop whispered, "I wanted to bring you this." In his hand was a lone marigold, slightly wilted.

"They're not in season." But she blushed in pleasure all the same.

"An Indian fellow had a lot of them. I thought it best to just get one."

Trude tweaked her in the ribs on the other side. Beside Trude was Buddy, watching the screen, his eyes unblinking, oblivious to the others.

The movie began. Joop whispered, "The mother is like Mrs. Falaise Cooper, no?"

As Jimmy Stewart adored Jean Arthur, she felt Joop lean into her, alongside her. If he could, he'd envelop her. She looked at the flower and up at his profile.

"*Why don't you write a play about ism-mania?*" Lionel Barrymore asked the woman who reminded Joop of Falaise.

"*Ism mania?*" the woman asked.

"*Communism, fascism, voodooism,*" Lionel Barrymore answered. "*Everyone's got an ism these days.*

Afterwards, walking to the pub, Joop took her in his arms and began dancing about. "Is this how they do the Big Apple?" he asked. He meant the dance everyone did in *You Can't Take It With You.*

Marigold laughed. "It's kind of like that. Come on, Trude, let's show 'em the Big Apple!"

"Shake it! Shake it!" Trude yelled, kicking her legs like the kids in the movie.

But when they sat down for drinks, the world caught up with the conversation.

Joop said, "Imagine if we were like in the movie, deciding not to build munitions, but to play the mouth harp, dancing the Big Apple instead."

Trude looked at them. "I don't understand why this happens and that nobody does anything."

Buddy shook his head. "I wish I knew why." It was impossible to keep the evening light. Finally, he asked, "So, uh, Trude, what are your plans after Oxford?"

"To become a legal genius, of course. Then I'm going to hold those fascist villains accountable."

"Trude will be an amazing lawyer," Marigold said.

Joop stood up. "Another round?"

Trude held up her glass for a refill. "Marigold is quite right. I will be an amazing lawyer. Because I'll tell you, Buddy. I love the law. You know, if it is properly applied, for every injustice, there is a remedy."

Buddy moved toward her, fascinated. "How do you know that?"

"Because of the economy and the world order, silly. What's happening in Germany is not going to go unanswered. When it's all over, it's going to make the Treaty of Versailles look like child's play. You'll see."

Joop returned to the table.

Marigold said, "Trude, tell Buddy how you know this."

Trude tapped her nose and smiled. "I have it on very good authority." She lit a cigarette, then exhaled. "Because Daddy's in the money world. They have certain insights, you know."

Buddy asked, "So are you gonna be the right honorable whatchamacallit?"

"Maybe. But I will say this." She leaned back. "After it's all over, I'm going to be there when they're held to account. Our family is located throughout Europe. And when this is over, I will be there. I don't care what I'll have to do—even be a charwoman for God's sake—but I am going to be present when those Nazis are brought to justice."

Buddy smiled at her. "Wow. You are really something, Trude."

"She is, isn't she?" Marigold agreed. "All I care about is the next movie musical, and here we have our own Nancy Astor, life-long member of Parliament."

"Somebody's got to do it." Trude turned back to Buddy. "Are you going to stay with CBS?"

"With all that's going on? I sure will. Then I'll continue in something to do with journalism."

Joop asked, "What are you going to do, Marigold?"

Marigold shrugged. "Take better pictures?" At the flash of disappointment on Trude's face, Marigold raised her eyebrows, "And I'll only take pictures of people who are happy." She held up her camera. "Say cheese, everyone!"

TRUDE AND MARIGOLD met up for tea a week later. Marigold handed her the photo. "Look what a cute couple you make."

Trude studied it carefully. The flash had dazzled them and Joop was beaming at the camera, yet Buddy and Trude were spirited, in that split second when one sees the other, oblivious to everything else.

Trude gave a small sigh. "Buddy's very nice. He looks a little bit like Jimmy Stewart, doesn't he? But I can't get mixed up with anyone."

"Why ever not?"

"Oh Marigold." For the first time, Marigold saw something in her friend resembling heartbreak. "What's happening in Germany is going to tear us apart."

* * *

"Mr. Murrow?"

"Yes Marigold."

"Before I came here, I worked for a relief agency at Woburn House. Uh, in light of the news last week, I was hoping sir, you might give me this Friday."

Ed Murrow leant forward and put out his cigarette. "What do you have in mind?"

"I'd like to photograph the children's arrival sir. I could photograph it sir."

He studied her for a moment and then smiled. "We work in radio, Marigold. Radio."

Marigold straightened her back. "Well, this arrival is only the first. I don't know if people understand how dire things are for those kids."

Murrow nodded. "Go on, you're doing great."

She realized he was waiting for her to make her case. Marigold added, "I've been given the chance to work with a proper photographer who's covering it, and um—"

"Yes?"

Her hands started sweating something fierce. She wiped them on her skirt. "If I can photograph it, then the next time, we can figure out how you can describe it, easily, on the broadcast. You know, because," She swallowed, "this is history, sir."

There were two photographers, Kurt and Gertie, who had worked with *Picture Post* before. Like Marek, they had been refugees and now they were British. Marigold's job was to assist them both. There were flash bulbs, tripods, countless rolls of film and various lenses.

The children's ferry would arrive at Harwich, two hours from London. From Harwich they'd make their way to Dovercourt Bay Holiday Camp. The day was bitterly cold.

Marigold looked out the window. The landscape was covered in frost. "I thought holiday camps were only used in summer."

"They are," Kurt answered.

"Does that mean they don't have heating?"

Gertie said, "Apparently, it's the best the authorities can do. One can only hope they'll be hosted before the taps start freezing."

Mindful of the others around them, Kurt and Gertie spoke in English. Marigold, for fear of getting in their way, preferred not to speak at all.

Harwich was mobbed by the press. As the children disembarked, cameras began clicking and reporters shouted questions. Kurt worked with two Leicas, which were just like Marigold's. "Stay close, stay close, Marigold," he said.

Obediently she loaded one camera, and handed it to him, when the other ran out of film.

Gertie, for her part, had planted herself in the arrivals lounge, her camera on a tripod, near some seats by a cloak room.

After a while, Kurt said, "Go check on Gertie, see if she needs anything."

Marigold worked her way through the crowd. Some of the girls had gathered outside the toilets. They glanced at her. They were all nearly her age.

She might have seen them ice skating at Central Park. Her heart beating, she said, *"Hallo! Willkommen in England!"*

This was met with silence. Then suddenly, the girls spoke at once, some in English that was much better than her German as well as some who didn't speak English at all. But a fatigued adrenalin washed over them, and the girls nattered about the trip, about boys, about fears and hopes.

One said, "I hope my family will speak some German."

Another girl said, "The one I'm going to doesn't have any other children."

"Do you think English boys are good looking?" Yet another posed this question as she studied the journalists and photographers.

"My parents will come for me as soon as this is over." The first one said.

"We were supposed to go to America, but we couldn't get visas. My father will bring my grandparents next month, I think."

MARIGOLD ANSWERED as many questions as she could and glanced over her shoulder. Gertie's camera was trained onto a little girl with long braids, who sat on a step holding a doll. Marigold watched Gertie say something to the girl. Whatever it was, it caused the faintest traces of a smile to appear and Gertie took the shot.

At Dovercourt Holiday Camp, those who had families ready to host them were quickly identified and the others watched them leave. By teatime, the excitement began to wind down and the press had thinned out. As Gertie and Kurt began putting away their equipment, Marigold gave her address to a pair of the older girls. "Write to me. When you come to London, we'll get together."

Someone took Marigold's arm and led her away. "How could you say that?" It was Miss Breen.

Marigold blushed. "Oh! Hello, I didn't know you were here."

"These girls have nothing." Miss Breen hissed, "They have no resources. How do you think anyone's going to be getting to London?"

"I was just—"

"You give them false hopes that everything will be, as you Americans so like to say, Hunky Dory, and it's not. For some of them the nightmare's just beginning."

Kurt caught Marigold's eye and waved her over, "Shall we?"

On the train ride back, she felt a pain as if she'd actually hurt those girls, injuring them with her ignorance. Gertie and Kurt were whispering in German. Marigold couldn't understand what they were saying, but Miss Breen was right. One could only imagine what would happen to those children. She pretended to sleep to keep any tears from escaping. So many more were still abroad and desperately needed to leave.

Winter

At Kings Road, there was garland along the mantle, a wreath and a tree. The smell of balsam, oranges and cloves filled the sitting room.

"Marigold dear, where shall we stand?"

Marigold set up the lamp over on the right, the place Marek always preferred it. She extended it so that everything was brilliantly illuminated, even though there were candles and the room looked so merry.

"Marek will tell us, Falaise."

"I say," Marek looked through the Rolleiflex, and moved its tripod back an inch. "We'll put Falaise in her chair of course, Buddy flanking her on the right. Zosia, grab that small bench, yes, put it front of Buddy, and Marigold and I will do the same on the other side."

Marigold ran around the tripod to peek through the lens. The edge of the Christmas tree was just barely visible.

"Come on, Marigold."

She sat down and Marek walked over to put his hand on her shoulder. "4, 3, 2, 1."

The women wore their finest, and the men were in dinner jackets. It was Christmas Eve 1938.

1939

Joop examined the movie listings in the paper while Marigold savored the last of her cake. They were sitting in Lyons Corner House, by a window overlooking the Strand. She watched a small group of Fascist black shirts, marching in lockstep, toward Piccadilly.

Joop put down his paper. "Hey." He gently put his hand on her chin and turned it away from the window. "I think something silly would be best, no?" With his other hand he dismissed the demonstration outside. "Current events are not so nice, now. I'd like something merry, yeah, merry. What do you think, Gouda?"

"I think you're right." She smiled at him. "Merry definitely works for me."

It was *Holiday* with Cary Grant and Katherine Hepburn.

The smell of wet wool, cheap scent and tobacco filled the upper balcony, and they squeezed into a pair of seats in the last row.

It took Marigold a moment to realize the newsreel's featured story was in New York, at Madison Square Garden. She recognized the auditorium with its audience facing the stage where there were three banners. One was the American flag, the other a portrait of George Washington. The third banner was a swastika. Marigold flushed and her throat went dry.

A procession with the Nazi flag made its way to the platform and the camera went into close up. The man carrying the flag looked at the camera. Tears of shame filled her eyes. She thought she might be sick. She stood up. "I just need the ladies room."

The movie was silly and it was lovely, but she couldn't shake the image of her own father holding that flag, walking through that crowd.

Standing on the street corner afterward, Joop pulled her close, "Do you want to go home?"

"No," she answered in a small voice. If Joop knew who her father was, then he'd despise her, at least as much as she despised her father herself.

Joop suddenly looked shy and uncertain. "Would you like to go to a bedsit?"

"What do you mean?"

"Uh, a friend, he has given me the key to his bedsit. It's in Elephant and Castle. Not so close, but not so far, either. Would you like to go?"

Suddenly embarrassed, she smiled and nodded. "Yes, yes I would."

"Ok then! We go to Elephant and Castle."

The room was shabby and smelled of old socks. Lying down next to her, he remained too polite to ask and she was afraid to tell, but being together with very little clothing sent her bad thoughts far, far away. It was nearly midnight, and she had to get back to Chelsea.

"Joop?"

"Hmm?" He tightened his arms around her and she leaned back against him.

She saw the shadow scamper along the floor. "Oh no!" She cried and sat up.

"Gouda, what is it?" Joop sat up and put his arm around her.

"I – I. I just saw a mouse."

"Ah. Well, then." He kissed her shoulder. "I will tell my friend to get a cat."

THE LAB at Broadcasting House was unusually busy. But Mr. Platt took her film and nodded, "See you at four then."

Marigold closed the door of the lab behind her and ran up the stairs, past the BBC suites and the canteen. She found an empty desk, a piece of paper and envelope with the CBS letterhead on top. She wrote the note, tears smarting at her eyes.

She wrote out her New York address on the envelope. She couldn't send it. Not yet. Marigold slipped the envelope into her purse and went to collect the film.

Spring

On the corner of Kings Road and Old Church Street, someone was bouncing a tennis ball. Back and forth, back and forth. It was Kit, the boy with the filthy knees and cheeky grin.

Hello!" He wiped his hair from his eyes.

"Hello." She knew she should give him a copy of the photographs she'd taken last summer. Some of them had turned out marvelously.

He pointed at her camera case. "You work with him?" He gestured back toward Lark Mews. She realized by 'him' he meant Marek.

"Yes, I do."

"So does me mum."

"Really? Oh. Is she Mrs. Hearne?"

"Yeah, that's right."

"Well, that's a coincidence."

They walked a few paces in silence until he asked, "What are you doing, Marigold?"

"Right now?"

Kit nodded as a reply.

"I'm walking back to my house. What are you doing?"

"I could show you something if you want."

"What?"

"It's at Cremorne," he said.

"Where's Cremorne?"

"It's on the Thames, innit?"

"All right, then."

They went down Cheyne Walk. Past the homes of Turner, of Whistler, the novelist George Eliot, past Chelsea Old Church, everything brick and ivy, trees and springtime.

"So, if it's something good, and you like it, will you give me some money?"

Marigold laughed. "Does your mother know you're doing this?"

"No fear! She'd have my arse if she did. I'm just being enterprising, like."

"Well, what will this thing be worth?" They made a right at the river and began walking west.

"It'll be hmm, would you say tuppence?"

"Okay. Show me what you've got."

Cremorne Gardens was an amusement park at the turn of the century but had gone to seed since the Great War. A few drunks were sleeping on benches, and litter was strewn near a waste bin. A formerly grand iron gate was half open and they walked through it toward the Embankment.

"Don't make a noise," the boy said. He added, whispering, "The mother's shy." Then he stopped and turned to Marigold. "You might want to take a photo."

"Really?"

Kit nodded. "I would."

She slipped the camera from its case and they bent down toward a thick azalea. Kit gently pulled the lower branches away. He crouched down and pointed toward the bush, mouthing,

"Look, in there."

Inside were three white puppies, nursing at their mother. Marigold gave a tiny gasp, and quickly took the picture, while the mother dog only growled a bit.

Walking away, Marigold said, "Who does she belong to?"

Kit shrugged, "I dunno. She doesn't have a tag. I call her Lulu."

"She's a beautiful dog. How do you think she's eating?"

Again, he shrugged. "I leave a sausage and bread most afternoons."

Before she could ask, he said, "We're not allowed dogs at the estate. Otherwise, I'd ask my mum." He paused, and attempted to snap, "like that."

Marigold had a good snap, so she did it for him. "You mean like that?"

"Yeah."

Marigold rummaged around in her purse. The envelope was still there. She moved it to the side and took out a tuppence. "That really was good. Thank you."

"Ta." He carefully put it in his pocket.

"You know, I'm going to give your mom some prints of those pictures I took last summer. I think you both would like them."

At this he blushed with pleasure. 'Cor. Thanks very much!"

AT THE MEWS, Marek said, "Here's a Jos-Pe tri color camera." The camera didn't look so different, really, from the Brownie she'd had in New York. "These are a few rolls of color film. Try it out. I'll get it processed for you. It's important to do new things, expand your horizons."

Joop arrived on a bicycle the next day.

When Marigold cleared a place for his bike inside the front door, Joop shook his head. "No, no. You will be my passenger," Joop's trousers were clipped around his ankles. He wore a newsboy's cap and a stripy sweater over his shirt and tie.

"Do I ride here on the bar?" The whole thing looked very uncomfortable.

"No, no. Marigold, you sit on the seat, and I will peddle. It's safer like this."

"I'm kind of heavy." The thought of a mishap in traffic crossed her mind.

He smiled at this. "You're not so heavy."

He tilted the bicycle toward her and she sat down, her legs

dangling over to one side. "Marigold you must keep your legs away from the spoke, yes?"

"Yes, Joop."

Slowly, he began to peddle, and he pulled into the center of the street. "My God!"

"Joop, what is it?" The camera was in its case around her neck, but if they should fall - suddenly it felt precarious.

"Marigold, you are so heavy!"

"Joop!" She hit him on the back, and he chuckled, turning left at the Thames.

"Where are we going?"

"Well, you said you have this color film, and I think a good place to use it is where there is a lot of color." Past the houses along the Embankment, past Cheyne Walk.

"Where?"

"You'll see, *kleng* Gouda."

The Royal Chelsea Hospital was set back from the Embankment on a vast green lawn. The residents were veterans who wore brilliant scarlet coats, with gold trim and black tricornered hats upon their heads.

"What is this?" Marigold watched the men moving back and forth across the green expanse.

"This is Oak Day." They got down from the bicycle and walked together. "It marks the time when Charles II hid inside an oak tree from the Parliamentarians who wanted to kill him." Joop locked his bicycle to a post in the fence.

"How do you know about this?"

"Tudors and Stuarts, Marigold. I wanted to read history, but then my father wanted me to work on numbers. So, no kings and queens of England, except for fun." Joop took two apples out of his saddle bag. They were a striking yellow and red. "Apple?"

"You haven't told me what your family business actually is."

"Guess."

"Dry goods."

"No."

"Porcelain."

"No, no. It's something you can eat. In fact, it's something I love."

"Chocolate."

He leaned toward her. "I bring it up all the time." He kissed her softly on the mouth.

"I'm afraid to ask."

"It's cheese. Cheese! Nothing better than Dutch cheese. *Lekker.*"

An old man in a scarlet coat approached them. "Are you here for the festivities?"

Joop said, "I regret to say we have no invitation, sir."

"Did your father fight in the Great War?"

Both of them nodded. "Well, that's good enough for me. Come on. If anyone asks you, say you're with Captain Lawson."

They followed him across the vast lawn. Marigold squinted at the grounds in the sunlight, as the elderly men lined up along the gravel. Spectators sat in folding chairs on the other side of the lawn. The center doors of the building opened, and a small military band emerged, in contemporary uniform. They began to play and the veterans moved forward in formation until given the command by an officer wearing black.

Marigold held up the camera wanting to photograph everything. Joop held her camera case and her purse, murmuring, "Look at the light on the portico." And, "Gouda, you must photograph that woman's hat."

The Duke of Kent was introduced and proceeded along the lines of veterans while the band continued to play.

Afterwards, Captain Lawson showed them around. "I was too old for the last one. But I served in the Boer War. That was my time."

"May I take your picture?" Marigold asked. "I'll bring you a copy if you like."

"Yes, you may." The old man drew himself up.

The red of his coat and the black of his tricornered hat, the green of the lawn, the blue of the sky. Marigold turned the aperture the slightest amount to the left, and then she turned it a fraction to the right. On the edge of the frame she saw Joop, standing in shadow. He was so tall and graceful and kind. She moved the camera back to Captain Lawson. "Perfect." She pushed the shutter. "One more." She advanced the film, "Joop, please stand with the Captain." Joop did so. The men smiled at her and then at each other. "Lovely."

It was dusk when they returned to Kings Road. Joop said, "I leave tomorrow."

She knew this day was coming, but it surprised her how much it hurt to hear him say it. "When will you come back?"

He shrugged. "I don't know. Cheese can take a lot of time."

"Cheese?"

"No. Truly it is Mathematics. Professor Meyritz is very brilliant and we will work together in Leiden."

"But-"

"It's what I've wanted to do, Marigold, since forever. And besides, Amsterdam is not so far away."

"No, no I guess not."

"Marigold—"

"Joop."

"You are-" He bit his lip and then looked away for a moment. She realized his eyes had filled with tears. "You are the New World. Everything shining, in color. Beautiful."

He kissed her and she leaned against him. Then he kissed her again and again. Joop stepped away. He put his foot on the pedal of his bicycle. "I'll write to you from the Netherlands!" And he rode into the night, back toward Sloane Square.

Kindness and laughter, his kisses and fair hair. She watched until he was a speck in the darkness, then turned to go inside. She didn't know whether her face was wet from his tears or whether the tears were her own.

Summer

MARIGOLD CLOSED THE DRAPES IN HER ROOM TO muffle out the King's Road city sounds. She crawled into bed as Trude slipped into the trundle beside her. Trude took her hand and whispered, "I'm a very serious person now, Marigold."

"You are?"

"Can't you tell?" Then Trude pulled the blanket up and closed her eyes.

Upstairs, Buddy's footsteps thumped around to the music he was playing.

"Yes, I can tell," Marigold whispered back. "Trude?"

"Hmm?" She could tell her friend was nodding off.

"Don't fall asleep yet." Marigold gently pulled her blanket down. "Trude, I need to show you something."

Trude opened her eyes. "What?"

Marigold turned on the light and brought out the envelope she'd addressed to her father, crumpled from being in her purse. "Read it."

Dear Dad,

I saw the newsreel from Madison Square Garden. I am so ashamed and so angry that this is how you see the world. It will be better for both of us if we no longer communicate at all. Whatsoever. This includes Mamie, too.

    Please do not try and contact me ever again.
Marigold.

Trude put the letter back in the envelope. "Oh Mari." Trude wiped the tear that had begun its descent down Marigold's face. "I have a stamp if you need one."

In spite of herself, Marigold smiled. "I do, actually."

Trude climbed out of the trundle and crossed the room. When she handed her the stamp, Marigold asked, "Do you really think there's going to be a war?"

"Yes. Yes, I do."

For Marigold, all that meant was that if Joop was in Holland and she was in London, there wouldn't be a way for her to see him again, at least not soon.

"And Mari."

"Yes?"

"There's something you should know."

Oh no. She was going to say she was in love with Joop. Marigold asked in the smallest voice she could, "What is it I need to know?"

"I've signed the Official Secrets Act."

"What does that mean?"

Trude sighed. "There are certain things I can't talk about now."

Marigold sat up. "Are you a spy?"

Trude didn't answer.

"Oh my God! You are. You are a spy."

Trude stretched her arms and folded them behind her head. "I really can't answer that."

Marigold threw a pillow at her. "I knew it! I knew you'd be a spy. Wow."

Upstairs, Buddy turned his record player off.

"I wish I were a spy," Marigold said. Outside, some traffic idled at a stop sign.

"Nah, you're too spontaneous to be much of a spy."

"Really?"

"Definitely."

ALL ALIENS WERE INSTRUCTED to update their registration cards, declare their addresses, and state their reasons for being in England. Outside the police station, the line wrapped around Lucan Place and back again. Trude and Marigold slowly moved forward, closer to the door.

Marigold said, "I think you should come in with me."

Trude shook her head. "No, no. I'm going to wait out here."

"Why? Don't you have to register?"

Trude raised her eyebrows. "My mother was British, so I'm not an alien. Besides, that man who came to college. We had a discussion about it."

"Was it"— Marigold paused for effect, and then shouted— "SECRET?"

Trude laughed. "I can't say just yet."

"Why?" Marigold put her hands on her hips.

"What?" Trude waived at a small child who moved with his parents to the front of the line.

"Oh, for heaven's sake." Marigold began laughing. too, "I'll not get anything out of you now."

On one side of the building some men stacked sandbags several feet deep. On the other side, where the people were, the line inched forward. Conversations in Italian, German, and French flowed all around them, and there were people speaking languages Marigold didn't recognize at all. Those with young children continued moving to the front. Behind her, Marigold recognized a couple who ran a restaurant down the street.

"What should I say my occupation is?"

"Girl Friday, silly." Trude looked up and squinted as if to count the barrage balloons that now littered the sky. "Then also write something about volunteering. I mean now that Woburn House is behind you."

"What should I do?" She wished she could come up with ideas the way that Trude did. She wished Trude would just go into the interview with her.

"Why not be one of those patrol wardens for Chelsea? Ask the constable. I'm sure that would go over very well in the interview."

"What are you going to do?"

"I can't say, Marigold."

"Trude, you've become a regular Mata Hari."

"Oh God, I hope not. You know she did get in a pretty dreadful muddle."

The man at the desk stapled one photo of Marigold to a card and then another to a form she had filled out.

He stamped both cards, then signed across one and handed it to Marigold. "Here you are, Miss McGrath. This grants you alien residence, Category C status. You are free to travel at will. Mind yourself and God save the King."

Afterward, they walked to Peter Jones to look at new dresses for the season.

"Marigold, being motherless is far more advantageous than I previously thought." Trude held up a chiffon frock in front of the mirror. It was beyond risqué.

"How do you mean?" Marigold admired one with a plunging neckline.

Trude examined the price tag and put the dress back. "There's no one to argue with about clothes or boys, or hopes, fears, and aspirations. There's so much less hypocrisy."

"What about your dad?"

Trude shrugged. "He's in Switzerland. Besides"—she chuckled— "I think he's terrified of me, to be honest."

Marigold laughed. "Ha! I can see why. Mata"—then she peered out from the dress— "Mata Hari."

SOME FIFTY PEOPLE who lived within a one-block radius of the drill were participating. They clustered in groups, chatting, discussing their chances should an air raid actually occur.

"Right!" A man wearing a helmet with *ARP* written across its front shouted into a megaphone, "Ladies and gentlemen! It is our civic duty to be apprised of emergency procedures should the unthinkable come to pass."

"Shh, shhh!" someone said.

The people looked doubtfully at him and at each other. There were now so many barrage balloons in the sky that it looked more like *Flash Gordon* than it did an impending air raid.

A little boy said, "Are we going for an ice lolly after, Mummy?" Which caused a few chuckles.

His mother shushed him, but the warden smiled and said, "If you do your work well, I am sure an ice lolly will be arranged. Isn't that right, Madam?"

A man shouted, "We'll need something a good deal stronger than that." To which there was much agreement.

The newsagent, Mr. Alwyn also wore a helmet and led Falaise to the area marked with a square chalked onto the pavement.

She said, "I really do not think this is necessary."

"Now, Mrs. Cooper, I wish that were true, but please believe me when I say that if fifty large bombs hit within a square mile, that there is a one in one hundred chance of survival. I should hate for anything to happen to you, so when the alarm sounds"— he pointed his arms very deliberately— "please run from the chemist over to this square and then drop to the ground."

Falaise lowered her ear trumpet. "Are you quite sure?"

"Yes, yes. I chose this role for you, because you will be carried by stretcher over to the ambulance. And with that, Mrs. Cooper, your part will be done. All right?"

Mr. Alwyn then crossed over to Marigold who stood with two other women, all wearing ill-fitting coveralls and helmets indicating they were with the ARP as well. "When the alarm has rung for ninety seconds," he said, "you will come here, and place a tourniquet onto the leg of this gentleman. Once completed, you shall assist him over to the chemist, which shall act as a shelter. Is that clear?"

"Yes, Mr. Alwyn."

The other warden shouted, "Places!"

"It's like a film set," the girl next to Marigold said.

The alarm sounded, as if from far away, and then grew louder and louder, until it was deafening. People ran one way, and then they ran the other, crashing together.

"Oy, 'scuse me."

"I beg your pardon."

"'Scuse me!"

"No, that's my position!"

"Oy, oy. Watch where you're going."

Seeing everyone fly into action became suddenly absurd, and Marigold began laughing.

"I say, are you going to wrap my leg or not?" The man on the ground tapped her leg.

"Yes, sorry." She knelt down and raised the gentleman's trouser hem. The helpless sock garter worked its way down his skinny calf. From the corner of her eye, she saw Falaise arguing with the boys attempting to put her on the stretcher. Behind Falaise, Mr. Alwyn still ran back and forth and back again, his arms waving, failing to impose order on his fellow participants.

The man at Marigold's leg squealed, "Oy, I'm ticklish!" and jerked his foot away. "Not like that. Oy!"

And Marigold began laughing again, her hands shaking, all of it unimaginable were they to find themselves performing the same task in New York City.

Back at the house Falaise was fit to be tied. "My heavens, that was dreadful. We must go to the Arts Club. I'm in desperate need of sustenance. And Marigold,"— Falaise gave her a stern look— "do change your coveralls. With the seat down around your knees like that, you've woefully little gravitas. For God's sake."

EVEN WITH HER G and T in the garden at the Arts Club, Falaise still found it all contemptible. "Clearly some ill-informed person is under the delusion that Britain might be invaded." The waiter approached them.

Falaise nodded, "Yes, please do bring us another round." She watched the waiter return to the bar then leaned back and closed her eyes. "Britain invaded. It will never happen. My heavens."

JULY ROLLED into August with its sublime weather and endless afternoons. Weekends at the Oust House watching Zosia grow ever closer to Alex Reilly made Marigold long to be with Joop. But he had his studies in Leiden now. Besides, it was better to say nothing, just keep it to herself. She'd made a mistake once before. She wasn't about to do so again.

The first weekend in September, everyone gathered at Zosia's for the end of the summer. They were tanned from the sun, gossiping about comings and goings in London.

Alex Reilly's little girl Emily had returned from her grandparents' and stood patiently as her father plaited her hair. "The way I see it"—Alex carefully twisted the hair between his fingers— "is that when things go to hell, which they invariably will, it presents the opportunity for certain fortunes, such as my own, to be restored." He fastened the elastic and gently tapped Emily's backside. "There you are."

Emily turned and kissed him on the cheek. Then she jumped into the pool.

"So, how will you do that, old man?" Marek sat on the pool's edge, his legs dangling in the water. Marigold knew that he found Alex to be sketchy, but Zosia would have none of it.

"Well, you know how those damn communists undid the conditions needed for business to be profitable. That, of course, and the crash, so—"

"Oh darling, I don't think we need to hash this out." Zosia brought out a pitcher of lemonade. "Marek is clearly oblivious and it's simply better to think about other things. Don't you agree?"

"Yes, I suppose. What are those other things? Little girls and puppy dog tails. Hmm."

Marigold pulled herself out of the water and watched Alex limp over to the table. He seemed flushed, from whiskey or tension, it was difficult to say. Alex filled his glass and looked across the fields toward his own manor house. Marigold wondered if Zosia noticed that Alex was always plotting how to make more money, to take advantage of an opportunity, things that sounded more like her father than she cared to admit.

That there had been no reply to her letter was more of a relief than anything else. She didn't have to be a genius to know that everything he supported was hateful and that the further away she was from him, the better. She wondered if she should begin pretending he was dead. She decided to ask Marek, but somehow, she didn't think he'd approve.

Buddy was in the deep end of the swimming pool. He shouted, "Marco!"

Then Emily and Marek shrieked, "Polo!" and dove underwater.

Marigold grabbed her towel and ran upstairs to her room. Supper would be in a few moments. There was still time to photograph the magic hour as Marek called it, when the shadows of early evening infused everything with that mysterious kind of light.

By eleven the next morning, Britain was at war with Germany.

PART III

THE WAR

Autumn
London

MARIGOLD DESCENDED THE NUMBER 11 AND PAUSED for a moment to readjust her gas mask, her helmet, and her handbag and camera. "It's just too much stuff," she muttered but then saw Kit running down the street toward her. She realized he was crying.

"Kit, what's wrong?"

He stopped and handed her a copy of the *Evening Standard*. "I don't know what to do."

Marigold read the announcement.

AIR RAID PRECAUTIONS FOR ANIMALS:
IF AT ALL POSSIBLE, SEND OR TAKE YOUR HOUSEHOLD ANIMALS INTO THE COUNTRY IN ADVANCE OF AN EMERGENCY. IF YOU CANNOT PLACE THEM IN THE CARE OF NEIGHBORS,
IT REALLY IS KINDEST TO HAVE THEM DESTROYED.

"We can't even have them at the estate! What am I going to do?" Snot and tears ran down his face. "I can't let them take her."

"Oh Kit."

"And me mum says I have to go with my class to Suffolk because we's going to be evacuated, then who's going to feed them? I hate these bloody Germans!"

"Come on."

Wordlessly, he followed her into the butcher who sold them some roast beef. They then walked together toward Cremorne.

"You know it's for lots of reasons that they've recommended it, right?"

"But that's not Lulu's fault!" She could tell he was about to start crying again.

"Of course not." She watched him feed Lulu and pet the puppies, his face twisted with grief. She'd ask Marek. Marek would know what to do.

"Oh no."

"We can't leave them there. It's just till we find them a home, Marek."

"You say that now, but unless you have some where for them to go…"

They continued working in silence, until Marek added, "The cat will be beside himself."

"But they're only puppies. Please Marek, at least for tonight."

He swore under his breath and then said, "Only if you stay with them. I'm going to my sister's. They'd better not get into anything."

"Thank you, Marek."

"I'm sure they need to be wormed."

"Yes, Marek."

"And go fetch some flea powder."

"Yes, Marek."

"Oh, for God's sake. Can we get to work please?"

Obediently she finished her tasks in silence. When he put on his jacket, she said, "Marek."

"Yes, Marigold."

"Do you think Alex Reilly might take them? He's plenty of room at that manor."

Marek gave her a look and then picked up the phone. "He's probably at Zosia's. Why don't you ask him?" Marek dialed the phone and then handed it to her. And indeed, Alex was there. She stammered out her request.

Alex replied, "Of course I will. Emily will be delighted. All for the war effort, eh?"

When she told Kit, he crossed his arms. "You won't let them kill them? Please don't lie to me."

"What? Kit, no! They're going to live in Sussex. I swear it. On a beautiful farm."

He sighed with relief. "I do wish we could have dogs at the estate."

"I know. But Lulu and the puppies are going to be ok."

"Promise?"

"Cross my heart, hope to die."

"Stick a needle in your eye?"

"Yup."

"That's a bloody stupid expression."

"Hey, somebody told me that 'bloody' is a bad word here. Is it?"

He looked at her and smiled. "Sometimes."

Under advisement of the government, during the first week of the war, four hundred thousand pets were put to sleep.

At first, the cinemas, pubs, and theatres were closed. Then, a few weeks later, they reopened. It was important that morale be kept high, and the citizens cheerful. Without entertainment, it was just too bleak. *Dark Victory* was on at the cinema on the corner of Old Church Street and King's Road.

It was the four o'clock show and not too terribly full. Zosia and Marigold squeezed into eighth row seats, grateful there wasn't a hat in front of them. Zosia nodded at the screen where Winston Churchill sat at his desk and looked out. He waved both hands forward as if gesturing to them directly. "*If words could kill,*" Churchill said, "*we should be dead already. But we are in a very different position from what we were ten weeks ago. We are far stronger than we were ten weeks ago. We are far better prepared to endure the worst malice of Hitler and his Huns than we were at the beginning of September.*"

"I do love Bette Davis," Zosia whispered.

"This isn't a tearjerker, is it?" Marigold wasn't sure she could take it.

Zosia patted her hand. "Oh darling, just watch it for the clothes. Bette Davis always looks marvelous in whatever she's doing. And besides, she plays an heiress. How tragic can it be?"

Churchill continued, "*I shall not attempt to prophesy whether the frenzy of a cornered maniac will drive Herr Hitler into the worst of all his crimes. But this I will say, without a doubt, that the fate of Holland, and Belgium, like that of Poland and Czechoslovakia and Austria, will be decided by the victory of the British Empire and the French Republic. If we are conquered, all will be enslaved. And the United States will be left, single handed, to guard the rights of men.*"

From CBS News:

THIS IS LONDON

"The other afternoon, I spent several hours underground studying the central control of London's air raid precaution system. One man can sit in that room and move ambulances, stretcher parties, gas decontamination squads and repair parties, just as though he had them on the end of a string. The nobs covering the walls resemble those in an army headquarters. The whole system is linked to local units by a direct telephone and if the telephones don't work, there are motorcycle dispatch riders standing by to carry messages. If London is bombed, one could sit in that room and by reading colored pins and disques on the maps, tell just where bridges have been blown up, where fire engines are needed, where additional ambulances are required and the position of reserve units that might be needed.

"It was quiet down there the other day, the elaborate maps on which one could follow the enemy approach of aircraft were clear. The telephone operators, young girls, who might have been college sophomores at home, sat at their instruments knitting, or reading. One was reading the *Life of Madame Curie*, another Tolstoy's *War and Peace*. The latest detective thrillers were also in evidence. Occasionally, they practice a little. The telephone rings, the operator takes down a message, passes it through a slot to a control officer, and in a few minutes' time, an ambulance brigade or fire engines go racing through the streets in a remote part of London on a practice trip. The whole scheme seems to be efficient and at the same time easy to operate. The Minister of Food will announce in the House of Commons the date for the introduction of rationing in Britain. And it is reported from Oslo that the

Norwegian Nobel Committee has reached a decision on its annual Peace award. It has been decided not to award a Peace Prize for 1939. I return you now to Columbia in New York.

— Edward R. Murrow, Columbia Broadcasting
System, November 29, 1939

* * *

ED MURROW's broadcasts were a huge success. And working on a show that everyone loved lent the office an exciting, urgent glamour.

When she wasn't working for Murrow, Marigold puttered with the Rolleicord, struggling to get the aperture just so, at the same time as framing a composition in its own perfect square.

At the darkroom in Lark Mews, she rinsed the prints one more time. "God damnit!" She'd overexposed half of the shots. What was even worse was that she was still chopping off everyone's heads. "Damnit, damnit, damnit, damnit!" Yet another roll of film wasted.

"Who the hell is that?" asked a woman in the front room. Marigold lifted her head. The voice was an American.

"Ha! It's Marigold," answered Marek.

Marigold came out of the darkroom. "Sorry."

The woman was blonde, with a face Marigold recognized from her mother's magazines, years ago. She couldn't pretend she wasn't starstruck. "You're Lee Miller."

The woman lit a cigarette. "I was once." Lee had been a model and a muse but was now a photographer in her own right.

Marek said, "Marigold hasn't quite whipped her Rolleicord into shape. As soon as she's mastered it, we're moving on to the Rolleiflex. Show Lee your contact sheets." Marigold handed some over to his guest. "Lee might help you more than I can."

Lee studied the pictures of Kit and his friends clowning around. "These are good."

"I've been using a Leica but would really love to work in square format. There's something with the Rolleiflex which is just more stylized."

"You took these using the Leica?"

Marigold nodded then handed her a few more. "These are with the Rolleicord."

Lee's smile was kind. "If you can work up the nerve and compensate for those five millimeters at the top, you could then do the photos of these kids with your Rolleicord."

Marigold opened her mouth to protest.

Lee shook her head. "No, no. Hear me out. Use the Rolleicord. Because when you do, they can see you. They can see you seeing them and it creates a stronger connection. It's something to do with our eyes and how we exchange energy. It sounds silly, but . . . Come with me on assignment next week. I bet you like fashion. Do you?"

Marigold nodded.

"Then bring the Rolleicord. I think you'll be surprised."

THE *VOGUE* STUDIO was in Hampstead. Marigold unloaded bags of lights, tripods, and various flashbulbs as traffic and pedestrians swarmed around them.

Lee scanned the area, murmuring, "Point of view, point of view." She looked up and down the street, over at the other buildings and then at the doorway where they would enter. There was no sign of the model. Lee asked, "Marigold. If you could do anything you want, anything at all, what would it be?"

Marigold answered without a moment's hesitation. "I would take a really great picture." Then she laughed, embarrassed. "Hopefully more than one. A lot of them would be great."

"Why do you want to take pictures?"

"Because, when someone sees something that I've

photographed, which I think is important enough to look at, then they're looking at the way I see the world."

"How do you see the world, Marigold?"

"I guess I see it much nicer than it actually is. You know? I see it the way I wish it was."

Lee nodded at this. "Ah, but then there's the tension of that versus what it actually is. You're a pretty girl. Is there any reason why you don't get in front of the camera?"

"Yes, there is." Marigold laughed again. "I don't like being told what to do!"

Lee nodded at this. "I don't like being told what to do either."

Marigold admired Lee's suit. It was clearly made for a man but altered to show off her curves. Lee's blonde hair was in a snood, over which rested a newsboys' cap to shade her eyes.

I should dress like that, Marigold thought.

A taxi pulled up and Lee waved. "Here they are. Remember what I said, Marigold."

"Point of view?" Which made Lee give her a thumbs up and nod.

Four different women emerged with garment bags, a portable typewriter, and briefcases. The tallest woman was so beautiful that she was unmistakably the model. Lee sent the others inside and said, "Right Jacqueline, hop back in the cab and then slowly emerge."

Lee glanced at a couple of men chatting just beyond them on the corner. She called, "'Scuse me, gents! Would you lend us a hand for just ten seconds?" Lee's charisma was such they obediently approached her.

Lee turned to Marigold. "We'll use the flash here. Now, what do you suppose is the most unexpected contrast in this moment the viewer might enjoy?"

"Uh . . ." Marigold held the flash where Lee indicated. "I don't know."

"What about indifference?"

"Excuse me?"

"Seriously. A gorgeous woman emerges from a cab in a street filled with men. But they are totally oblivious to her! Now why would that be?"

Marigold looked around and then saw them. "Because they're looking at the barrage balloons."

"Good! That's very good. That's what we'll do." Lee looked into her camera.

"Gentlemen!" Lee gave them a dazzling smile. "When this lady leaves the cab, please look up at the sky and search for any pesky activity beyond the balloons."

The men gave Lee a curious look, then wordlessly they nodded and did as they were told. The model got out of the cab. The men were oblivious, searching for activity up above. Lee took the picture.

As the men continued to look at the sky, the model walked into the building, and the men completely ignored her. Lee took another shot and advanced her film. "Marigold. Remember"— Lee smiled at her— "what did I say?"

"Point of view, Lee."

"That's right." Lee laughed.

None of them knew that the enemy was indeed lurking, waiting for the moment when barrage balloons would not be enough.

By December, Ed Murrow decided Marvin should report from Amsterdam.

When Marigold learned this, she knocked on Marvin's door. "Uh, Miss Breckenridge?"

"Marvin, please."

"Would you mail a letter for me when you get to Holland?"

Marvin arched an eyebrow. "You're not giving away state secrets, are you?"

Marigold laughed. "No, but the Dutch are allies, aren't they?"

Marvin said, "They're officially neutral. At least so far."

Marigold handed her an envelope addressed to Joop. Inside it were three pictures. One was their kiss on the Eiffel Tower. The second was from the Royal Hospital with the veterans in their red coats. And the last was in the peniche, when Marigold had held the camera toward a mirror as she looked in the viewfinder and Joop looked at her. Their shoulders were bare, his arm resting upon hers. On the back, Marigold had written *Merry Christmas*.

She left Marvin's office, thrilled at the thought of his opening the letter. But in the corridor, outside Mr. Murrow's, a small group had gathered around someone who was sobbing. It was his secretary, Miss Campbell.

Marigold whispered to Buddy, "What happened?"

Buddy shook his head, "It's her brother. He's missing in action."

Everyone became hushed, unsure what to say.

That afternoon, the bus was delayed and Marigold decided to walk. When the siren sounded, she quickly descended to the underground and sat upon the *Times* to keep her coat tidy. The platform quickly filled up. An hour passed, and people chatted to each other, quietly, waiting patiently. When they got the All Clear, a train arrived to great applause.

A man shouted, "How do you like that, Gerry?" Which made the crowd cheer and laugh.

During the next week, Ed Murrow called everyone into his office. "What we need is a break. Let's get out of town and take the team to Amsterdam. We'll check on Marvin and find out what's really going on. What do you say, gang?" To which everyone cheered and began planning the trip.

Winter

"So, my dear, once again, England is in this dreadful predicament." Buddy was working, Zosia and Marek were helping with refugees, but Marigold had stayed behind with Falaise. "You know, this is the twenty-third Christmas that my boys have been angels. Ronny, he was the elder, is the reason I know Zosia. They were betrothed."

"I didn't know that."

"She came just before the war started, and when they met, they fell desperately in love. Then he joined up. Of course, Ronny and Thomas, my younger son, enlisted together. They shipped out at the beginning of January 1915." Falaise sighed. "I never saw them again." The older woman looked at her, the life vanished from her face, haunted by loss and grief. "Their father, well, he was a dreadful alcoholic. The only reason I'd married him was that he touched me rather skillfully. Of course, things were very different then. But once the boys were . . . gone, well, he just died one night, drowning in his own vomit, the coward. Christmas can be such a difficult time for a person, do you not think?"

"Falaise." Marigold went and knelt before her.

She looked so sad, Marigold wanted to wipe her tears, to send them away and forget all about it. "Falaise, why don't we stretch our legs? The night is so wonderful during the blackout."

Reluctantly, Falaise agreed, and they made their way along Cheyne Walk until someone growled, "Who goes there! Friend or foe?"

"It's Marigold, Mr. Alwyn."

"Oh. Is that you, Miss McGrath? And Mrs. Cooper! A very happy Christmas to you, dear lady."

"Why, Mr. Alwyn. Good heavens, why thank you."

"Don't stay out too late now, ladies. All kinds of unsavory types out and about, even on Christmas Eve."

At this, Falaise gave a small laugh. "I say, Mr. Alwyn, you do know how to tempt a girl."

Walking back, she said, "That was a good idea, Marigold. A little fresh air, and a bit of a flirt with that charmer, the news agent. I do like Mr. Alwyn. Isn't he lovely?"

Amsterdam

It was a large grey house, between two others that looked much the same, only a few feet from a wide canal. Marigold took a deep breath and swallowed. Hands trembling, she pulled a chain and heard the bell ring inside.

Not two seconds later, Joop stood in the doorway, a pair of ice skates over his shoulders.

His gaze was impassive, and then suddenly she was in his arms. "Gouda! Gouda." He kissed her hair and her ears and her cheeks. "Come inside." He called out something in Dutch and then followed it with, "Mother!" he shouted. "There's someone I'd like you to meet!"

There was warmth and laughter. In a room at the end of the corridor, a pair of women sat with two small children, surrounded by toys and blocks. This had to be his mother and older sister, Bette.

"Of course, you will stay with us for lunch?" his mother asked.

Another sister who was younger than Joop joined them. "I'm Flortje," she announced. They walked back through the corridor and Marigold noticed the photos on the wall. One was clearly from a play or a film. Marigold realized its cousin was on the wall at Mr. Ganz's camera shop on 83rd Street.

"I've seen another photo from this same production."

"Have you?" Joop's mother stopped in front of the picture. "That's me. It was in Berlin. I was an actress then."

"Do you remember the photographer?"

"Only vaguely. I was about your age at the time. There was quite a bit going on."

"He owns the camera shop I use in New York City."

"Does he? Well, the world is a small place, isn't it? How extraordinary."

Everyone gathered at the table, the little children making a ruckus while Bette ignored them one second and cajoled them the next. Joop's father was the last to enter and he smiled at Marigold, seeing Joop hold her hand throughout the meal.

"And what will you do this afternoon?" asked his father.

"We'll skate on the Keizersgracht," Joop said.

"Oh, but I don't have a pair of skates," Marigold said, thanking God she'd be spared that humiliation.

"You can use mine," Flortje offered.

"Oh, that's very kind but—"

"What size are you?"

"I'm a thirty-eight. I'm sure your feet are much smaller than mine."

"No, no. I am thirty-eight, too!"

Outside the house, Marigold's knees began knocking as she laced up the skates. "Joop, I'm not much of a skater."

Joop crouched in front of her. He put his hands on her knees. "Marigold, together we will be Fred and we will be Ginger."

"Not Sonja Henie?"

He straightened up. "Now don't get carried away!" He held his hand out to her, then firmly wrapped his other arm around her waist. "Lean upon me." His skates started going every which way. "Wooah." He righted himself. "Just kidding. No. I like Fred and I like Ginger."

And so it was. They moved up and down the ice, singing their favorite songs, as he held her so firmly it was impossible to fall.

Afterward, they went to a café filled with other students. Everyone at their table chattered in Dutch until they noticed Joop answering only in English. "This is Marigold," he announced. "Marigold is from New York."

"New York!" one of them said. "What must that be like?"

Another said, "I went to New York once, when I was only little of course."

"You have a lot of Jews there, don't you? I'm Jewish and I'm going to emigrate as soon as possible. But getting a visa is now very difficult."

Another girl said, "But we don't have to worry about the Nazis coming to Holland, right, Joop?"

Another boy answered, "I think we should worry."

Joop said, "All that we've got is our cheese and our chocolate."

"No, we have beer."

"Oh, that's true, and Ginnever, too."

Joop continued, "We don't have anything for them. We were neutral last time. We're neutral this time."

"And the refugees?"

"That's what the Red Cross is for."

Marigold sipped her cocoa. The camp at Dovercourt Bay came to mind and she watched Joop's jaw tighten.

Someone else said, "The refugee agencies have had to pick up the tempo, I daresay."

"And you?" Marigold softly asked Joop. "What about you? Have you picked up the tempo?"

"When Professor Meyritz and I discussed the statistical outcomes of the pending events at such a tempo, it would make your head spin. That's the expression, yeah?"

"Yeah, that's the expression." She squirmed and failed to push away the ache in her heart that came from not knowing when she'd see Joop again.

It was late by the time the café closed for the night. The evening air was clear and cold.

They walked along the canal until they came to her hotel. A doorman in an elaborate uniform stood guard at the stairs. Joop whispered, "Do you think anyone will stop us if I accompany you?"

"No, they won't," she whispered back.

Rather than take the lift, they walked the three flights, their ice skates over their shoulders, silently knocking against their coats. She opened the door to her small room. The moon illuminated everything. Joop placed the skates by the door and took her coat, then stepped out of his boots. Suddenly, somehow, he'd taken off all of his clothes, standing before her in his long johns and heavy woolen knitted socks.

Marigold began to laugh and then stopped herself, realizing how much she loved him and that what she really wanted to do was to burst into tears.

"Gouda," he said. He took her hand, then kissed it and placed it on his chest. "Why are you laughing?" His voice and his smile were tentative. "Is it you're going to start crying?"

"I . . . I . . ." she was afraid she was going to hyperventilate. "It's because your socks are so ridiculous!"

"Ridiculous?" He shook his head as if shocked, then lifted her, placing her over his shoulder as if she were a sack. "Ridiculous? These are the socks my Oppas knitted me! They are the warmest socks I own."

"Who is that, your grandfather?"

"No, my nanny!" Laughing they fell upon the bed and she slipped out of her own clothes leaving her unremarkable socks upon her feet over the silk stockings she'd taken such care to wear in order to delight him.

It was grey the next morning. Marigold awoke to feel Joop's lips upon her neck and then her collarbone. He moved toward her breast then her belly, sliding the belt of her garters aside, and licking her naval. Time stopped. His tongue was inside her, his hands holding her hips.

"Joop." His warmth melted every sad fiber of her being and she started to come. "Joop."

"Ik hou van jou," he whispered. "I love you."

Then he was inside her, moving his hand to press against the bone of her pelvis. This time when she came, she watched his face as he came, too.

Downstairs, he helped himself to breakfast while Marigold conducted the business of checking out. A taxi to the station and then only minutes until they parted again, for how long was anybody's guess.

The cabdriver said something she didn't understand and Joop answered in the affirmative.

Looking out the window, all she could think was how much she wanted Joop to stay next to her, with his ridiculous socks and tender body to keep her warm. She stole a glance at him. He was staring straight ahead, lost somewhere in his thoughts.

The rain was freezing. Inside, the station was mobbed. She looked up for the platform information and then, below the sign, she saw the children. There were at least a few dozen. Standing with them were several adults, all of whom seemed to be on the edge of uncontained anguish.

Marigold froze to the spot. Joop saw her take it in.

"Gouda." She turned away from the children to look at him. He put down the ice skates and held her tightly. Then he took a step backward, "Gouda, with this war," He shook his head and embraced her again.

"What is it, Joop?" He let her go but could not meet her eyes.

Finally, he said, "We don't know what's going to happen." Joop struggled to peak. "Please, please. Do not wait for me."

"What?" Everything stopped. "What do you mean?" He was saying it had been a mistake.

"You don't have to . . ." He shrugged. "You must be free to have happiness . . ." He seemed unable to continue.

"I thought." Mortified, the blood rushed to her face. "I thought you . . ." It was like with Alan. More anger than shame began to pour out of her. "Goddamnit!" An old couple standing nearby turned to look at them. Marigold inched closer to Joop. "And Goddamn you."

Joop reached out to her, but she jerked away. "How dare you?" She spat out the words, "You think you can just raise my skirts, because I'm a Yank? Well, go to hell, Joop. Just go to hell."

She brushed off his arm and strode toward the platform. She would not look to see if he watched. She stepped around bewildered children, numbers hanging from their necks, some of them crying, struggling with their suitcases and surrounded by weeping parents as young women helped them board the train. Suddenly, Marigold had a terrible headache. This upset with Joop was nothing compared to what these families felt. She kept moving forward, searching for the right train car. Her head pounded from the sounds of the parents and children, the shouting of rail workers, and intermittent trains' whistles.

The truth of it was that working with Murrow, Marigold hadn't done a thing to really help anyone. Her own mother, Evangeline, had been a refugee. What would she have told Marigold to do now? But Marigold already knew the answer. She climbed aboard then turned to see if Joop was watching. But he had already gone.

Dear Mrs. Krumbull,

I've thought a great deal about the disservice I did to Woburn House last summer and indeed those people involved in its mission. Since that time, I've had the privilege of working for Mr. Edward R. Murrow at CBS but watching the newsreels of late has led me to write this letter to you.

Last week I was in Holland and watched a Kindertransport board the train and finally saw, firsthand, what it is like for those who must say goodbye. If you would give me another chance to be of service, I would be so grateful to be doing something that actually matters to people at this time.

You might say, "Well, what good are you? You've already shown that your indifference to paperwork makes your efforts little more than perfunctory." But what I should like to propose is taking portraits of the children, as I assisted the photographers Mr. Hutton and Miss Deutsch at Dovercourt Bay. If you thought it suitable, perhaps I might do this once they've settled at Camp Kitchener or any of the other places they'll go after they arrive in Britain.

I've been working as a photographer for Mr. Murrow's team at CBS and have become somewhat proficient in the darkroom, too. Please find enclosed a few snapshots I took of children living at the estate down the street from my home, as well as a few on that day in December when I last saw Miss Breen. Photographs would provide some comfort to any of the family members who are still able to receive correspondence, as well as a record for the children's time at the English facilities themselves. I know there's an arrival of children by train this coming Friday. If I might be of any assistance in any way at Liverpool Street, I would be very grateful to provide it.

I hope you'll say yes.
Your humble obedient servant,
Marigold McGrath.

Falaise nodded. "I think that's very nice, dear. Just the right tone of humility."

Marigold handed it to Buddy. "What do you think?"

"Yeah, looks pretty obsequious to me."

* * *

IN THE EIGHTEEN months since Marigold had been at Woburn House, the refugee agencies had all moved to Bloomsbury House in Great Russell Street. The facilities were larger and the energy more intense. More than twenty thousand letters now arrived every week from those seeking assistance to get their families and friends out of harm's way and over to Britain.

For his part, Colonel Mayhew seemed unchanged. He took a sip from his tea and said, "Miss McGrath, Mrs. Krumbull told me

151

about your very helpful offer. What is it that you propose to do exactly?"

"Uh, Colonel Mayhew sir, I know my time here was . . . that it didn't end well, but um, I read there's a transport arriving at Liverpool Street today, and I wondered if I could be of assistance with that?"

"Oh?" he called into the next room. "Miss Breen!"

Marigold looked at the floor. She couldn't imagine what Miss Breen might say.

She heard Miss Breen's voice. "Yes Colonel?"

When Marigold looked up, Miss Breen was still speaking. "It's a very kind offer and we will need all the help we can get." She handed Marigold a folder. "You'll be given the list of the children who actually made it onto the train, from which point we'll ask those who are collecting them for the names of those they'll be hosting. If all goes well, it shouldn't take more than an hour or two."

"Would it be helpful to take their pictures?"

Colonel Mayhew considered this. "Perhaps. If a child is in such a state you think it would be best not, then don't. But for the rest, their pictures will be a record of their safe arrival. So, chop-chop. The train arrives this afternoon!"

The crowd at Liverpool Street overwhelmed every space in the station. All trains from everywhere were delayed. Lady Lyon, who was leading the boots on the ground, had set up a card table on the edge of the platform. Families who had agreed to foster the children hovered by the table. At last, at last, the train pulled along the platform.

Slowly, the children emerged from the train. They looked much younger than the group at Dovercourt. But they were smartly turned out, their parents having clearly wanted to put their best foot forward. Some faces were curious and open, others were in shock, their faces streaked with tears.

Marigold took a discreet step back. The Rolleicord hung on its strap around her neck. She looked down at the viewfinder and adjusted the aperture. The picture came into focus. The train. The platform. And an endless line of children. She pushed the button and wound the film.

"Oh my God." A frazzled looking chaperone approached her and lit a cigarette. "You're with us, right?"

Marigold nodded.

She handed Marigold the list. "It was appalling."

"What do you mean?"

"At Hannover, not two stops into our journey, the bloody gestapo had each and every one of these kids get off of the train and empty their suitcases. And the little ones—well someone's going to have to do a great deal of washing to clean up. But still" —the chaperone took a drag and exhaled— "we're here. They're going to be safe."

Marigold knelt down by a little girl standing alone. The number 53 hung from her neck. "Was heist du?"

"Irene." She looked about seven years old.

"Möchtest du, dass ich Ihr Foto mache?"

The little girl recoiled in fear. "Warum?"

"Für deine Eltern."

"Meine Eltern sind im Gefängnis."

Prison. Irene's parents were in prison. It was impossible to even imagine such a thing. Marigold took a deep breath and forced herself to think of something to say.

"Oh! Well, perhaps you . . ." She wished she spoke better German. She turned to the chaperone. "Could you help me please? Just ask her if she'd like to have a photo for herself?"

"That's a bit misguided, don't you think?" With a sigh, the chaperone asked if she wanted a photo in German. "Willst du für seine Kamera posieren?"

The little girl named Irene looked doubtful.

"You can take one of me first." Marigold held up the camera and said. "Es könnte spass machen!" *It will be fun.*

At this, Irene reconsidered. She gave Marigold a little smile. Marigold looked into the viewfinder, and as Lee had described, she then looked at Irene and made sure that Irene registered this. A shy smile made its appearance. Marigold pushed the button and advanced the film. "Now your turn."

Thanks to Marek's endless supply of film, Marigold's camera was the perfect deflection for the children's apprehension of what was to come. As their numbers began thinning, those awaiting collection began to pose, first alone and then together, with rail workers and the chaperones and, finally, clowning around as much as circumstances permitted. It was clear that Marigold's taking pictures helped them to relax and know they were safe. She had enough German and the older ones had enough English they were able to negotiate the few moments that were caught for posterity.

WHEN SHE SHOWED Marek her contact sheets he began laughing and said, "Well done. You are a clever girl. Let's show them to Stefan."

Stefan Lorant had two magazines. One was called *Lilliput* and the other was *Picture Post*. When Marek brought Marigold and her photos to him, Stefan said, "I already have more of these kids' pics than I know what to do with."

"Just have a look." Marek handed him the folder.

Stefan looked at one, and then, smiling, he looked at another. Soon he was chuckling and laughing. "These are wonderful, Marigold. Really. Listen we'll run them in *Lilliput,* but I won't be able to give you a credit."

"You won't?"

"What is your status here? I mean to work."

"Oh. I . . . I don't know."

"So let's just run these pictures, shall we? Really marvelous."

AT THE NEWSAGENT, Mr. Alwyn said, "*Lilliput* magazine? Yes indeed." He handed her a copy. "Here you are."

Marigold opened the magazine and blushed. "Look Mr. Alwyn, these photographs are mine."

"Are they?" He peered over and studied the pages. "Well done, Miss McGrath! Very well done."

"Look, Mari." She and Trude were arm in arm, walking down King's Road. Along a wall under construction were advertisements for *Lilliput*. Normally, the covers were illustrations, but this time, the magazine was advertised with a photo instead. The photo used was hers. A little boy and girl holding their suitcases, standing on either side of a bobby, who was crouched, so he was the same height as the children, his hands on each of their shoulders. His expression was gentle. The children looked back at him, both of them curious, yet vulnerable and brave.

"Give me your camera." Trude said. "We should take your picture with this."

Marigold looked up and down the street to see if there was anyone else was looking at the ad. There didn't seem to be. But still, there was the strange peaceful stillness that came from having done and made something, even though no one else knew that she was the one who had taken the picture.

"Smile," Trude said.

It was strange, but oh, so pleasant, too.

PART IV

THE ENGELANDVAARDER

Amsterdam
Spring

Joop gave the small volume back to the librarian. An original copy of *Letters of Euler on Different Subjects in Natural Philosophy, Addressed to a German Princess*. He loved this book and would visit it in the library whenever he was in Amsterdam. He thought about Marigold. She had been so angry the last time he saw her. Perhaps, if he could get her a copy of this, it might help her to understand the complexity of his feelings. He felt as though his entire life was filled with this need to make sense out of all the conflicting problems and situations that exist even in the face of extraordinary joy and harmony. Or was it the other way around? Ah well.

The man looked at his library card. "Kasander. Are you related to Judge Albertus Kasander?"

"I am his son."

The man smiled at him and stamped the library card. "I know who your father is. I heard him speak a few years ago. Will you go into the law as he did?"

"No, I am more of a maths person."

"Well, we need good maths people too." The librarian nodded. "Good day, Mr. Kasander."

Joop crossed the street and untied his bicycle. The afternoon light was long and tinged with gold. It promised to be a beautiful evening. He thought about Marigold and what she might be doing. Then he reminded himself there was no use musing over such things. Britain was at war. At least that wouldn't happen in the Netherlands. Germany had no bone to pick with the Dutch.

Their relations had remained neutral all through the Great War. Joop cycled faster, picking up speed. Besides, Germany and the Netherlands had signed the neutrality guarantee in '39.

His friend Piet had invited him to go sailing at Zandvoort that evening. And Joop agreed because he didn't want to think about things until Monday.

It was a Thursday night. They'd brought the boat in and sat on the edge of the dock.

"Drink up!" shouted Piet, "American girls are a dime a dozen."

"That's not true."

"Ok, maybe not. But you will bounce back. There are plenty of fish in the sea."

"No. That's not true either."

"Ah now, come on."

They'd been drinking for a few hours by then and Piet pushed Joop and Joop pushed back hard. They fell into the water, laughing even while Joop was crying. But the North Sea was so freezing, so cold, that Joop said, "Come on, you bastard, let's get out of here."

They staggered up to the shore. The night sky was unusually clear.

"What do you think is going to happen?"

"It will be like last time." Piet put another log on the fire. "We'll keep our noses clean and the Krauts will leave us alone."

"Right."

"They'll leave us alone."

"Says you."

"Joop." He handed him the whiskey. "Drink up. You need to take your mind off this."

They nodded off by their campfire and slept past dawn while countless parachutes brought the Nazi invasion to their country. When a pair of war planes roared overhead, they woke suddenly. The planes grew smaller crossing the North Sea.

"Oh Christ." Joop thought of Marigold and everything he

loved about England. Then the planes grew larger. They had turned around and were headed back.

"Joop." Piet grabbed his sneakers and began running toward the small shipyard. "Come on!" Joop quickly followed.

They threw themselves down just as the bullets rained overhead. Whatever Joop had thought, clearly had been wrong. Whatever he had believed, Joop realized he was very much mistaken.

Four days later, the Germans leveled Rotterdam, destroying twenty-four thousand buildings and displacing eighty thousand of its citizens. The German offensive had begun. As soon as the Queen and her ministers fled into exile, the Netherlands offered its surrender. The German occupation of the Low Countries was absolute.

* * *

IN THE WEEKS THAT FOLLOWED, it seemed that every day was sunny and rain came only at night. Stunned by the invasion, Dutch citizens were thrust into a state of muted shock. Some were sympathizers who were only too happy to accommodate the German occupation, but there were patriots, too. There were also opportunists, black marketeers, and resisters. Some of them were communists and some of them were Christians. Then there were the Jews.

BEHIND THE HOUSE on Keizersgracht was a large terrace and garden. Resting on a chaise longue with his eyes closed, it was possible to forget the events of the last weeks, indeed whether anything was different at all.

"Joop." His mother put her hand on his shoulder. He had dozed off while studying. But now, with his eyes open, it was impossible to think about anything but the last weeks. "Joop," she said again and sat down beside him. "You know I met your father just after the war."

"Yes, I know."

"And things were very chaotic then. I had grown up in a family that was—"

"They were in the theatre. You told me this already."

"But Joop, what I didn't tell you, because it didn't seem important then"—she took his hand and held it firmly— "it's important now, because, because . . ."

"What?"

Her voice dropped. "My parents were Jewish." She looked at Joop and the love in her gaze pushed away any possible response to this. He knew his parents had secrets. But that this should be one of them— It was hard to believe this was the first time she had discussed this. "I think it's one reason your father has always been so concerned with the plight of Jews here and in Germany. Um," She softly cleared her throat as if something had caught her words. "And because we chose, most definitely, to not be religious, it didn't seem to be something we needed to discuss with you."

Joop closed his eyes. He wanted to pretend the conversation

wasn't happening. But his mother remained at his side, still holding his hand, not letting go.

Finally, he asked, "Do the girls know?"

"Not yet."

Over the years, he had often not understood his parents, but now, this was beyond anything—

"Are you going to leave?" he asked.

"No! Why?"

"Mama."

"Joop. This is my country. This is your father's country. They can't make us leave."

He moved to pull his hand away, but she kept holding it. Sighing, he finally relaxed and they leaned into each other, as if he were still a little boy. There were birds chirping in a small fountain under a flowering tree. The dog changed his napping position on the flagstones.

"With your father as a judge, he's been assured we'll have certain protections. Certain privileges. He's—well, he has to resign, of course, but—"

"What? When did that happen?"

"Yesterday. That's why I decided to tell you now. I've written to Bette. I'll speak with Flortje this evening."

* * *

In Leiden, Professor Meyritz said to Joop, "We could use your help." The professor made no secret of his contempt for the NSB's rapid expansion and collaboration with the Germans. "You know the situation will not grow less urgent."

There had been whispers and meetings, students organizing— how to forge documents, how to hide Jews, how to kick those Goddamn Nazis out of their country.

"Think carefully before you decide anything, Joop." Professor Meyritz tapped tobacco into the bowl of an enormous pipe.

When Joop didn't answer, the old man said, "Then you must

163

think carefully again, before you take any action. Pass me that, would you?" He gestured to a gold lighter on top of a pile of papers. Joop had left England specifically to study with Professor Meyritz and until that awful day, he believed himself to be happy, at least when he was working on formulas and calculations.

As for Marigold, on the day she came to the house, his father had insisted, "Do not keep this girl on a string if there's going to be a war." She had been in the other room at the time, collecting Flortje's skates and his father had been adamant. "You must let her go. Think about it, Joop. The kindest thing is for there to be no false hopes, no pining over something that will most likely be destroyed." And yet Joop couldn't stop thinking that perhaps his father had been wrong. But still, Joop had let her go and it was awful to think about her. It was much better just to focus on the math.

"What are you going to do?" Joop asked.

The professor shrugged. "I'm an old man. I'm not too concerned for myself. As for my wife, well"—he gave a small chuckle— "up until Rotterdam, we were hopeful for an American visa. But you, Joop. The Germans play for keeps. They'll think nothing of stealing, no, I mean killing, our best and brightest. By whom I mean you, and those like you. You must work very hard to stay alive. This country will need you once this war is over. Now let's get back to work."

* * *

PIET BROUGHT the beers to their seats outside the tavern. Two German soldiers conducted surveillance by the small bridge across the canal. Piet gave them a look then lit a cigarette.

"I never thought of myself as loving violence before." He spoke so softly that Joop had to lean forward to hear him. "The way I see it, there are two avenues open to us."

"Yeah?"

"Either we join the Nederlandse Unie, or—"

"What? They're going to cooperate with the Germans."

"No, it only looks that way. Their mandate is to preserve Dutch culture. So we don't become Germans! And besides, Nederlandse Unie will prevent those fucking Dutch Nazis from securing office. Or"—he took a deep drag of his cigarette and nodded toward the Germans—"we kill them."

"Hmm." Piet was Jewish. And now, astonishingly, Joop was too. There was a term for it. Mischlinge. Joop asked, "Why not do both?"

But who was he kidding? Joop was not a killer.

His father, despite being a judge, had always been a man of few words. But since the invasion, he'd become a virtual mute. Joop made his way over to the courthouse. Here too were German soldiers, stationed at the door.

He ran up the steps two at a time. The door to his father's chambers were open. He had started the business of packing.

"Joop. To what do I owe your visit?" Piles of folders and briefs were everywhere.

"Mama spoke with me."

"Ah."

"I've been doing some thinking."

He studied his son. "At the tavern?"

Joop nodded. "It shows, hunh?"

"Only when you slur." Then he smiled. "And sway."

"Well, I was hoping for some friendly advice."

"As luck would have it, I'll soon have enough time to give you all the advice in the world." The judge grabbed his hat. Both of them nodded toward the Germans at the door and exited the building. Outside, the air was soft, promising another beautiful evening.

Joop said, "The North Sea crossing is one hundred miles to England, isn't it?" If he could just get to England, then he could fight.

His father answered, "You know I've heard that fishing boats can make it there in less than two days." They stood at the curb, watching several German army trucks navigate the traffic.

"Really?"

The judge nodded. "Apparently, some of them still do. In spite of the war."

Father and son looked at each other for a long moment. The judge added, "For some men, they do it because of the war."

The traffic light changed. Neither of them said a word.

London

By May, everyone had someone who was caught in the appalling turn of events. Three hundred thousand French and British soldiers were trapped. If they weren't evacuated, the whole thing would soon go belly up. Then there'd be a German offensive into England.

Marigold could not push Joop from her mind. She studied the photos at the houseboat. How their skin touched, his arm draped across her shoulder, his smiling at the mirror as she looked down at her camera was too painful. She had to clamp down the memory's happiness. Her eyes grew red from crying. Was he all right? Had he become a soldier? What if he'd been in Rotterdam? Or in France?

The photos at the Chelsea Hospital were in color and Joop had been right. It had been the perfect place for that film and camera. How was it possible her broken heart actually hurt so much? She put the photos down as a sob began tearing at her throat and placed the pillow over her head. Why did he let her go?

Buddy knocked on the door. "Mac."

Oh god, she thought. Not now. "What is it?" She sat up.

"Mac, come on."

"Go without me."

"No, you come too."

When she didn't answer, he added, "We need to get stuff for Falaise."

Groaning, she laced up her shoes and followed him downstairs. The wireless was blasting from the living room. Buddy slipped in and turned it down.

"I think she's napping." They went down to the street level and onto King's Road.

"Why am I here? You don't need me to go with you, Buddy."

"Yeah, I do." They walked on in silence. Finally, he said, "This is a real hard day for Falaise, and I think we should discuss it." He stopped and turned to her. "You know how her sons died, right?"

"It was in the last war."

"They died in France. Both of them, at the Somme." By which he meant the months long battle with more than a million casualties.

"I didn't know."

They resumed walking.

"You're not the only one with heartache, my friend. We've got to be here for each other."

"I just can't stop—" They arrived at the grocer.

"Yes, you can."

He held the door open for her and followed her inside. "Get a handle on this thing! Look to see how you can help someone besides yourself. Because It's only getting started. The Krauts might be here in a matter of weeks. What are you going to do then? Sulk in your room?"

"That's not fair."

"Yes please?" the woman at the counter asked.

"I'll take six of those fine-looking oranges and how about some shortbread biscuits." He handed her a ration card.

"An excellent choice sir." The woman nodded and began bagging the fruit.

Buddy turned back to Marigold. "None of it is fair, Marigold. Not one single bit of it."

From CBS Radio:

"The Allied rear guard is still holding Dunkirk against increasing German pressure. Heavy German field guns are pounding the beaches and efforts to remove more men are continuing. According to Mr. Anthony Eden, more than four-fifths of the British expeditionary forces have been evacuated.

"The Air Force claims at least 125 German planes have been shot down in the Dunkirk area during the last two days. Today's score has given us thirty-five Germans down and eight British fighters lost. Yesterday, I spent several hours at what may be tonight, or next week, Britain's first line of defense, an airfield on the southeast coast. German bases weren't more than ten minutes flying time away. . . I talked with pilots as they came back from Dunkirk. . . As the ground crew swarmed over the aircraft, refueling motors and guns, we sat on the ground and talked.

"Out in the middle of the field, the wreckage of a plane was being cleared up. It had crashed the night before. The pilot had been shot in the head, but had managed to get back to his field. The Royal Air Force prides itself on never walking out of a plane until it falls apart. I can tell you what those boys told me. They were the cream of the youth of Britain. As we sat there, they were waiting to take off again. They talked of their own work, discussed the German Air Force with all the casualness of Sunday morning quarterbacks discussing yesterday's football game.

"There were no nerves, no profanity, and no heroics. There was no swagger about those boys in wrinkled and stained uniforms. The movies do that sort of thing much more dramatically than it is in real life. They told me of the patrol from which they'd just returned. Six Germans down, we lost two. . . I return you now to Columbia in New York."

— June 2nd, 1940 Edward R. Murrow, This Is London

Marigold straightened her belt, her helmet, her gasmask, camera, and purse. Whenever she was in uniform, it always seemed she clunked, clunked along like a cow with its bell. Walking to the Arts Club, she resolved to give up the camera and handbag.

Falaise was in the club garden, sitting near a willow tree. She turned to Marigold, and her face was impassive, her eyes hidden by dark glasses.

Falaise tapped the seat next to her. "I worry about you, dear. Really." She sighed. "We don't know what's going to happen."

"Well, I think we should hope for the best." Marigold unloaded her stuff and leaned back.

"Yes, but my dear. Your father and I have corresponded and"

—

When had Falaise been in touch with her father? Marigold opened her camera case. Her face was suddenly flushed. She took out the Rolleicord and fiddled with the lens.

"Really dear, he believes the Germans will invade."

"Why does he think that?" Marigold nearly choked on her words. "I can't imagine—"

"He seems to have it on good authority."

"I'm sure he does." She thought of him huddling with the American Bund, relishing the thought of invading England.

"He wants you to return to New York. It will be for the best, dear."

Marigold slipped the camera back in its case. "Somehow, I doubt that very much." She stood up and willed her legs to stop trembling.

"Now don't be disagreeable."

Marigold picked up her gas mask and strapped it over her shoulder. "I have to report to Mr. Alwyn."

"What about your duties with Mr. Murrow?"

"He understands that my volunteer work must come first. He supports my doing this." Her mouth went dry considering what it really meant, simply walking around until something was blown up or worse. It was so nerve racking it made her sick. She straightened her back. "As you can see, Falaise, I have 'rounds this evening."

At Central Command she ran up the stairs. There was a sad looking water closet just on the landing beside the office. Mr. Alwyn's voice carried into the corridor, instructing the group for the evening's patrol. Marigold slipped into the loo and locked the door. Her fingers trembled as she pulled her gear out of the way, just in time to kneel over the toilet and vomit.

The next day at Bloomsbury House, she found Zosia at a desk, sorting through the endless letters seeking help.

Zosia looked up. "Listen Marigold, the idea is to evacuate as many children as we can. At this point, at least here in Britain, it doesn't matter what their status is—they need to go somewhere out of harm's away. Your first lady, Mrs. Roosevelt, is behind the United States Committee for the Care of European Children specifically to get Jewish children out of the continent, but they'll take those who are in Britain, too."

"How can I help?"

"You're going to chaperone the first crossing."

"What do you mean?" Zosia was surely mistaken. Marigold was going to continue working with Marek.

"You'll go back to New York with them." Had Marek said something to Zosia without telling Marigold? Only the day before he had said how much she contributed to the studio.

Marigold took a step back. "Oh, no Zosia. I can't do that."

Zosia looked up from her desk. "Why on earth not?"

"Because, because . . ." She couldn't mention Joop. Besides their relationship was over. He'd said so himself. Nor could she say that the idea of seeing her own father was so repugnant that she'd just as soon volunteer for the frontline rather than go back to New York.

"I'm . . . I'm not returning to the States."

Zosia didn't speak for a moment.

"I'm helping here. I'm—Marek is helping me—"

"Marek is helping you do what?"

"He's helping me with my photos of kids for *Lilliput* magazine. Stefan Lorant said, when I'm ready, he'll feature some in *Picture Post*." She could barely speak now. "It's going to create the attention that's needed for the British." What was it Lorant said? Her mouth was dry. "To be sympathetic toward refugee children." Her voice trailed off.

Her palms were wet. Marek, Lee Miller, Stefan Lorant. These people had taken a shine to her and were teaching her how to take pictures. Not just photos, but great pictures! She couldn't leave now.

"Marigold," Zosia spoke very gently. "That work is being done by many, many accomplished photographers already. I don't think anyone is in dire need of your contribution in that department. And as a matter of fact, Stefan Lorant is being deported. Now, come on."

"What? Marek said that he's friends with Churchill. That's he's very important!"

"Both of those things are true. But Stefan is also disliked by some powerful antisemites."

"What do you mean?"

"England has antisemites, too. They're not just in Germany. What's happened to Stefan Lorant is very wrong. I heard he's moving to America. So, Marigold, I think the last thing you need to worry about is publishing your photographs."

It was then Marigold realized Zosia didn't think she had the chops. The hollowness of disappointment began to puddle around her heart. Had Marek said as much? As if reading her mind, Zosia added, "My brother is very generous, but Marigold—"

"No."

Stick up for yourself, Marigold, the voice inside her warned.

"I'm not going. I'm sure there are a ton of Americans who'd be only too happy to go back because I'm going to stay here. Britain is my home. I live here now. It's my home and I'm going to defend it."

Summer

The summer became strange, people confused, uncertain how to act. Before Dunkirk, everyone shrugged, it was just a phony war. It seemed too much fuss, what with ration cards, lugging one's gas mask everywhere. Now, no one knew if it was business as usual, or if the world was coming to an end.

And there remained the unspoken question, where were the Americans?

Falaise stockpiled canned goods which now filled the corners of each room. Children who'd been evacuated to the countryside returned, giving their parents what for if it was suggested they should leave once again.

But for Marigold, the places to work on taking pictures became endless. There were refugees in Bristol, refugees in Essex and even as far as Devon. Setting up her camera, her teachers' voices echoed in her mind.

"It's the speed of the film, Marigold," Marek reminded her.

"Remember, with the Rolleiflex you can't go in too close. Think about the entire composition," Lee Miller added.

"Catch the humanity, the life on each face," Stefan Lorant declared. "For every twenty pictures, three of them might be good."

"For every one hundred pictures, there might be two of them which are great. *Picture Post* wants the great ones," Marek said, handing her more rolls of film than she could carry.

"Where are you getting all of this?" Marigold's eyes widened at the endless volume of his supplies.

Marek raised an eyebrow. "Ministry of Information, dearie."

ARRIVING AT DOVERCOURT BAY, or the Calgarth Estate in the Lake District, Marigold would present her letter of introduction from Stefan Lorant.

"But you look so young," was always the response.

"I stay out of the sun," was her standard reply following whoever it was to see the children in the lunchroom. Marigold's German was both good and bad enough to make people laugh, so the young refugees took to her more often than not.

She visited farms, where the children earned their keep working in the field. She went to Quaker Schools which now enrolled refugees, and a small school where German Jews learned performance and art. There were schools that had once been in London, and now evacuated, were dotted along the coast.

"These are marvelous, Marigold." Marek examined a contact sheet with a magnifying glass much like a jeweler's. "Make sure your aperture is focused on the story you want to tell. Not this foreground here."

"Try and capture their inner thought the moment they look at the camera," Lee Miller said. "You only have a second to catch their reaction to that instant."

Marigold returned to visit the locations again. With the refugees' genuine, spontaneous welcome, she soon found, thanks to Marek's endless supply of film, that the shining flash of a child's personality was as potent a story as the tragedy of their circumstance.

Grudgingly, Zosia had to concede. Marigold's pictures were wonderful.

* * *

SHE READ THE POSTCARD, even as her heart contracted, unsure whether to laugh or cry.

Dear Marigold.

Much has changed here since I last saw you. I think of you always. The way that
*   we left it, I am not surprised if you don't think of me now. But I just wanted to*
*   send you my love. With best wishes, JOOP.*

It was a picture of a windmill amongst a field of tulips. But it was sent with an English stamp, and the postmark was from London. It was better to shrug it off. Perhaps it was a joke.

* * *

"I SAY!" Falaise was downstairs, cooing with delight. "That's a very smart uniform."

"Thank you, Mrs. Cooper."

"I'll just let her know you're here."

"What's that?"

"I said—"

But Marigold was already on the landing, and there he was, in uniform, a black beret fastened to the epaulet of his jacket, a leather strap diagonally across his chest fastened to the belt around his waist.

Bursting with happiness, she could see it wasn't a joke after all. "Joop." She was afraid she might swoon.

"I am hoping you'll come to have tea with me."

Marigold glanced at the floor to catch her breath. She looked up. His uniform was very handsome. "Where should we do that?"

"At the Savoy?"

Falaise watched this keenly, her ear horn angled so she didn't miss a word. "Oh my dear, tea at the Savoy would be perfect this afternoon. Then afterwards you can walk along the Strand, maybe take in a show?" It was miraculous how sometimes Falaise heard every single word and didn't miss a thing.

A taxi was waiting on the side street. Joop opened the door and climbed in behind Marigold.

"You certainly took your chances, didn't you, Joop?" They had yet to embrace but she'd be damned if she were the one to buckle first.

"Americans say, luck is the residual of skill and preparedness, don't they?"

"What's that got to do with having a taxi?" She tucked her hands under her knees to keep from hugging him.

"I had to be prepared. In case I was lucky, and you said yes."

AT THE SAVOY, in the room where they served tea, there was a delicate, cage like structure. It rested under a large glass cupola. Inside the cage sat a trio of musicians who accompanied the clinking of cutlery upon plates amongst the murmuring voices of uniformed men and elegant women.

Joop and Marigold were shown to a table near the cage and a waiter marked their ration cards.

Joop said, "We would like everything, yes please."

They were brought tea and cakes. Then a trolley filled with scones and jam and cucumber sandwiches appeared. Finally, the waiter bowed, leaving them alone.

Marigold asked, "How did you get here?"

"A British trawler picked me up from a Dutch fisherman." Joop popped a sandwich in his mouth and chewed. "The water was very cold! When I got ashore, I was arrested, interrogated, and then brought to Her Majesty."

"The Queen of England?"

"Ha, no, Queen Wilhelmina! She's just in Belgravia." He smiled. "She's currently recruiting."

"Is that when you sent me the postcard?"

"Yeah." He nodded happily. "I was training and couldn't get away."

Before she could stop herself, Marigold said, "I thought you broke up with me."

"Gouda." For a moment neither of them spoke. Finally, he whispered, "As a man of honor, I cannot—"

A waiter said, "May I interest you in more hot water, madam?"

"What? Yes, thank you." The waiter replaced the larger silver pot of water.

Joop murmured, "I cannot ask you to wait."

"But I prefer my tea stronger."

"No, Marigold." He put his hand on hers. "When I go, I might not come back." The music suddenly stopped. Her ears roared. She wondered if everyone was staring, waiting for her to start crying. She took a deep breath. What would Trude do? Something sophisticated, for sure.

She gave him a little smile. "What a strange thing to say."

The band resumed playing. It had just been a pause in the song.

She glanced around the room, then attempted to make an ironic smile, terrified she'd burst into tears. "Are you a spy?" she asked. She thanked God no one was watching them. Her question sounded ridiculous, hardly sophisticated.

Joop shook his head. "How can a man who loves cheese be a spy? Honestly, you American girls have the craziest ideas."

She opened her mouth to answer, but then realized the band had stopped again. Now the roar in her ears was, in fact, planes overhead.

Sirens blared, and waiters rushed around the tables. "Ladies, gentlemen, please make your way to the shelter downstairs." The sky flickered bright white like lightning.

A massive boom shook the chandeliers overhead.

"Come on, come on." Joop dragged her under the table. He counted, and on the number five another explosion rumbled, this time further away. They crawled back out. The room was deserted, glasses and food having tumbled to the floor. Joop opened a door out onto the terrace. Black smoke billowed toward the left. Over to the right, they raced down a set of stairs, underneath the hotel.

Joop pounded on the door.

It opened a small crack. "This way, this way please."

It was a basement. Sandbags lined the walls. Folding chairs and card tables had been placed throughout. A waiter led them past those who only moments ago were taking tea.

There was another deafening boom. The room darkened and the earth shook. Gradually, the lights began to brighten. Everyone remained silent as a fine shower of dust covered their shoulders.

The musicians were over in a corner. The violinist said, "One and two and . . ." He began to sing her very favorite, *"If I didn't care . . ."*

Joop led her to the chairs closest to the music. He put his arm around her shoulders and softly, he sang along. They were safe now, but the thought that they might become trapped, or even killed was in the back of everyone's mind. But no one gave way to showing it.

She willed herself to remain calm. "I'm going to Sussex tomorrow."

Joop crossed his arms. "What will you do there?"

"I'm helping with the evacuation."

A waiter approached them yet again, this time with a tray. "May I interest you in a sandwich?" Marigold wondered where on earth the food came from.

As if reading her mind, the waiter said, "We have a kitchen, here, down underground."

"Oh." Joop offered her one, "Marigold?"

She nodded and held the sandwich in her hand.

Joop took one for himself. He opened his mouth with an enormous bite.

Marigold watched him while he chewed. "What kind is it?"

Joop had a look and smiled. "I think you know."

* * *

AN HOUR PASSED and then another. The lamps overhead swayed in the rumbling as the mortar dust continued to fall like snow. By now, the band was chatting amongst itself, but the waiters kept checking on all of their guests.

"Will you be here when I come back?" Marigold whispered.

"I don't know."

"I wish you could stay." Damn, the tears began falling. Damnit, she had to get a grip. No one else seemed to be crying.

"I'll ask the queen." He wiped the tear from her cheek.

"What?"

"She's the boss. She tells me when I can stay or when I should go."

"She does not."

"Yes! I assure you. I will say, Your Majesty. Marigold, my American goddess, needs me to stay. Please, Your Majesty, make it so."

She poked him in the rib and then he said after a moment, "My parents and Flortje are still there. The situation is not good, Marigold."

"I'm sorry."

"Gouda," he murmured. "Hey," and kissed her softly on the mouth. The relentless pounding continued. Joop bowed his head, chuckling to himself.

"What?" she asked.

"It's just occurred to me that cheese tastes not so delicious when kissing."

"Oh Joop." He put his arm around her, and she leant against him, marveling at how she was bursting with happiness even as rockets exploded along the Thames, destroying their world in a war that was just beginning.

* * *

MARIGOLD RANG the door at the Guinness Estate. Streams of children ran past her, down the pavements making their way to the buses, which would take them either directly to the country-side or over to Charing Cross.

Kit came out to the vestibule and swore under his breath, "I'm not bleeding going."

"Why not?"

"I left before and stayed with those—you know, in Suffolk. I'm just not going!" His nine-year-old ire was just getting started. "It was useless. I need to be here with my mum. Who else is going to—what if they come and I'm not here?"

Marigold didn't answer.

"Who's going to protect her? Who will look out for my mum?" He narrowed his eyes, tough as nails, but still, a little boy.

Finally, Marigold said, "If they come, and you're in Sussex, she won't have to worry about something happening to you. Then she'll leave London and join you. But, Kit, she has to work in the meantime."

"I'm not going." He tried a different tactic. "Besides the Krauts aren't going to come. We're not going to let them." The grounds of the estate were now swarming with children, teachers, parents, and every kind of volunteer imaginable.

"Where is your mum?"

"She's with the ponce."

"Do you mean Marek?"

"Yeah."

"I don't think that's a very nice term."

"*I don't think that's . . .*" he mimicked her and then added, "silly Yank."

"Oy!" she warned him, tapping his shoe with her foot.

Which made him smile, and softly echo "Oy," tapping her shoe in return.

The Number 11 would leave in ten minutes. It was the last bus she could take for the train to Sussex if she was going with those children.

"Look." Most of the families had left already. "How about if I make you a deal?"

"What?"

"Maybe you could stay at the Reillys'."

"Who?"

"Uh, he's someone um—"

"Is he your boyfriend?"

"No! No, no. He's the boyfriend of Marek's sis- of someone else I know. And his place is great. You'd love it."

"Can Pat come?"

"Who's Pat?"

"He's a mate."

"But isn't he going to someone they've made arrangements with?"

Kit didn't answer.

"I'll ask."

Kit looked at her.

"Okay? I'll ask. That's all I can do. But I think you'll want to go."

"Why's that?"

"Lulu's there."

And remarkably, Alex Reilly agreed. The boys could stay with the caretaker and his wife in the cottage on the edge of the grounds.

* * *

AT THE TRAIN STATION, the various plans for evacuation collapsed amongst the tears and histrionics of saying goodbye yet again. Hordes of weeping mothers and wailing children moved every which way while rail workers swore, watching the volunteers juggle the impending chaos and waiting for all hell to break loose.

Kit's mother, Sara, stood with one hand on his shoulder, her mouth a closed line, waiting for some kind of order to emerge. Marigold stood with her clipboard.

A woman approached with two little girls, dressed identically, holding hands. They all gave her a guarded look.

Marigold put her best foot forward. "Hello. Mrs. Brown, is this Sally? Is this Dora?" What Marigold really wanted to do was just take pictures. She sighed. It would have to wait. "Girls, you're going to Hawkhurst, is that right? Here, we'll be in this car. Yes, Mrs. Brown, I'll be their chaperone, that's right. I'll see that they get to the family. Yes, yes, I will."

"Mrs. Holcombe, how nice to see you. Is this Antony? Yes, I'm travelling with the children. Yes, I'm there to make sure no one is left stranded!"

Finally, there was the cry, "All aboard!"

The train began to move. Gradually, the children settled into the rhythm of the journey and Marigold took out her camera.

"What's that?" a boy asked.

"It's a Rolleicord." Marigold held it out so he could have a better look. "Can I take your photo?"

"Oh, take mine, miss!" said a little girl.

"Yeah, take mine, too, please," said a boy.

"And mine!" shouted another.

It was the last stop of the afternoon. Mr. and Mrs. Blossom drove up in a small van, and the boys were thrilled to ride in the back. With them were the three puppies and their mother, Lulu.

Autumn

The following days passed in a blur. Marigold was too in love to notice the breadlines, the sandbags, or which ration cards were needed where. She forgot her keys on the bus. She left her purse in a cab. She poured the wrong developers into the trays.

What was important was whether that blue satin tea length was still available, and if she could find the right shade of lipstick for tomorrow's night out.

Newsreels and the BBC didn't seem important at all now.

Buddy shrugged. "You amaze me, Mac."

She handed the camera to Marek.

He adjusted a lamp. "If you would lean closer to the window, your lordship. That's perfect." They were in Whitehall, inside a minister's chambers. The man did as Marek requested.

Marigold sighed. Even going to Dovercourt Bay and taking the kids' photos felt unimportant, compared to Joop's arms holding her, dancing at a supper club.

"Marigold, wake up!" Marek snapped his fingers.

"What? Oh sorry."

"Where is your brain, you silly girl?" He spoke in a whisper, so the MP couldn't hear them.

"I just, I just—"

"You're not here to daydream, Marigold. Get your head together." In a louder voice, he added, "We'll need B-1 film and please move the umbrella thus." Marek nodded to the MP. "Mr. Smithson, if you could just lean more to your left, sir, that would be very helpful. Thank you, sir."

BACK AT THE Mews he said, "Whatever it is that's preoccupying you is undoing all the good work that you accomplished this summer."

"It is?"

"Photographs which indicated your budding talent are now languishing in the pile of foolish teen, young girl I-don't-know-what."

"Oh, well." She smiled weakly. "Joop is back."

"Then use it. This is a time to work twice as hard." He dropped his voice. "Use sexual energy to make your photos"—he smiled—"electric."

Marigold took the Rolleicord back out. She photographed people laughing. Standing in doorways, emerging from trains, holding hands, at the pub, in the park. Photos of the sky, above and between things.

Marek examined the prints back in the darkroom. He shook his head. "It isn't enough for these to be snapshots. It's not about a lucky moment. The world is three-dimensional, Marigold. Take the world around you, and collapse it, into two dimensions. It's about composing and controlling the frame."

"Yes, Marek." She looked at the prints. He was right of course.

* * *

THE DRESS WAS WRAPPED in tissue in the box Marigold had under her arm. It was marvelous, and impossible to keep from skipping at the thought of wearing it. Marigold glanced at her watch as the streetlamps went on and the shop lamps reflected on the wet pavement. She just had time for a bath, and to paint her nails, too. Seeing Joop, feeling the satin on her skin, on her waist, Joop touching it as he placed his arms around her. Dancing . . .

She saw Mr. Alwyn tend the box hedge outside his shop. He was silly, but so kind really.

"Mr. Alwyn!"

He straightened up. "Hello, dear!" he said. "My, you're looking well today."

"I have a date with my young man." She gave him a little curtsey and a wave, about to keep moving when the sirens blared. Marigold froze and looked at the sky.

Mr. Alwyn grabbed her. "Come inside, come inside!" he commanded, pulling her through the door. "Get down, get down!" The sky turned black. Her heart racing, they crouched down. The contents of the shop rattled. There was an explosion, and the earth seemed to tilt. A crashing rumble deafened the sound of Mr. Alwyn's inventory falling off shelves. Everything was still. Another siren gave the all clear. Trembling, Marigold put her hand out. The box was still by her side.

"Miss McGrath." Mr. Alwyn was standing over her. "Are you all right, Miss McGrath?"

"Yes, Mr. Alwyn." Everything in the shop was in disarray on the floor.

"Right." He held out his hand. "We must help the others." She shakily got to her feet. "That's right. We'll leave your box here. Let's get our helmets."

The thick smell of burning fuel permeated everything, even through their masks. Cautiously, they made their way toward the black smoke in Cheyne Row. The Church of the Holy Redeemer's crypt was a favored shelter. It was large and clean, much more comfortable than most of the others. Some volunteers and the warden, Mr. Thorpe, were already there, moving in and out of the smoke. Everything seemed fine at first, but when she got closer, Marigold heard the faint moaning. Those who had sought shelter were trapped inside by the rubble.

"We're coming! Don't panic," Mr. Alwyn called down to them. "Everyone stay put. Stay put!"

"We've a gas leak down here!" someone shouted.

Mr. Thorpe said, "I'm going in." He made his way down toward the crypt and called, "How many are you?"

A man said, "Nearly a hundred."

"Right, don't panic. We're on our way."

Fire trucks, Royal Engineers and an ambulance arrived.

"Bring them over here," Mr. Alwyn said to Marigold.

Marigold made her way to the side of the church. Its wall was blown away, the sacristy leveled. She stepped over vestments and chalices which had fallen into the street. Further down, was a crater where a bomb had exploded upon contact. Several bodies were scattered amongst crushed gravestones and a flattened mausoleum. She gingerly stepped over the debris back toward the trucks. Her job was to bring survivors some blankets and tea, not this. Not this!

A fine rain made everything slick under foot. It was impossible not to slip, nor to recoil from what might be limbs or bodies, it was too dark to tell.

A small cry came from somewhere on her left.

"Over here, over here!" Marigold called to the trucks, but they did not hear her. She waved her torch at them, and shouted, "Over here!"

Marigold heard the cry again. "Where are you?"

"Help." It sounded like a child.

She moved her torch over the stones. "I'm coming, stay there. Stay there. Call to me again." There was nothing.

Marigold knelt down. The rubble cut through her stockings. "Call to me again, so I can find you."

"Here. I'm here."

"We're going to get you. We will. I'll bring the men." Marigold stood and ran, shouting to the volunteers, "Hey! Hey. There's a child here, in this rubble here. Come please!" She ran back to the pile. "What's your name?"

There was no answer. She knelt down to where the voice had come from. "Tell me your name." She placed her ear next to the rubble. The Royal Engineers had given strict instructions to not move anything alone to prevent any more stone falling or another explosive detonating. "Come on," she whispered, "please answer."

Finally, finally. She thought she heard something. She said

again, her lips nearly touching the stone. "My name is Marigold. What's yours?"

* * *

IT WAS SUNRISE. At 275, the door on the landing was open. Marigold peered into the sitting room. Joop lay on the sofa, his back to her, still in his uniform. Like a monument of a soldier at rest.

As if by magic, he turned over and opened his eyes. She was covered in dust and grime and blood. In her arms was the box with the dress she'd intended on wearing.

He stood up and gently took it from her. "When you didn't show, I thought you broke up with me."

Her lips were cracked and her throat felt like sandpaper. "No such luck, pal." The cat wandered in and rubbed against her legs.

"I'll run you a hot bath, and make you a Dutch breakfast."

"What's that?" she croaked, "Something with cheese?"

"That's what I love about American girls. You are so clever!"

"Joop." All of Marigold's pluck dissolved and her knees buckled. There was only the grief from being unable to stop seeing what had happened.

"I'm here, Marigold." He held her and she began to sob.

"We were too late." Marigold wept. "I heard her, but we were too late."

AT NOON, she sat alone in her dressing gown. The sunshine was bright on the terrace. The thought of leaving the house terrified her. But the thought of remaining there was just as bad.

"My dear," Falaise said gently, "we must go about our business and conduct our affairs as if there is nothing, nothing in the world that affects us."

"But—" If only they had found the little girl before. If only a thousand things had gone differently than they did.

"No, Marigold. Do not give those monsters the satisfaction. I, for one, will not."

Henrenhurst, Sussex

The afternoon light had begun to fade. The door to the manor house was open. Music played from the wireless and Kit saw Lulu run inside. He ran after her straight into the tall man taking aim with a rifle. Kit gasped.

"Hullo."

Kit blushed furiously. He'd been told not to bother Mr. Reilly, not to snoop around the big house. But he'd done his chores, and school wasn't for another two days.

The Blossoms seemed kind enough, but all Mr. Blossom wanted to do was work on his carvings, and all Mrs. Blossom wanted to do was crochet socks. Then Pat had taken ill, come down with tonsilitis or something, and his own mother had collected him and taken him back to the city.

Lulu licked Kit's face, knocking him over, making him laugh. She seemed as happy to see Kit as he was to see her. In fact, if Lulu hadn't been there, the whole thing would have been nothing less than dreadful. But somehow, having this little dog and her pups at his side changed everything.

The man gave him a quizzical look. "Aren't there supposed to be two of you?"

Mr. Reilly was as handsome as a movie star, really. Dark eyes and hair. Only a little bit frightening. Kit noticed his limp. Mr. Blossom had told Kit that Mr. Reilly had been a war hero. He wondered if the limp was from that.

"What's your name?"

"Uh, I'm Kit."

"Hullo Kit. How are the Blossoms treating you?"

He had to make sure Mr. Reilly gave him a good review.

"Very well, thank you, sir."

"Good man."

In the cabinet behind Mr. Reilly were at least twenty rifles, much like the one Mr. Reilly was holding. "This is my gun rack. For grouse hunting and such. What do you think?"

Kit thought they were lovelier than anything he'd ever seen. Ever. "It's brilliant," he whispered. Then he noticed that along the far wall there were even more, and by the doorway were several crates, one of which was open. Those guns were surely for the military. He'd never seen so many before in his life.

"Do you want to hold one?"

"Cor, yes please."

Mr. Reilly gestured to the rifles he said he used for hunting. "Tell me which one you fancy, and I'll set you up." He showed Kit how to load it and how to fire it. Then he said, "About these others, and the ones in the crates particularly, we say nothing. Got it? This stuff is top secret, and we don't want loose lips sinking ships and whatnot. Do you understand?"

"Yes, sir. I understand."

"Let's try your gun out, shall we?"

They walked across a field and Kit was slightly terrified but thrilled and dazzled at the same time. Despite the limp, Mr. Reilly moved with purpose and authority. When they came to a shed at the edge of a field, he had Kit bring out a wine crate filled with empty bottles.

"Here," he said, "let's put these up. Some target practice, what."

Obediently, Kit balanced the bottles along the posts of the fence.

"I'll have a go, and then you do the same, right?" Mr. Reilly took aim and fired. The glass smashed into a thousand pieces. "Now, Kit. Find the bottle through the iron sight. See it?"

"Yes."

"Good. Cock the gun, find the bottle, then squeeze the trigger, but mind the kickback!"

Kit did as instructed. The recoil walloped just where his arm pit met his shoulder and it hurt like the dickens, but he hit the bottle!

"Well done, well done indeed. Let's go again."

After a few rounds, Mr. Reilly asked, "Where's your father then, Kit?"

"He's dead, sir."

"Ah. Well, that's beastly, isn't it? Terribly sorry."

"He died in Spain."

"Did he now?"

Kit didn't know if his father had really died in Spain, but it seemed the best reason to give for his not coming back from there, and for not having a father. Whenever he offered it up, people became thoughtful and didn't ask any more questions.

"Terrible business, war." Mr. Reilly said. "Just dreadful."

Afterward, the sunlight changed into shadow as they walked back to the house. Mr. Reilly said, "Did you enjoy yourself?"

"Oh, yes, thank you, sir."

"Good, because bear in mind, lad, should I ever find you in my lodgings, without my invitation, be advised, I will shoot you dead." Mr. Reilly smiled. "And I'm not joking."

London

Leaving the cinema, even during blackout, it felt as though everything was normal. Trude said, "I thought the way he went after the assailants was utterly credible."

They had just seen *Foreign Correspondent*, but Joop wouldn't comment.

Marigold said, "I could never do it. I wouldn't do it! They were armed. To be left alone in a field. That's crazy."

"I don't know, I would chase him," Trude said. She was in uniform, unable to discuss anything about how her days were spent. "The question is whether we race toward danger or not."

"But why would Joel McCrea just go after these men?" Marigold asked. "Is it to impress Fisher's daughter?"

Buddy shook his head. "Nanh. He's chasing the story. He's chasing the story to its conclusion."

"But where are the police?" Marigold asked. "How long can it take them to come back?"

"They are quislings!" Joop could barely keep from shouting. "The assailants are quislings."

"What are those?" Marigold asked.

He took her arm and tucked it under his. "They are citizens who collaborate with the occupying enemy, Marigold. In Holland, we have lots of them."

They walked in silence in the dark, until Joop said, "I think it's time we go dancing."

Elbows bent, hands touched, feet shuffled, and hips shimmied. The trumpet wailed, Joop shouted, "YEAH! We are jumping at the Woodside!"

The saxophones held back and forth, back and forth. "Come Yankee goddess! We shall dance!" He picked her up and spun around till she shrieked with laughter, "Yeah, yeah, yeah!" And everyone on the dance floor shrieked and shouted, too.

It was crowded, and impossible to move, really. Soldiers and their girls, or young men like Buddy, who was in the corner yelling with Trude, their heads bent in serious discussion. Finally, Marigold saw them from the corner of her eye as Joop spun and swirled and dipped and wove her, and the crowd was applauding, then began dancing once again.

Gradually, the music calmed. The crowd swayed slowly as the vocalist crooned, "*If I didn't care, would I act this way?*" Joop sang along either looking deep into her eyes, or with his head back bellowing out the words for all the world to hear.

Afterward, he asked, "Elephant and Castle?"

She nodded, then glanced at Buddy and Trude, who were now dancing very close. Somehow, Trude looked up, and smiling, waved Marigold away. Outside the revelers poured into the street, with only taxis' cat-eye slits for light.

Anxious to cross the Thames before another raid, Joop grabbed her hand. "Let's hurry, Gouda." And they ran across the bridge.

PART V

ONDERDUIKERS
(IN HIDING)

Santpoort, Holland

Autumn

"Christ!" Joop sat up. "Christ, Christ. Jesus Christ." It was cold and everything hurt. He unclipped his fastenings and shoved the parachute into his rucksack. It really hurt to breathe. Had he cracked a rib? He prayed to God he wouldn't have to do that again. He stretched back out and took a deep breath. The air was different here than in England. He patted the soil. He'd been dropped in Santpoort, not so far from Amsterdam. It was good to be home. He thought about the orders he'd received before leaving England.

"I know who your father is." The general had smiled. At the time, Joop wondered if the general meant that he knew that his father had been forced to resign because Joop's mother was Jewish. Did the general know that his parents had decided to stay and wait out the occupation?

The general had continued, "As you know, the bombing of Rotterdam not only displaced eighty thousand people, but it also leveled the American consulate, destroying all the visa applications to the United States. Anyone from Holland hoping to make it to America is now back to square one."

They were standing in that room in Belgravia, at 77 Chester Square, next to Queen Wilhelmina's study. "In addition to establishing contact with us here, your job is to provide assistance for those Dutch citizens whose departure is deemed urgent. We currently know of three cells for escapees and those looking to leave. You will connect those people with those routes. But first, you must offer van Hamel whatever support he requires."

Joop closed his eyes, recalling the general's orders in that rarified corner of London, even as they could hear Queen Wilhelmina's voice through an open door. She was thanking some other Engelandvaarders for joining the cause. Joop had met her once before. He'd been nine years old when she'd made a royal visit to his school. But now, lying in a field at two-thirty in the morning, with his mission in front of him, it felt impossibly surreal. A few stars peeped out from the clouds.

Maybe he'd convince his family to go into hiding, too. His parents had insisted they wouldn't, as a matter of principle, that they were protected, that nothing would happen. The sky began to fade, and some seagulls hollered for him to get up.

Groaning, he hoisted the rucksack onto his back and considered the next order of business. First, he had to make contact with England. Then he had to assess the forgeries being produced to get the Onderduikers safely out of Holland. Lastly, he had to determine what could be done for Lodo van Hamel.

Santpoort was barely inland, and Joop loved the milky brightness of morning at the coast. He was dressed simply, like any ordinary villager. He headed toward a nearby cluster of buildings and saw an older woman emerge from a bakery. God, he was hungry. Could she be relied upon? Or was she already a traitor? He wasn't ready to risk finding out, so he nodded to her and kept walking.

Eventually, he arrived at some railroad tracks. Half a dozen people were gathered at what must have been a stop. He didn't see anyone who looked his age. They were mostly older or else they were children. The Germans had been very clever, absorbing anyone who might have presented trouble or resistance. When the train came, Joop pulled his cap over his eyes and boarded with the others.

Inside, there were some young men making their way through the cars. They were state police who were now officially part of the Nazi occupation, and only too glad to pledge allegiance to Hitler.

"Papieren," one said.

Another one with an Alsatian shepherd followed close behind.

Joop handed him his documents, forged of course, with the name Jan Kremer. The soldier gave him back the little book.

"Danke." Joop nodded, surprised that his heart was hammering so. He put the documents away and exchanged glances with the dog. His friend Piet had a dog like that. He should find Piet. That's what he'd do. Piet would know what was going on. He would find Piet first.

"WELCOME HOME!" Piet gave him a solid hug. "I was afraid you disappeared."

Joop shrugged. "Not me, old man. I just had to take a break."

Piet and his granny seemed to be all right, but their dog, Dolly, was very thin and the hair around her nose had grown white.

"Lie down, Dolly. That's a good girl," Piet told her. She did as commanded and lay her snout on her paws, waiting for better things.

They climbed the stairs to the attic, where Piet had set up his radio. Radios had been confiscated and destroyed by then, but still, he'd made alternate arrangements. A piece of wood, some salvaged wire, a rusty razor blade and pencil were enough to construct a "foxhole" receiver.

"Nice innovation," Joop said.

"We have to be careful, but it works well enough to get *Radio Orange*," Piet said, then he laughed softly. "Our German friends would not be very happy if they knew about this! Haha. Ah well." He shrugged. "What am I supposed to do?"

"Well, I'll tell you what you might do." Carefully, Joop removed the transmitter from his rucksack. "Uh, one of my responsibilities is this."

Piet glanced at Joop, then folded his arms. "Is this going to get the Krauts out?"

"If we use it properly, it will."

"Well, then. By all mean, let's find it a place of its own."

With the transmitter situated, Joop sent a message to British intelligence at their SOE office. Then he took off his headphones and rested them next to the box. He and Piet had placed it on a desk behind a bookshelf that hid a secret staircase, under a blanket inside an armoire behind another blanket. Amsterdam was full of such bookcases. They concealed passageways and attics, rooms where servants and hermits and crazy relatives had once lived. Now they were filled with the Onderduikers, desperate to hide from the Nazis, waiting it out until they could escape or the occupation ended. Then they'd be free to carry on with their lives.

Piet's granny had delicious stew and homemade bread for them in the kitchen. She asked Joop, "Do your parents know you're here?"

Joop shook his head. "Not yet." As soon as he spoke, he realized he'd created yet another deception that would depend on this old woman's ability to remain discreet. He added, "It's safer if they don't."

"I heard your mother"—Piet cleared his throat—"I heard your mother took in the Ossenbruggens." Mr. Ossenbruggen had been the Kasanders' accountant, and the Kasanders' house on Keizersgracht had an attic just like Piet's.

"And you?"

"We toe the line. There's talk of forming a Jewish committee to protect our interests, so they don't just—it's about keeping everyone safe for the moment."

When he had left London, the SOE had provided Joop with several hundred ration cards. He took a huge handful out of his rucksack and handed them to Piet's granny. "Thank you for supper. I hope these come in useful." She took his hand, and he felt a lump in his throat.

"Come here," she answered. Joop had known Piet and his granny nearly all his life. Joop bent down and she kissed him on the cheek. "Take care."

Joop whispered, "Thanks again."

That night, he watched the house on Keizersgracht. With the strict curfew, the streets were nearly deserted. Everything was blacked out. He wondered how they were behind those curtains. If their own dog was all right. If Flortje was all right and whether his older sister had managed to escape with her family. Indeed, if there was anything he could give them to ease the coming months. The door of the house opened and his father emerged with the dog. Joop watched them walk down the street, unaware that he was just across the canal, fighting the urge to start crying. He rubbed his face with his hands then quickly made his way to the next stop.

* * *

"I CAN'T TELL THE DIFFERENCE." Joop held a card in each hand. They appeared to be identical.

He was on the other side of town at the house of a group called C6. C6 was considered to be one of the most militant resistance cells, and if Joop were honest, he was a little bit intimidated. C6 had known to expect someone, but who it would be had remained a mystery. That night, it was Joop.

"These are the originals." One of the men pointed to various ration cards, passports, and travelling authorization papers. Then he gestured to the other end of the table, which was covered with more of them. "These are the ones we've made."

Joop compared another set of the originals against their forged replicas. He shook his head and shrugged. "Really, I can't tell the difference."

"That's the idea!" laughed one of the men. "It's quite a bit of work, let me tell you." A pair of brothers who had assisted in the forgeries beamed from ear to ear. They looked younger than Joop.

Another man, Gerrit, seemed to be in charge. That Gerrit was a communist didn't matter. He was a doctor and a bit older than any of them and his ideas were radical, uncompromising. He'd fought in Spain and was unquestionably brave.

"If it's not direct, meaningful sabotage, then assassination is the only way," Gerrit said. "Eliminate those in charge—both Nazis and our Dutch collaborators."

"But there are so many collaborators," Joop said. "Are we just going to kill the lot of them?"

Gerrit shrugged. "Maybe not, if we're successful with sabotaging enough rail lines and roadways. Create mayhem, keep them off balance. They'll be so exasperated dealing with us, they won't be able to execute whatever it is their strategy is supposed to be."

"And those who need to get out?" Joop asked, "what are your thoughts on that?"

Gerrit shrugged. "Well, we're going to need money."

Joop placed ten thousand guilders on the table. "Will this be enough?"

The men stared at the banknotes. Joop knew they didn't need money to ensure their commitment. But still, he gestured to the cash. "This can't be the reason we don't prevail."

They had to be confident that the British were equally fierce and unwavering in their support. And to understand that the queen herself had a hand in it, that there would be no reason for the resisters to ever surrender, not for one moment. If the cash and the food began to run out, the fear that an occupied people would simply give up and give over was terrifyingly real.

"We are going to prevail," one of the brothers said.

"And Lodo?" Lodo was a dashing naval warrior who parachuted in as the first Dutch agent in this war. Completing his mission, Lodo had been waiting for a seaplane back to England, when he was captured by the Germans.

"Lodo's at the Orange Hotel." Gerrit sighed. The reputation of the Orange Hotel was such that no one spoke of what went on there.

"He's the main reason I'm here." Joop gestured to the mountain of leaflets, identity cards, and rations. "I mean I'm here for these, but I need to make contact with Lodo." Joop glanced around the room. He hoped they couldn't tell that he was not brave.

"Well, interestingly enough you're about the same size as young Theo here." Gerrit gestured to one of the boys. "You can wear our little SS offering on its maiden voyage."

Theo brought out a box, revealing an impeccable SS Shutzkommando uniform. Its polished buttons gleamed against the black fabric, everything freshly pressed. Joop glanced at Theo. He wasn't much older than Joop, and like him, resembled a typical Dutchman with blonde hair, blue eyes. He was also Jewish.

"Did you register?" Joop asked him.

"No. Why should I? It isn't anybody's business."

Joop considered this.

"Besides, if I did"—Theo slipped on the SS uniform's hat—"I wouldn't be able to wear this, now, would I?"

Joop fingered the red badge; it was perfect. "Who's was this?"

"We got it from the Streifendienst." Those were the patrol services who walked the neighborhoods, ensuring everyone was in line. Gerrit chuckled. "We also have two more just like them." He pointed at the cash. "You know, with enough of this, everything is still negotiable."

Joop's flawless German and Aryan looks, ensured no one would ever challenge him in that uniform. He would contact Lodo and then take the first group of Onderduikers out of Holland to safety. But the question of how he would hide them in plain sight took more than a little courage. Then Joop remembered that he was not brave. He was not brave at all.

The Orange Hotel was the name for the prison located in Scheveningen, a beach town on the edge of the Hague. Joop rode the train from Amsterdam, then collected a bicycle at the station, his SS uniform carefully packed inside his knapsack. He'd been given the name and address of a woman whose cottage was on the dunes near the center of town. The woman had two children. A boy who was fourteen and a girl who was twenty.

"I'm Jan Kremer," he told her. All of them knew it was better that they not know too much about each other.

After their supper, Joop and the boy went out to the beach and walked along the water's edge. The skies and sand were endless. They were very close to where Lodo had waited for the seaplane but had been arrested by the Germans instead. The tide was out, and they went far, far from the strand and its row of shops and houses. Joop felt that if the tide kept receding, he might walk back to England and to Marigold.

The boy said to him, "Jan's not your real name, is it?"

"It is for now," Joop answered.

"DeeDee"—by whom the boy meant his sister— "is with the movement, too."

"It really is better if we don't talk about that," Joop said. After a while, he added, "You're going to see me in a Streifendienst uniform tomorrow. I'll need you to pretend everything is normal. Can you do that?"

The boy nodded then asked, "Why?"

Gerrit had said the boy's father was in prison, just like Lodo. "Where's your dad?" Joop asked him, softly.

"In Scheveningen." By which he meant the Orange Hotel.

"That's the reason why. They put him there because we're fighting a war, and we have to win it. So, I'm going to pretend to be one of them. It's how I'll get information. I have to pretend I am the enemy."

Joop considered his spectacles. He wasn't much use without them, but he looked more convincing if he didn't wear them. The boy stepped back and Joop turned around for a final inspection. "What do you think?"

The boy shook his head. "If I didn't know better, I'd want to kill you."

"Ha! Thank you very much."

Shining boots, clicking heels, supreme arrogance. The flunkies at the gates let him in without question. He claimed to be from Central Command to interrogate prisoner Ludwig van Hamel concerning radio transmissions and the like.

"Sir," he said to the officer in charge. He handed the other man a series of requests and forms, all of which were forged. The man glanced at them and Joop's heart was in his throat, waiting to be found out. The officer nodded and told a guard to lead Joop down the corridor to an interview room.

Inside was a table with two chairs. On the table were two glasses, a pitcher of water, and an ashtray. Joop took off his hat and sat down. He was sure there was a peephole somewhere and he knew he'd have to keep it together, not betray too much. The door opened and a wreck of a man shuffled inside.

Joop nearly cried out but then steeled himself and lit a cigarette.

"Sit down," he said in German.

Lodo sat. His right eye was bulged shut, crusted with infection and blood. His nose had clearly been broken; the swollen skin on either side was blue. Joop waited. Lodo said nothing.

Finally, Joop said, "Cigarette?"

He watched Lodo take the cigarette, his hand and fingers a mangled mess from God only knew what.

As he lit Lodo's cigarette, he murmured in Dutch, "Lil Wil and Big J send their love."

Lodo's good eye flashed at this. It was the nickname for the queen and princess, whom Lodo had transported to Britain. "Do you have a message for van't Sant?"

Lodo nodded. "Are you the magistrate's son?"

"Yeah," Joop spoke as softly as he dared.

"I know who your father is," Lodo said. "My dad brought several cases before him. Did your parents get out?"

Joop shook his head and said in German, "I'm asking the questions!"

"They have the codes," Lodo said. "I don't know whether it was Hans or Jean, but I think Jean probably collapsed. When they keep this up for a week"—he gestured to his face and hand— "it's only a question of time."

Joop filled a water glass and passed it to him. Lodo drank it down then whispered, "But they don't have the transmitter."

Joop raised his voice. "Within six months, the Reich will have eliminated all degenerates from the Netherlands! You mark my words. The next generation will only know the Dutch as some quixotic ethnic group, who were absorbed for the greater good of Germany."

A smile briefly appeared on Lodo's bloodied face. "Quixotic. I like that," he murmured. He took a final drag on his cigarette, adding, "It's in Ede. With Mrs. van Lier." He coughed and said, "She owns the general store."

Then Joop lowered his head to collect his hat. "I'll tell your family that you're here." Joop was not a believer, and yet he whispered, "God bless you, Lodo." Then he called for the guard and raised his arm, "Heil Hitler!"

That night, Joop walked on the beach and screamed at the sea, sobbing at the wretchedness of it all.

Joop sent transmissions from Piet's house, using the SOE's established code making the last three characters of every sentence into random errors. This was the sign that the message was authentic.

London responded that they were sending more agents and shipments at the next new moon.

After the transmission, Joop made his way to Gerrit's where the first group of

Onderduikers would be selected. They studied the list. It was his old math professor and family.

At C6, Gerrit explained the plan. "We have a car and will do the initial run at dusk, so that it's early enough for there to be services and whatnot. We get them situated and then Joop will take them through Belgium and into France. From there"—the professor was an old man; the thought of him climbing mountains seemed very unlikely—"we'll figure it out. If we make it to Paris, they'll go onto Marseilles and get out from there."

Joop decided it would be better to go back home dressed as SS. When his mother opened the door, he thanked God she'd once been an actress, because if she hadn't concealed the myriad of reactions he knew she must be feeling, it would have been enough for all of them to be arrested.

His parents were very thin, and Flortje looked terrible. His older sister, Bette, had left with her husband for Canada only weeks before the invasion. Why Flortje hadn't gone with them remained a mystery for Joop.

"You really must go."

"It's out of the question," his mother said.

"Well, then, at least Flortje."

"I'm not leaving them!" Flortje was adamant. "I'm working with the Children's Relief Fund in Leiden. And I . . ." Her voice trailed off.

"What?"

"There's a boy," their mother added.

Joop crossed his arms. "Oh, for God's sake."

"Shut up! At least he's helping people, not racing around dressed like a Nazi."

"Flortje." Their father was in the doorway. "That's enough. Joop, we should all eat."

At supper Joop said, "You must go to France. I won't stand to hear any more either way."

"Oh, Joop. For heaven's sake." His mother shook her head.

His father asked, "Why France?"

"Our contacts are established there. Then getting you to Spain or Switzerland will be that much easier."

"And those we leave behind? What kind of unity does that demonstrate for everyone else under siege? We can't all be in exile, Joop."

"How will I know you're all right?"

His father answered, "I should ask the same of you, son."

THE IDEA WAS to slip away on an afternoon, just as it was becoming dusk, when the streets were full and all kinds of people returned from school or the office. Professor Meyritz, his wife, her sister, and three teenage boys were the passengers. Someone had found them Nationale Jeugdstorm uniforms, and with Joop dressed in the borrowed SS outfit, they resembled quislings of the highest standing. A sleek black car with swastika flags idled outside the alley behind Cornelia Street. Everyone piled into the back where Joop was waiting inside, an envelope with forged identity cards for each of them in his hand.

If they were caught in this endeavor, it would be the Orange Hotel for all of them. The boys and men would be sent to labor camps, the women and girls to Westerbork. Joop and Theo most likely shot. It was that simple.

The town of Ede was a hundred kilometers due east. It was the wrong direction if one were fleeing, so it wasn't the first place the authorities would look. Still, the rationed petrol gave them little room for error.

By nightfall the landscape changed, and the long flat expanses became ragged, edged by trees, obscuring the low moonlight. Narrow openings in the folds over the car's headlights lit the road, which curved into the forest.

They turned onto a dirt path that led to a clearing behind an old barn. Theo parked the car and removed the swastikas while everyone changed into clothes like the locals wore. A tarp was placed over the car. They walked the last twenty minutes to the center of Ede, which was known for holiday houses and hiking. It was just after six. The light in the general store was still on but a closed sign hung from the door.

Joop rang the bell, and a small woman emerged from the back. When she opened the door, she kept the chain on the lock.

"Mrs. van Lier?"

"Yes?"

"I'm Jan Kremer. I've brought my cousins. We're hoping you have space in one of the cottages for them."

The guys at C6 had done their homework. With rations and careful hiding, these families would be safe. Then, when the new route had been established, Joop would bring them to Belgium, and walk them through France until they reached Paris. Whether they'd go over to Spain or to Switzerland was up to the Maquis in France who were still working on that detail.

"Who sent you?"

"The Starling family," which was the password he'd been given.

She smiled and opened the door. "Please come in. Come and get something to eat first. I have just the cottage for them."

While the group sat down to soup, Mrs. van Lier brought Joop to the larder. Inside it were sausages and cured hams, bags of coffee beans, sacks of potatoes, and jars of pickled greens.

"Thanks be to God we still have some inventory," she said. Massive wheels of cheese and sacs of flour were on the shelves. In the far corner of the larder, what appeared to be a wood pile was in fact a decoy. Mrs. van Lier tapped the wall, which released a latch from the other side, revealing a small alcove, inside of which was Lodo's transmitter.

The depth of Joop's sigh surprised even him. He smiled at her, embarrassed. He hadn't realized he'd been holding his breath for the better part of a day.

She placed her hand on his back. "You probably need a moment."

"Yes. Thank you."

Mrs. van Lier had to be sixty years old. The guys at C6 had told him she'd started smuggling families out of Holland in the week after the invasion. In addition to Professor Meyritz's group, several dozen were hiding at other houses she rented to holiday-makers in season. And there was no doubt that if she were caught she'd be executed. Joop could see that inside this small woman was in fact a fearless giant.

"Mrs. van Lier. These are for you." He handed her an envelope filled with ration cards and cash.

"God bless you, Jan Kremer." She smiled again. "You're a very brave young man."

London

By November, Marigold's routine had become nearly normal. Sunday afternoons, she met families at Charing Cross to escort children out to Sussex. Mondays she spent in the darkroom at Lark Mews, and Tuesdays in Dovercourt Bay, photographing refugee children. During the rest of the week, she was either scouting for Ed Murrow or accompanying Marek on his assignments, holding various cameras, lenses, and the like. Time was a whirlwind, hectic, and exhausting. Because when she wasn't doing any of these things, she was making the rounds with air raid wardens, knocking on doors, reminding people to pull their blackouts closed.

Then, the sirens would begin. Nearly every night. First, the incendiaries fell, lighting the sky as if they were delicate harmless fireworks. If one managed to use the stirrup pumps or throw sand on them in time to put them out, they were only pesky creatures out of a sinister fairy tale. Sometimes, she saw groups of men and women extinguish the incendiaries in their evening clothes, even as they laughed and drank cocktails.

Otherwise, the incendiaries caught fire, wreaking havoc. Then she'd turn the corner and behind some barbed wire was a building's gaping wound, revealing a home torn apart by those very same explosives.

"Who goes there?" the warden demanded in the dark. Only the naked tree branches were illuminated by the moon.

"It's just Marigold, Mr. Alwyn," she said. "Is everything all right?"

"Right as rain my dear, considering the circumstances." He gave a terse chuckle.

"I'll see you in the morning, then, Mr. Alwyn."

"Indeed, you shall. Give my best to Mrs. Cooper."

IT WAS Thanksgiving that Thursday and the Murrows invited the Americans they knew to join them.

"Bring your Dutch fella," Mr. Murrow said.

"I wish I could, but he's . . . um, fighting."

"Of course," Mr. Murrow said sadly. "Of course, he is."

Sussex

Winter

ALEX REILLY TOOK AIM AT THE WINE BOTTLE. "Rationing is just a bore!" He pressed the trigger. It smashed into a thousand pieces. "It's not for the likes of us, is it Kit?"

"No sir." Kit's insides jumped the way they always did when the bullet hit its target. But he managed to hide the jump and remain still, as if it were nothing.

Alex Reilly stepped back. "Your go."

Kit took aim. He'd learned how to hold the gun steady, not wavering, nor letting his hands begin sweating. "It's not for the likes of us at all." Kit pressed the trigger. The bottle exploded just as Alex Reilly's had. Both he and Alex burst into laughter.

"Well done," Alex Reilly shouted. "Very well done indeed."

Alex Reilly's daughter, Emily, came home from school for the holiday. She was a few years younger, but still, Kit didn't find her as boring as he found most girls.

When they first met, just after Kit arrived, Emily had said, "I'll show you the horses." He'd seen them already but was too polite to say so. After the stables, she had continued with their tour. "This is our library. Sometimes Papa has a movie, and we can watch it on this wall." She showed him where the projector was kept, and with it, reels upon reels of film.

"This is my favorite place." Emily had ended the tour by showing him the goldfish pond. "The cat likes it too." The weather was still warm then and they sat, watching the cat take in the last of the sunlight.

"Papa told me that Lulu and her puppies came from you," Emily said.

"Well, yes. I suppose so."

"Was that because everyone was killing their dogs in London?"

Kit thought it best not to get into that. "No, Mr. Reilly got them beforehand."

Emily asked him, "Do you think it was right for everyone to kill their dogs?"

Kit shook his head. She was the first person he'd met who openly discussed it.

Emily continued, "My grandad said they did it so the Germans wouldn't hurt them or eat them should they invade."

"Did your grandad have a dog?"

"No," she laughed. "He has a canary!"

"I don't think we have to worry about the Germans hurting or eating our dogs here. If they should invade, I would just kill them."

"The dogs?"

"No! The Germans."

Which made Emily laugh. When they ran with the dogs back to the house, she turned at the door and said, "See you at supper, then."

Now, it was nearly Christmas. Kit mused how life in Sussex had turned out to be not so bad. He still lived with the Blossoms in the caretaker's cottage, but when Emily was home, he ate supper with her at the manor house.

During the week Emily stayed at the abbey for school, while Kit walked to the grammar in the center of the village. Some of the lads at school were all right. Often, they'd track the Spitfires and Mosquitos coming and going from the airstrip a few miles down the road. And for Kit, surprisingly, life was rarely dull. He did miss his mum, though. There was just no denying it. He wondered if she was being careful enough, working as hard as she did, or her being at home, alone as she was.

That evening, Marigold and Miss Zosia, who was Mr. Reilly's lady friend, were also at the manor house when Kit arrived.

He watched everyone exchange greetings, and, embarrassed, stood off to the side.

"Darling!" Zosia said, seeing Emily.

"Zosia!" Kit watched Emily give Zosia a kiss. "Hello Marigold," Emily added shyly.

"Hi Emily." Marigold stood next to Kit and poked him in the ribs. "Hello there, stranger."

Kit blushed. "Hullo."

As they followed Zosia and Emily into the dining room, Marigold added, "You look wonderful."

To which Kit shrugged. "Yes, well."

"No, you do. You've filled out. I have a note for you from your mom."

"My mom," he mimicked her.

At supper, Alex Reilly announced, "Ladies, I have a little something I came across recently, which I think might delight you both." They were several pairs of silk stockings, nearly impossible to find since rationing had begun.

"Wow." Marigold breathed. "Thank you so much."

"Oh Alex, darling"—Zosia opened one of the boxes—"you are clever. How on earth did you find these?"

He smiled. "It's important to be connected." He winked at Kit. "What, with all this austerity, one can hardly begin to function. Cigarette?"

THE NEXT MORNING, everyone piled into the car for a brief trip to London. Kit and Emily rode with Marigold in the back. Within a few minutes, Emily had nodded off.

Marigold looked over at Kit. "You seem very happy here."

"Yeah." He shrugged, always the cool customer.

"I know your mother is over the moon that you're coming back."

He briefly stole a glance in her direction. "Do you think it's better if I stay with her this time?"

"Kit, it's impossible to say. If something were to happen to either of you—And it would be because you were supposed to be safer by staying apart. I don't know the answer."

"It's odd that, isn't it?"

"What?"

"Now that everything's about this war, there isn't a sensible answer for almost anything. Bad things can happen even if you're trying to be good. And good things happen even when everything's become horrible. Why is that?"

"Beats the heck out of me, Kit. If you knew the answer to those questions, you could be boss of the world, I daresay."

"I like that, boss of the world. But wouldn't that make me sound a bit like a Hitler?"

She laughed. "Yeah, it would, actually. Just a bit."

WHEN THEY ARRIVED at the mews house, Kit's mother was just sweeping the doorstep. Alex Reilly pulled up and everyone climbed out of the car. Kit ran to his mother, and she gave him a fierce embrace.

Zosia said, "Mrs. Hearne, please. Do spend Christmas with us this year. There will be more than enough room in Sussex."

"That's very kind of you, miss, but Kit and I will have some catching up to do."

Alex Reilly added, "You should come. You can visit without any of us interfering. That way you can see what he gets up to, how he is managing."

"Thank you, sir, but—"

"And the threat of a bomb is so greatly diminished out where we are," Zosia added. "I know Marek would insist upon it." They all stood there awkwardly until Zosia asked Marigold, "Where is my brother?"

"He's in Scotland, with the Ministry of Information."

By now, Mrs. Hearne had put the broom away and was buttoning up her coat.

Alex Reilly glanced at his wristwatch. "Well, the invitation stands. You're very welcome."

A small blue truck entered the mews, pulling up beside Alex Reilly's Bentley. The driver leaned out of his window. "Afternoon, gov'ner."

Then Alex turned to Zosia. "I just need to see a man about a horse."

Emily asked, "Are we getting a horse?"

Zosia laughed. "No, it's an expression."

"Close your ears, poppet, "Alex said. "Let's not pick up any fag ends."

"What does that mean?" Marigold whispered to Kit.

"Fag ends, you know." Kit mimed smoking a cigarette. "Picking up a fag end."

The man with the truck loaded boxes and crates into the boot of Alex's car. Kit looked away and then from the corner of his eye watched Marigold observe the scene. He wondered if he should tell her about Reilly's seemingly endless deliveries. He glanced up at Reilly, who was counting out a large stack of five-pound notes. When the boot was closed, Alex handed the money to the man.

Kit saw Marigold's eyes widen. When she looked back at him, Kit shrugged and shook his head.

"HAPPY CHRISTMAS, HAPPY CHRISTMAS, DEAR!" Falaise waived from the back seat of Alex Reilly's car as he drove away down Old Church Street. With the exception of Buddy and Marigold, everyone had gone to Sussex.

Marigold went back inside and climbed the stairs. She gave a small shiver. It was dreadfully chilly.

She placed more coal in the grate and blew on her hands. It was Christmas Eve. She had never worked on a holiday before.

But it was only fair. People had families, and volunteers were needed for the patrols. She heard Buddy climb the stairs.

"Hello!" he shouted.

"I'm in here."

Buddy came into the sitting room carrying a large package. "For crying out loud Marigold, where's the heat?"

They stood over the box on the landing. Buddy placed a coin in the slot and turned it. Nothing happened. He softly swore, "Goddamnit."

Marigold could see his breath when he spoke. "We'll just have to keep our coats on, I guess."

They got a small fire going and sat by the grate. Buddy opened his package. "Hey, look what I got from the old folks at home." He took out an enormous muffler someone had knitted and wrapped it around his neck. Smiling, he rummaged through the package. "Oh, boy, look at this!"

"What, Buddy?" She tightly hugged herself to keep warm.

"Did you ever try a Moravian cookie?"

"No, what's that?"

He handed Marigold a tube filled with wafer-thin ginger-snaps. She tried one, "Oh my goodness. Buddy, that's delicious."

"Yes indeed. Buddy'll take care of you. Moravian cookies, all around!"

They opened two bottles of milk and ate every last cookie in silence.

Then Buddy stood up. "Okay. Come on, Mac, let's go to church."

"What? Oh no, thank you, Buddy."

Buddy was expected at CBS for a twenty four hour shift, and Marigold needed to change before reporting to the APW at Central Command.

"Gotta sing carols at Christmas, Mac. You know it'll make you feel good!"

Wearing her uniform, she grudgingly followed him to the

Church of the Holy Redeemer. The hole in the crypt had been mostly repaired and the sanctuary was full of people.

And Buddy was right. Singing carols did make her feel better. But when they got to "Silent Night," Marigold thought about Joop and wherever he might be. She thought about the bombing of the crypt and the people who had died. She thought about the little girl, calling for help from under the rubble. But Marigold knew to keep singing, even as the tears ran down her face.

Mr. Alwyn had set up a feast at Central Command. Christmas crackers and paper hats, chocolate biscuits and fizzy apple cider.

"Mr. Alwyn!" Marigold asked, "How did you get all this?"

"Haha, even I have contacts, my dear. Happy Christmas." He toasted the workers. "Thanks to you, we keep Chelsea safe, and with your help, we shall win this war. Happy Christmas, all!"

SHE WALKED HOME AT DAYLIGHT, and saw Joop sitting on the doorstep of King's Road. In his arms were several packages, but he'd fallen asleep against the door frame. Marigold nudged his boot gently with her shoe. "Alstublieft?"

Joop's eyes opened. "I didn't miss Christmas, did I?"

Whereupon she sat down beside him, her heart leaping with joy, to tightly hold him, and cover him with kisses.

"Marigold, I have to go soon." He looked so grave, she almost didn't recognize him.

"You don't want to come in for breakfast?"

"I don't mean that, Gouda. I mean I have to go back to Holland."

"But why? Your queen is here."

He shrugged and whispered, "You know I have to do it."

"When, Joop?"

"I don't know. I won't be able to say when."

"Oh." Her helmet and gas mask, his packages and gas mask,

and the two of them sitting in the doorway made her want to take their picture. But her camera was inside.

"Joop."

"Hmm?"

She slowly kissed him and then whispered, "We have the house to ourselves."

"We do?"

She nodded and then kissed him again. "Let's celebrate Christmas."

By evening, he began to resemble his former self. They huddled by the small fireplace, naked, save for the blankets over their shoulders. "Gouda, this New Year's, yeah, we're going to celebrate in traditional Dutch style." He said this as if the Germans had received the memo, that everything was calm, and that people had returned to their ordinary lives. "So," he said, "this is for you." He handed her one of the packages. It was a white rabbit fur jacket.

"Joop! Thank you!" She dropped her blanket and put it on, "How do I look?" she spun around in front of him.

"You look Lekker. You look mooi. I hope you like it." She sat next to him and he wrapped his arms around her, stroking the rabbit fur.

"I love it. How ever did you find this?"

"Alex Reilly of course." Joop shrugged. "It seems he can get anything."

Those crates in the back of Reilly's car, the silk stockings that were now in her bedroom drawer flashed across her mind. She turned and kissed Joop on the mouth, pushing those thoughts away.

On New Year's Eve, the blackout drapes inside Chester Square were closed. But when Joop and Marigold entered the ballroom, the party was in full swing with handsome officers in dress uniform, beautiful women in glamorous gowns, music, and dancing.

"Goudsbloem," Joop murmured, saying her name in Dutch,

"here is someone I want you to meet." He led her forward through the crowd, then whispered into her ear, "And don't forget to curtsey."

Standing beside her, Joop bowed deeply. "Your Majesty. May I present, my very dearest friend, Miss Marigold McGrath?"

Queen Wilhelmina was not a young woman, but when she smiled, her eyes conveyed a liveliness that saw everything. "Miss McGrath, Lieutenant Kasander has told me so much about you. Thank you for the support you give to our brave soldier, upon whom the Netherlands depends."

"Your Majesty." Marigold curtsied, shocked that she didn't keel over.

"Now tell me. When will the Americans join the effort?"

"I just don't know, Your Majesty. But I can't wait for them to decide. So, in my own small way I already have."

"I'm glad to hear it. Miss McGrath, here is a token on behalf of the Dutch people." The queen placed a small pin in Marigold's hand. "Lieutenant Kasander will explain its meaning." And with that, the queen moved on, turning her considerable charm toward other soldiers and their dates, very much like themselves.

"What is this?" It was a tiny enamel daisy.

"It's a marguerite. It is the symbol of Dutch resistance." He pinned it onto her chest. "Wear it always and we will win this war."

1941

BRITAIN'S SPECIAL OPERATIONS EXECUTIVE WAS located at Baker Street. The corridors were hushed and Joop waited outside the office with a frosted door much like a schoolboy waiting to see the headmaster. He glanced at his watch. He was due back in Holland by the end of the week. But still—

The office door opened. A young man in uniform peered out. He said, "They'll see you now."

Joop followed him into a rabbit warren of rooms, inside the last of which were two men. "Lieutenant Kasander, please explain to the general what it is you do."

"Well, sir. My role is to assist with the lines of communication. There are many people involved, such as who can pass on the word, a message, who can create the documents, the papers and passports, find the connections. And there are those who cannot serve in any capacity other than to help the Onderduikers move between one house and another, one village and another. They play a valuable role, too. Then there are soldiers. The idea is how to get those allied soldiers who are parachuting down, or those who've been shot down, anyone running away, really, over to a safe place. That is what I do."

The general had been examining papers at a desk. He looked up at Joop. "Commander Marx brought your concerns about the transmissions being corrupted to my attention."

"Yes, it's very perplexing, sir."

The general remained silent for a moment, then asked, "What evidence do you have, lieutenant?" And continued reading the papers on his desk.

"It's just a hunch, sir. I can't explain it, but I am convinced that someone besides our Dutch agents are receiving messages from the SOE."

The general said, "I see."

Commander Marks handed the general several transcripts. "The evidence for that is SOE has been receiving messages that are flawless in their transmission. Under the current circumstances, that would be impossible sir."

"How so?"

Marx continued, "We use the poetry code and each of us has a specific series of errors to indicate which one of us is communicating what. How is it that so many of the transmissions from Holland are perfect? That doesn't make sense."

The superior officer's expression was impassive. "Well, thank you, Lieutenant Kasander. We'll take this under advisement. And good luck."

In spite of this, the SOE continued with the poetry coding, oblivious to what had to be a security breach. It didn't make sense. Too many agents had disappeared. Or if they hadn't disappeared, why was it their transmissions were consistently flawless?

Joop's rucksack was replenished with forged documents, ration cards, and cash. His weapon was cleaned and he was given a large supply of bullets. He was given enough food that if he became stranded, he would be able to get through a few days.

He climbed into the truck, which brought him to the air base where he strapped on his parachute. After supper, a plane flew him to the drop point. The door opened and he was given the signal. Joop raised his thumb and saluted. Then he jumped into the night.

Amsterdam

It was sometime between three and four in the morning. This was always the best time for Joop to walk through town. It was quiet and he could think. Usually, he would pass by the house on Keizersgracht and watch his family's home from across the canal but tonight was different. The strike the day before had become ugly. It had been to protest the unceasing harassment of Amsterdam's Jewish citizens by the Nazis. Joop had been wearing the German uniform at the time, and somehow, he got caught up in having to play the enforcer. It had deeply shamed him.

But now, his uniform was hidden away, and the streets were quiet.

He saw a group of men in the distance being shoved into the back of a truck. He knew where they were going. It was either Kamp Schoorl or Scheveningen. From there, they'd be sent to Germany or Poland. It made his stomach burn. Joop headed to Piet's house. The whole thing made him sick.

Joop had a key and slipped in the door without making a sound. Instead of barking, the dog wagged her tail. Joop slipped off his boots and she followed him upstairs to the attic. The early hours were the best time to transmit a message, as the airwaves were usually clear and he could send his communication through without hassle. Still, he had to be careful.

Piet was in his pajamas when he made an appearance at dawn.

"What do you say, comrade?"

Piet's yawn was the answer.

"Here, I brought you something from England." Joop removed a small bottle of beer from his rucksack.

"Lekker! How did you get that?" Only the Germans had access to alcohol now, so beer was very hard to come by.

"The Brits take good care of me." Joop had a bottle for himself, too. They opened their beers and toasted, "Proost!"

"Nothing like a war to start drinking at breakfast." Piet licked his lips. "My God. That is delicious."

The sky turned pink as they sat in contented silence. Eventually, Piet said, "You should know about last night."

"Uh oh."

Piet sighed and said, "Well, it's good, but then it's very, very bad."

Downstairs, his granny put some music on the victrola. Piet said, "She loves her Caruso. It helps her get through the occupation."

"Should I finish my beer before you tell me?"

"No. You'll need it after I tell you."

"What happened?"

"Someone killed a kraut two days ago. So, the Germans returned the favor."

"What do you mean?" Joop suddenly felt nauseous. He knew what came next.

Piet drained his beer. "Uh"—his voice began to tremble—"they rounded up all of the guys in the next street, Joop."

"What happened?" He wondered whether Piet had any idea that Joop had been there.

"They lined them up and had their families come out so they would see what happened next." His hands shook and he tried to roll a cigarette. "They shot them." Piet was now weeping. "Then yesterday, we had a strike. Four hundred more men were arrested."

Joop guzzled his beer to numb his shame, then took a deep breath and said, "Piet. Piet."

Piet wiped his eyes and lit the cigarette. "I thought that after a year, that somehow, things would shift. But it's only getting worse, Joop."

Joop rubbed his face with his hands. He wanted to see his parents, to make sure they were all right. Downstairs, the record started to skip. They waited for Piet's granny to move the needle, but she did not. They heard her mounting the stairs. Then she opened the door. With her were two policemen. The dog barked furiously.

"Shh, lie down," Piet said.

"Pieter," she said. "These men want to interview you." Thank God, they'd already concealed the transmitter.

The policeman looked at Joop and said, "Papers."

Wordlessly, Joop handed him the forged ones.

"All right, Jan Kramer."

Piet had not heard Joop's alias before. When his friend looked askance, Joop remained silent. "You come, too," the policeman said. "We like catching two birds with one stone."

THERE WERE ABOUT two dozen men in the truck. On the way to Kamp Schoorl, they compared notes. Some were petty thieves, others accused of being in the underground. Several had refused to report to their assigned work duty, and a couple of them were communists. A third of them were Jewish.

At the camp, a guard said, "Strip."

Silently, they did so. Another guard took their clothes, their shoes, their identification, everything. Then someone turned the hose on them.

Stay still, Joop told himself. Completely still. It was February and several of the men were older. They did not look as if they could stand rough treatment for long. Joop averted his gaze and stayed silent.

At dusk they were directed to the registrar and given clogs, socks, underwear, and old army uniforms, none of which fit.

The registrar said to Piet, "You're number 325411." He was

handed a jacket. On the front was that number. To the left of the number was a yellow triangle over which was an inverted red triangle, meaning a political prisoner who was a Jew.

The registrar said to Joop, "You're number 737244." Next to the number on Joop's jacket was only the inverted red triangle, signifying a political prisoner. Joop realized it was because he wasn't circumcised. *Remain calm*, his mind instructed him. *Remain calm*.

The barracks were cold. He wondered how many of the older guys would actually last. That night, Piet whispered, "What are we going to do?"

Joop murmured, "We'll not say a word. Do you understand, Piet? Don't say a word until it's time."

"Time for what?"

Joop mouthed, "Escape."

Roll call was at six the next morning. Within moments, it was clear that roll call was a chance for their captors to have a good laugh. "Hats on, hats off!"

"Turn to the left, to the right. Lie down!"

The ground was wet. "Twenty squats!"

A prisoner staggered, and the guard shouted, "You don't like it eh? Tell me then, how you like this!"—kicking and beating him until he lay unconscious before the others.

The next day, someone protested, and he too was beaten, then hogtied and placed in a concrete lined hole to sit in his own excrement. A guard laughed at the men struggling to contain their horror. "What? We'll let him out at the end of the week."

A steady rain began falling and the temperatures at night were below freezing. Another guard said, "If you think it's so bad, I'll put you in the hole, too. You'll see, it's a fine accommodation."

Prisoners were assigned different tasks. Piet and Joop were directed to repair the rose garden, a barbed wire enclosure where prisoners were sent to stand for however long suited their captors. Some stood there for hours, others stood there for days. The knots on the wire cut their fingers and hands. One of the inmates being punished warned them, "Just you wait. It's gonna get worse."

Which was true.

Joop knew. They had to get out of there.

Kamp Schoorl was not far from the coast, about an hour north of Amsterdam. The question was how the hell were they going to escape. The sadism of the guards was unlike anything Joop had ever seen, but then again, because so many detainees were arriving every day, perhaps the opportunity to leave lay there. Somehow, he'd pose as one of them, which he'd done so often that it was almost second nature. Then he'd steal a truck.

Steal a truck. How was he going to manage that? He watched two guards walk the perimeter of the camp, a pair of dogs at their side. He watched the new arrivals, coming in trucks, more and more each day.

Depending on the guards' whim, the morning roll call could last hours. That meant they'd have to disappear before it started. But then, when their numbers came up, all hell would break loose. But so what? Joop thought. No one would think to look in a truck. Particularly if he'd done away with the truck's drivers and indeed, substituted himself. None of these people looked at him and knew him and what he looked like. They thought that they did. But none of them saw him. Not one.

It became critical to stay out of trouble and not be put in that rose garden, nor in, God forbid, one of those concrete holes. He'd had the foresight to keep some of the barbed wire when repairing that work. The next order of business was to determine when those guards got the trucks. They'd have to be ready and waiting for them.

The guards got drunk at night, and Joop and Piet crept before dawn into one of those trucks. At roll call the next day, their two numbers were missing and the alarm was sounded. The search began.

Joop and Piet were in the back of a truck waiting for someone to come inside. Then the first one entered. Joop stretched the barbed wire around the man's throat and pulled it tight, breaking his skin as he strangled the guard. Joop's own blood ran cold, watching his victim's eyes bulge out of his head, a look of holy terror as he met his maker at the hands of a dirty prisoner.

Fingers trembling, Joop and Piet stripped the corpse and removed the truck's keys from a pocket.

Joop put on his clothes and waited for another guard. When the second man came, Joop did it again. He would not let Piet do such a disgusting thing.

Piet looked at him and said, "I would do it! I would do it, Joop."

And Joop answered, "Fine. You decide what we'll do with their bodies," wanting to scream and vomit, because more than anything, he did not think himself a killer. Yet there were two men who were dead at his hands.

Joop started the truck. His hands were wet. Afraid they'd slip on the steering wheel, he wiped them on the dead man's trousers. Every fiber in his being buzzed. It felt impossible to breathe.

By now Piet was also in uniform and sat on the passenger side. The guards at the gate stepped forward, their dogs' tongues panting, pulling on the leads. Joop glanced in the rearview mirror and saw the rushing to and fro of guards looking for the escapees. He swallowed to keep the bile in his throat from rising any higher.

The gate slowly opened. Joop and Piet casually waved the Nazi salute as their truck left the grounds, heading toward the main road.

They drove east out of Kamp Schoorl, not daring to pull over nor stop until they were twenty kilometers from Ede.

"About the bodies," Piet said. He had removed the guards' tags and dressed them in their own prison uniforms. "They will be us." They dragged the guards' corpses into the front seat. There was a can of petrol in the back. They doused everything. The truck, the bodies, the engine. Piet lit a match.

Then they ran until it felt as if their lungs would burst.

Finally, they arrived at the general store of the heroic Mrs. van Lier. She opened the door to find them gasping, emaciated in their victims' German uniforms. They didn't need to say what they'd been through.

"Mr. Kremer," she said. She put her hand on Joop's arm. "You're safe now. Come sit by the stove. You both look famished. I'll get you some soup."

It was the fourth of March, 1941.

London

Marek bent down before he turned the key in its lock. "Look at these lovelies, Marigold." Yellow and white buds peeked through the earth. "Even as we kill each other, these glorious creatures appear, indifferent to our shit."

Marek rarely spoke like that.

The day before, they'd waded through the wreckage of a school. The all clear had just sounded, and they'd put the cameras aside to help distraught parents pull limbs and bodies from the ruins.

"Gently, gently," the wardens had called out, fearful of timbers crushing survivors.

Finally, it was time for Marek to take photos for the government which would not be shared with the public. Handing him film, holding the flashbulb, Marigold worked, deftly determined to help without nerves or hesitation, bitterly grateful the pathos muted her response. All of it was too terrible to even weep.

When it was over, it began to rain. They returned to Lark Mews, developing in silence the film Marigold couldn't bear to see.

"Don't turn away." Marek gently admonished her. "This is what happens in war. Part of our job is to record it."

Then Marigold nodded, taking notes, as he explained how they should label the contact sheets, and pictures which featured bodies that were identified.

Everything was placed in a large brown packet. Marigold wrote Ministry of Information across the front. She watched Marek wipe his face with a handkerchief. He held out his hand to her and she took it. "Marigold," he spoke just above a whisper. "We just witnessed the most terrible day in many peoples' lives. Losing their children like that." He shook his head, still holding her hand. "If something should happen to you, I wouldn't get over it. I know I wouldn't."

But now it was Friday. The smell of burnt flesh and explosives washed away, and the pavements reflected sunshine.

Marek loaded his Rolleiflex. "First, we'll head to the Ministry, take a few candids followed by tea at the Ritz, my girl. I daresay you've earned it."

Walking beside him, her arms full of camera bags, she didn't need to fret about Joop. He had his work, and she had hers. Many of Marek's pictures were appearing in papers all around the world. Then he had others to exhibit at galleries or for sale by his dealer once the war ended.

Despite the tower of sandbags outside its windows, the chandelier and marble floors at the Ritz remained elegant. They sat down, placing their equipment just under the table. "Zosia brought me here once."

"Did she? That saucy minx didn't say a word. When was that?

A waiter approached them.

"Before. When things were just picking up with Alex Reilly."

The waiter stood, silently waiting.

Marek handed him their ration cards. "Two cream teas, and which do you prefer, Marigold, Darjeeling or oolong?"

"Oolong, please."

"Excellent choice. And a Grants, whiskey. Neat. For both of us."

Marigold chuckled. "I think Zosia brought me to chaperone, really."

"You? A chaperone?" He lit a cigarette. "It's like bringing a lamb to slaughter, Marigold. That sister of mine, I say."

She cast her gaze down when the food arrived and Marek sized up the waiter, who returned the frank smile. Matchbooks were discreetly exchanged.

Marek turned back to her and watched her slather jam upon her scone. "Rations are a bore, but we've still got strawberry jam."

Being with Marek, chatting about this or that summoned life in all its color and pushed the war into a cupboard whose door could be locked and the key thrown away. She gave him her best smile, then sighed, and took a lusty bite. It was so delicious. "I'd be lost without it."

"Now listen, little one. You've acquitted yourself well. I think you have genuine talent." His praise was always measured. Marek was not one to flatter.

But as Marigold chewed, she beamed with pleasure, hoping he didn't notice her blush. Awkwardly, she swallowed, "Thank you."

He leaned forward and dabbed at her mouth with his napkin. "Just a few stray crumbs. We can't be caught with jam in the wrong places, eh?"

Marek's affection was always spontaneous and natural. She couldn't recall her father ever being like that. The week before, when someone had mistaken Marigold for Marek's daughter, he had answered, "Even better than that, she's my protegee."

And Marigold had thought, "I wish you were my father," as she adjusted the light, then handed him a camera.

Marek refilled her teacup, "I don't like to see you mooning after your Dutchman. There's nothing we can do about whether he's here or there."

"I know. You're right."

"So, tomorrow's your birthday." He had a sip of whiskey. "I spoke with Falaise. We're going to have supper at the Café de Paris. I'll meet you there and we'll have a table next to the stage. Let's have Buddy come, too. God knows you've earned it, Marigold."

"And Zosia?"

He waved his hand. "She's off with that blackguard, Reilly. Honestly, desperate times call for desperate measures, I suppose."

A NEW HAIRCUT, just above her shoulders and her nails painted bright red. Walking home, a young woman's reflection glanced back at her. Marigold was becoming someone she wanted to be. That there was no birthday greeting from America meant almost nothing. She was a woman now, in possession of her wits, as Falaise would say.

Marigold placed the white rabbit jacket over her shoulders, and Falaise beamed with approval. "My dear, but you're lovely."

Falaise herself was resplendent in a long velvet cloak. "Here's a little something to wear with your beautiful blue frock. Happy birthday, dear." It was a ring with a diminutive sapphire in its center. "My father gave this to me when I turned twenty-one. It belongs on a twenty-one-year-old's finger."

Even Buddy looked smashing in his white dinner jacket. Their taxi crawled along the Embankment in the dark.

Falaise said, "You haven't been to the Café de Paris, have you, dear?"

Marigold shook her head. "No, this is my first time."

"Oh, my dear! It is splendid. You will love it."

There had been raids during the night, but the Café de Paris was more than twenty feet underground. There was no way their revelries could be interrupted.

Approaching Piccadilly, Marigold realized that Falaise, being slightly deaf, hadn't noticed the sirens. But then there was a clap and the flash of blue light.

Suddenly, traffic appeared from nowhere and people were everywhere. Wardens with their whistles, rumbling and screaming on the edge of Leicester Square.

A roar, then another clap.

"Let's get out of here," Buddy paid the driver. He helped Falaise out of the cab. Bits of buildings and incendiaries fell from the sky. They ran, ducking for cover under a hotel's awning. The sirens continued, deafening.

The Café de Paris was just across the street. Fire trucks lined up outside, water spraying on neighboring buildings. Everything grew silent. Another siren gave the all clear.

It was then Marigold saw the people, tinged with soot and blood. Some were in rags, their evening clothes blown off them in the blast. Bodies were being carried on stretchers.

"Oh!" She turned Falaise away to face the hotel. "We must go inside."

"All right, dear." They went through the doors. People were still moving in every direction.

Someone shouted, "Make way, make way."

The stretchers followed them into the lobby, flooding the entrance. Marigold's heart began to slow, until it moved in tandem with her breath. Where was Buddy? Where was Marek?

She could see the Café de Paris entrance through a large pane window. Buddy was helping rescuers carry a woman whose leg was gushing blood. She realized Falaise was watching over her shoulder.

Falaise said, "Oh my dear. Oh my dear." The doors of the hotel's dining room were flung open. Bodies were everywhere and linens were pulled from tables to bandage the wounded.

Falaise grabbed Marigold's hand. "Marigold. Look at me. Look at me!" She touched Marigold's chin and turned it toward her. The sounds of the room seemed to melt into silence. But when Falaise spoke, Marigold heard the words, "Nothing we do will change what has happened." Falaise's voice was increasingly muffled as if underwater. "Be sure you have yourself in check." She touched Marigold's cheek. "Take a deep breath, Marigold."

Marigold did. The noise and the chaos returned.

"That's it."

Marigold hadn't realized her face was wet.

"Now, find Marek. He must be looking for us. Please go make enquiries."

Marek was in the ballroom at the back of the hotel. Marigold studied his face. He appeared to be asleep.

His words, "Don't look away, this is what happens in a war," played over and over while the warden assured her that Marek would have died instantly. He'd been pulled from a table alongside the orchestra. When the bomb hit, the warden explained, Marek must have been standing, because his back had been blown clean away, leaving only the shell of his dapper handsome front.

WHEN SOMEONE ASKED about the studio, Marigold stepped forward, "I'll take care of it."

It was after the funeral. Alex Reilly had bundled Zosia into his car, taking her away from the source of her grief. As usual, the key was in the tin behind the African violets at Lark Mews. Their small pool of color had grown riotous overnight, and the cat meowed, ready for his breakfast. Everything was as it should have been, with only one exception.

As the days passed, Marigold logged rolls of film, filed prints, and cleaned lenses. She prepared the solutions and developed some pictures. She hung up the prints and turned out the red light. She fed the cat and arranged the cameras the way that Marek liked them, ready to shoot at a moment's notice.

On the tenth day someone knocked at the door.

"No one's here!" she shouted.

It was Joop. He crossed the room and she was in his arms.

"I'm sorry I missed your birthday," he said.

Suddenly the sobbing tumbled out of her even though the words wouldn't come. She couldn't say it.

"I'm sorry, Gouda," From the way he embraced her, she understood that he knew. "I am so sorry." Her sorrow erupted, but Joop's large hands kept her safe.

"Marek-" She almost choked on the word.

Joop's large hands stroked her back."

"Marek-" then it came, as a muffled scream into his chest. She stopped crying and his breathing against hers slowly calmed her heart. Yet the rage would not leave, and she trembled to keep from screaming again.

When he finally lowered his arms, she was still trembling and said, "I am done with this war. God damn them. They killed him. They killed Marek."

It was only at dusk when she pulled the blackout and turned on the light did she notice the gash on Joop's face. Tenderly, she removed his glasses. When she touched his cheek, he winced. The gash was over an old bruise that was still yellow and mauve.

"I have to go back." He was so thin, and his blonde hair nearly shaved off.

She was afraid to ask why and knew that she shouldn't, but she did anyway.

He sighed and rubbed his face. "Gouda, Marigold. You know I speak German."

She nodded.

"What I do involves that. The Germans think I'm one thing, when actually I'm another. They have to think that I am German." He groaned and put his arm over his eyes.

"Please." She put her hand on his arm. "Don't go back." She couldn't tell if he was weeping. "Please stay here now. Can't you stay here this time?"

"I wish I could. But if I stay, we won't win the war."

"Why?" Now her own tears were smarting behind her eyes again. Damnit.

"Gouda." He held her hand. "Because, a German soldier was killed, and they came and rounded up twenty Dutch boys. All of them younger than we are. Because I was pretending that I was German—I had to." He sighed and looked at her. "Then there was a strike. In protest. And it was good." He started to laugh bitterly. "And, then uh. I was arrested, Marigold."

"What happened?"

"I won't tell you about the rest of it."

She heard someone close the door of the house next door, and footsteps making their to the main street. A dog barked in the distance. It occurred to her that it was probably the only dog left in London. "I hate this fucking war. I do! And where are the

Americans? Where is my country? Where are they?" She hated to think of what he had done. "Please Joop." She couldn't let him go back. "The queen needs you. She needs you here."

"No, Gouda. She needs me to report to her here. Then I must —I cannot talk about it." He kissed her gently and said, "Promise me."

"Anything, Joop."

"Marigold. We are going to win this war. I will win it for you, the country, and even the queen. But you must promise me one thing."

"Yes?"

He held her face in his hands. "Promise, you will not wait for me."

"God damn you." Marigold slapped him as hard as she could. "Goddamn you straight to hell!" She crossed to the door and opened it. "Get out. Just get out and do not come back."

They stared at each other for one brief moment. Then he was gone.

The cat rubbed her legs and meowed. Marigold picked up his bowl and saw a mouse run between the floorboards. She opened the kitchen drawer. Marek's gun was in its case, just as always. She checked it, then pointed at the floor and fired.

She hated mice. She just did.

IT HAD BEEN a fortnight since the Café de Paris. Marigold gingerly placed the last of the prints into their portfolio. The final roll of film had been of the Foreign Secretary, Anthony Eden. Marek had caught Eden's singular good looks, his moody glamour. Some of Marek's portraits were so arresting that they more resembled movie actors than they did government officials.

Some of those pictures would be kept back and not sent over to Downing Street. Marigold placed the portfolio in her rucksack and began the bicycle journey to the West End.

At a red light, she glanced at a pile of rubble in front of the hollow shell of a building, its interior exposed, haunted like a phantom. That was when she saw three little girls skipping toward the rubble. It was raining lightly and one of them had her umbrella open. Another was in Wellingtons. They couldn't have been more than nine or ten years old. The light turned green, but Marigold remained, her foot on the curb, watching the girls.

"Over here!" One gestured to the others and they began to climb the rubble.

Marigold's heart was in her throat.

"Like this!" called the lead girl, who gracefully leapt off the rubble onto the pavement below. The other two followed suit and Marigold was transfixed, watching them, seeing the ruin of war behind them. The clouds were moody, the building behind them tragic, but the girls were indifferent, leaping and dancing. Marigold took out her Rolleicord. She removed the lens cap.

She called out, "Can you jump together? At the same time?"

"You mean like this?" And the girls leapt, the three of them holding hands, laughing, their feet off the ground, joyous for a moment, despite the cruelty of a wretched, vicious war. Marigold took the picture. She moved her bicycle closer. She wound the film and took another one and then she took another.

Spring

"Bring your pj's," Buddy had advised. "We all do now." And it was true. What with the gas mask, ARP helmet, her camera, and everything else, making it home across town was far more complicated than simply having one's toothbrush and a change of clothes at the ready.

The blackouts were pulled shut and the room thick with smoke. Was it Daphne from CBS or Daryl from the BBC who'd invited everyone over? The place was so overrun with revelers it was impossible to tell. Marigold had had way too much to drink by then and it didn't make a difference anyway. She spied Buddy across the room, deep in conversation with some Irish girl he fancied.

It was midnight. The party was in full swing and so loud that when the sirens and rumbling began it took several seconds to realize what it was. At first it prompted wildness and whooping, but then the room grew quiet. Only the thickest of skins could ignore blast after blast.

Marigold took shelter under the dining table. It was by far the most reassuring space in the room. She stretched and then realized that someone had put a record on the phonograph. The bombs continued falling and the floors began to shake. "*If I didn't care. . . ..*" She considered Joop's bravery and his generosity. Love is kind, she realized, and Joop was always kind. Love is generous, she knew that was true, and there was no doubt about it, he was generous to a fault. Joop. She hadn't said she loved him.

A man in spectacles on the other side of the table crawled over to where she lay. He looked nice enough. He was already in his pj's. They were flannel with a polite stripe.

"I want someone to hold you, when you're in need of holding," Joop had said.

"Oh my God," said the man.

"Don't be afraid." Marigold reached out and patted the man's hand.

"How can you say that?" he asked.

She sighed. "Well, I'm more afraid of mice than I am of death."

"I'm terrified of death."

She laced her fingers in his. "Really?"

"Hmmmhmm."

"Wow," she replied. Joop had said he wanted someone to hold her. "So," she inched closer to him under the table. "How about . . ." There was a fearsome roar and the walls shook. Bits of ceiling plaster hit the table, crashing dishes that were still there. "To take your mind off this racket . . ." Bulbs in the chandelier exploded, falling down on the floor around them. "Why don't you kiss me instead?"

"Gosh. I think I will." The floor shook some more. His hand was on her cheek, and his tongue was fully upon her.

"I mean, if we have to die, how would you rather go?" One could hear the bombs drop on the next block. "In a shelter, or making love to a woman you don't even know?"

He kissed her in response. God, she thought, I am really drunk. She wrapped her legs around him, declaring, "If we have to die, let's die doing this!"

He laughed, "My goodness. I don't mind if I do."

By dawn everything was still. Marigold looked at the sleeping form beside her and crawled over to the window. The light on the Thames was more beguiling than ever. But the houses across the river on the South Bank had vanished, levelled by the raid in the night. Black smoke whispered from the crater where a pub used to be. Several alarms were sounding and some fire engines came barreling down the Embankment. A girl across the room coughed and then sat up to light a cigarette. Marigold found her shoes and quickly left the building.

Walking along the river, she realized that every moment, every second that man had touched her, she'd been thinking of Joop. Joop's kindness and his humor. At the King's Road, she let herself in and ran up the stairs. "Falaise? Falaise!"

The house was empty. Marigold washed herself clean and put on her uniform. She sat down with a pen and paper. Her head was thumping, really. How could she have been so childish and stupid? Joop only wanted to be honorable.

Dear Joop,
Please accept my apology for my beastly rudeness the last time we met. I failed to grasp your very generous kindness and want to assure you that I grasp it now. I am thus releasing you from any obligation, should circumstances mandate that you behave differently than you might have, were we a couple and there wasn't a war.

She found it difficult to swallow, letting him go in so many words. But she certainly didn't want him gallivanting to and fro—Marigold thought of the man in his flannel pajamas under the table. She didn't even know his name. So, wasn't she the one who was gallivanting now? Oh, Joop. Marigold took a deep breath and continued writing.

Joop, in addition to the sentiments above, I should like to add that nothing would make me happier nor give me greater joy than to see you safe and sound and to drink tea with you, once again, at the Savoy.

~~Sincerely,~~

~~Love,~~
~~as ever~~
Your,
Marigold. XO

Straightaway, she took the letter to Chester Square. A puzzled looking clerk said, "We don't normally take the post for our soldiers. That is done at—"

"Please. I've met the queen already. Lieutenant Kasander introduced us. I know she has a special interest in him."

"Ah." He didn't look as though he believed her, but he did smile when she tapped the marguerite pinned to her lapel. "Her Majesty gave me this."

"Ah yes." The clerk smiled. "It's our Dutch symbol of resistance."

"So please, if there is someone or some way that Lieutenant Kasander is receiving letters, don't you think it kindest that this one be included? It's only words of encouragement."

She had been careful not to seal the envelope. Censors were there for a reason after all.

The clerk shrugged. "It might be months until he sees it."

Marigold looked at the clerk. She didn't speak, but she said in her heart, please know that I love him. He deserves some words of encouragement.

Somehow the clerk seemed to understand. "I will see that he gets it."

"Dank u wel." She left the building and burst into tears.

AT BREAKFAST, Falaise declared, "Buddy you're so handsome in those pinstripes! I do love a man in a pinstripe suit."

"Falaise is right," Marigold agreed. "You look terrific."

"Thanks, Mac."

Outside on King's Road, they walked in silence, enjoying the

Spring weather. Finally, Buddy said, "Mac, will you do me a favor?"

"What's that?"

"Would you put in a good word with Trude?"

"What? I thought she liked you already."

"Well, I'd like to get to know her much, much better."

Marigold laughed. "What about those English birds, you know, British crumpet?"

"Well, I'll tell you Marigold. Trude may be the smartest, most unusual person—present company excepted of course."

"Of course."

She smiled up at him. Suddenly he seemed much, much younger than she. She pat Buddy's back. "I'll put in a good word. Are you busy tonight?"

"I'm working late. I'll be home by eleven."

"Well, I'll tell her to stay over. Make sure you're still wearing those pinstripes. You really do look terrific."

"YOU DON'T THINK Buddy's family is like those *Tobacco Road* people, do you?" Trude asked.

They'd just come from that film. She and Marigold stopped at the corner. The night was overcast but otherwise mild. Trude lit a cigarette and they walked along, past the Houses of Parliament, along the wide street, everything deliciously peaceful, glad to be girls, just making their way home.

"I'm sure they're nothing like that. His father's a reverend or something."

"He does sound like them, though," Trude said.

"I'll tell you this, Trude. I've learned a lot from Buddy, not the least of which is we shouldn't judge a person by their . . . their—"

"Yes?"

"Oh, you know what I'm going to say." She gave her friend a stern look. "You're not too much of a snob to give him a chance, are you?"

"I'm not a snob!" And they both laughed and linked arms. Several taxis idled at the corner, waiting for a fare.

Trude headed toward them. "Shall we just grab a cab?"

"No, it's so lovely out. Let's walk." They strolled another couple of blocks, enjoying the night air. There hadn't been any raids since April and Marigold's relief that the attacks might be over was palpable. The clouds parted for a moment and the barrage balloons shifted so that the moonlight shone upon them. Sandbags lined the street, and the park's black iron railings were wrapped in barbed wire. It was a perfect evening.

"Buddy should be home by the time we get there," Marigold said.

"Do you hear that?" Trude asked.

A buzzing sounded. At first it was faint. Then it grew louder.

"Oh God, no," Marigold groaned.

"Come on." Trude threw down the cigarette and grabbed Marigold's hand. Together, they ran lightly down the street.

"It's like that time in Central Park," Marigold said.

Trude smiled, "Last one there is a rotten egg!"

The sirens had begun and the home guards' whistles were blowing. As if from nowhere, the street was suddenly full of pedestrians darting in one direction or another, as if they'd break into song and dance, caught in the middle of a movie musical.

A warden called out to them, "Come on, come on, girls. Get a move on."

The underground was just up ahead. Machine gun bullets hit against the pavement and a bomb whistled before hitting its target. The sky lit up, first white then orange. The deafening noise of one explosion, then another, smoke and dust billowing out everywhere.

The crowd raced into the underground's escalators, which were stationary, and then down a flight of stairs, which were mobbed. Down one floor, then another, the lights flickered and went out. There was a collective moan of barely contained panic.

Yet everyone stood still and held their breath, counting to themselves until the next moment of contact.

"Steady, steady," said a man behind her. She could smell his pipe tobacco and the dank of a wet wool coat. Someone flickered a lighter and held it high above the others. The crowd looked up at it and then somewhere, a lantern illuminated the passage. Slowly, everyone stepped forward. At the second landing, they silently waited for the others to descend.

Come on, come on, Marigold thought. She wondered where Trude was and briefly looked over her shoulder. Trude met her gaze and nodded. The crowd stepped forward, then stopped when the earth began to shake, the air filling with sweat and fear. The lights went back on and they descended again, past another platform already filled with huddling bodies. There was a roar. Some tiles fell from the ceiling.

"Keep moving, keep—" The voice was muffled in the whooshing and the roar, Everything went black again and they fell, crashing against each other, against the stairs and the stone.

A searing pain in Marigold's arm dazzled her. She wondered if her hand was blown off, but then sighed, realizing she could wiggle her fingers. They were warm and sticky. She tried to move her body but couldn't. The pipe tobacco man was on top of her, his dank coat scratching, crushed against her skin. Marigold's mouth filled with blood. Her fingers clawed against something to squeeze herself out from under him. But then they gave way, because what she was holding were his entrails. Gagging, Marigold spat out a piece of tooth. Everything was still.

* * *

"Big Ben is solemnly chiming the hours tonight, despite the bombs which last night struck the tower on which the great clock stands. Much of the glass was ripped from the face of Big Ben and the masonry above was badly burned. But the damage is reparable. Buildings which are a part of the

very substance and symbol of England were damaged in last night's heavy raid. Among these were the houses of Parliament, Westminster Abbey, and the British Museum. The raid on London last night was one of the heaviest so far. For the fourth time in this war, the offices of the Columbia Broadcasting System were made uninhabitable."

— Larry LeSueur, This Is London, May 11, 1941

* * *

NAZIS BOMB WIDELY

Seven-Hour "Blitz" Hits Every Section of the British Capital

London, Sunday, May 11 — London went through a grueling Nazi air raid the past night that British officials early today described as heavy and approaching in intensity of those in April. Damage and casualties were both great.

This third bad "Blitz" within a month, following an attack by the British Royal Air Force on Berlin over Friday night, bore the stamp of the blows upon the city the nights of April 16 and 19. . . The raid alert lasted nearly seven hours. The "All clear" sounded when the pale light of day was already beginning to show the extent of punishment London received. . . Miles of London's streets at dawn today bore the unmistakable traces of a heavy "Blitz." Pavements were strewn with glass fragments, stone and bricks every which way and innumerable splotches of sand where incendiaries had been snuffed out.

— New York Times, Sunday, May 11, 1941

It took Buddy and Falaise days to find her. When she was well enough to speak Buddy came to the hospital and sat beside her bed. He had a pen and notepaper with him.

"You don't have a choice, Mac. You must write your dad, just as a matter of decency." So carefully and formally, they composed a letter stating the facts, and they agreed that Marigold would leave it at that.

Then there was the letter to Trude's father in Switzerland. "How should we start this?" Buddy whispered.

For Marigold there was no answer because the grief from losing Trude was more than she could bear. She closed her eyes to keep from sobbing. Everything hurt so. Her ribs made it feel impossible to breathe. When she opened her eyes and turned to Buddy, she saw the notepad on his lap was covered in tears. He looked up, embarrassed, and shrugged, "I so wish, Mac—"

"Me too. I wish it, too."

He tore the tear-stained piece off the pad, ready to start again. Marigold watched him put the pen down. Buddy moved to sit on the edge of her bed. He covered his face with his hands and wept like a baby.

Weeks passed before Marigold's ribs healed enough for her to stand or sit down unassisted. A flurry of telegrams came from her stepmother, but there was nothing from her father. She did not hear from Trude's father either. Someone at the hospital assured her the authorities would have seen to those details.

A dentist capped her broken tooth and diligent exercises from a therapist meant she'd restore the use of her wrist. As for the end of her little finger, everyone agreed. For that to be the lost appendage was just a stroke of luck, really.

"You're not the worse for it at all," the doctor said as he removed the stitches.

Marigold tried not to wince. "No, I guess not." It had never occurred to her that a finger so small could hurt so much.

"My dear," Falaise exclaimed a month later. "Think of it as a badge of honor, like a dueling scar, I daresay."

"And my gloves?" Marigold was less convinced. The throbbing still continued. Still losing the first two joints of one's little finger was preferable to the alternative.

"We'll just tuck it in, with a stitch." Falaise's arthritic hands were surprisingly nimble. She bit off the extra thread with her teeth, and with a small pair of scissors from her sewing box removed the offending fabric. She tossed it into the rag basket. "There." She handed the glove to Marigold. "Give this a go."

Marigold held up the glove. "But Falaise, this is the wrong hand!" To which they both started to laugh.

"Oh dear. Oh dear." Falaise took her in her arms. Marigold hugged Falaise, tightly sobbing into her shoulder until eventually her injured finger throbbed a little less.

By and by, instead of throbbing, the little finger merely twitched.

Summer

Marigold sat on the terrace at King's Road, muted by grief, while Falaise and Zosia looked on, sipping their tea, full of their own thoughts.

"No doubt it's shell shock," Falaise observed.

For Marigold, it was the business of before, full of dreams, friendships, and loving Joop. Now that was done, a large part of it gone. It was July by then, but grief still crushed her chest. It felt impossible to move.

Zosia finally lured Marigold back out to the country. "It's important to do something, darling. It's the only way you'll get back on your feet."

At supper that night, Zosia said, "Emily's au pair has just left them. I am sure Alex could use the help." She added, "Do you want me to ask?"

When Marigold didn't answer, Zosia placed her arms around her, adding very softly, "Marigold, I've lost someone, too."

Which only made the ache that much worse. "I know! I don't know how to—"

Marek. How were they supposed to go on without him?

Zosia wiped her own tear from her face, said, "You must find something to do."

And so July passed at Alex Reilly's manor across the field from Zosia's oust house. Marigold filled Emily's days with collecting things to draw, chattering with Kit, and taking photographs. It was just something to do, away from London, away from the people who died.

"I'M WORRIED," Zosia said in August. "You're still too listless."

In response, Marigold offered a half smile.

Alex Reilly thought a moment and said, "I might have the answer for Marigold. I'll introduce her to someone at the abbey. It's a unique place, Marigold, and they've taught my Emily a thing or two as well."

"How fascinating," Zosia said. "Marigold, darling, what do you think?"

"I think I should like that very much." Humbled by their kindness, Marigold knew, that without Zosia and Alex, she would have been lost.

HENREN ABBEY WAS in a village where there was one pub, one hotel, a newsagent, a post office, and a tearoom. That, and the direct train to London. The abbey itself was very old. Medieval arches and flying buttresses overlooked an ancient battlefield from before the Magna Carta. Then, during the sixteenth century it became a private home, and remained so until the Great War, when it became a girls' school. In 1941 there were forty-five pupils, all girls, aged nine to fourteen, who were effectively raised as if it were a convent.

The headmistress said, "We're Church of England of course. And yes, we're very observant. The girls attend chapel twice a day and have hymn practice besides." She pronounced 'girls' as 'gells'.

Marigold looked down, Trude had always said 'Gells', sending up those who spoke that way. Marigold didn't know whether to laugh or cry. She looked back up as the headmistress was still speaking.

"With so many women in the war effort, we're short staffed

more often than not. Miss McGrath, I believe you would do splendidly as our junior matron."

BUT THE JOB hardly felt like work, and she soon found herself wandering the abbey's grounds, imagining ancient ghosts, only to turn a corner and find a gaggle of giggling girls. Somehow, seeing her made them roar with silliness, having a great old time over nothing at all. For Marigold, it brought to mind New York and Trude, and she looked forward to the encounters, caught in a moment's joy, where there seemed to not be a war, anywhere, in the slightest.

Sussex

Autumn

"Wakey, wakey girls. Rise and shine. You've had your time. I've had mine." When Marigold made the two quick rings of the hand bell, she still sensed the space where the end of her finger would have been. To have lost a detail so small but that loomed so large was a distraction in and of itself.

Marigold wiggled the remaining third of her finger and pulled back the drapes. Sunlight poured into the frigid room.

Small bodies reluctantly rose from their beds. "Oh Miss Mac, I can't get up, I just can't!" wailed a creature who snuggled deeper under the covers.

"Yes, you can. It's a beautiful day outside. Everyone dressed, please. You have ten minutes."

Emily Reilly stuck out her head from under the blankets and smiled at her. Emily's smile always summoned Trude and possibly saved Marigold from herself.

She continued to walk along the corridors, ringing the bell and opening doors, saying, "Good morning! Good morning!"

Then sleepy faced girls in crocodile lines filled the great hall, and the head matron sent them to the dining room row by row, in silence.

Afterwards, they tidied their rooms, said their prayers, and headed off to class. Georgie, the senior matron, used this break for a cigarette and a cuppa just behind the cloakrooms, where the staff had their space to gather and gossip.

"You'd be very pretty with a bit of pancake." Georgie attempted to be helpful. "Before this wretched business, I ran the Revlon counter at Selfridges. I daresay, a good many girls looked just smashing after a visit, and they didn't have the same attributes as you."

Truly, all of the women gathered around in an effort to be kind, all of them discreet, somehow already apprised of her story.

"There's a gardener's shed where you might set something up," the bursar said. It was a dilapidated shack with a corrugated roof. But it did have a cement floor, running water, and a basin over which hung a lightbulb. Marigold pulled on its cord and the bulb came on. "It can be your studio." The bursar smiled.

"You might do a photography club with the gels," suggested the headmistress.

Within days, the necessary chemicals and boxes of donated film arrived at the gardener's shed. A sign was painted, Photography Club and hung on the door. As the weather changed, the girls mastered their Brownies during languid afternoons studying light as Marigold discussed how one thing worked and then another. They modeled wearing scarves and garlands from school plays and learned how to process their own prints. Much of it ended with all of them laughing with the spontaneous delight of just being girls and learning something fun. Only the roar of Spitfires and Mosquitos from the local airstrip indicated anything was amiss.

Emily stayed at school four nights per week rather than the customary five. Her father preferred her to be near following the loss of her mother. The headmistress was happy to oblige, because Alex Reilly had been most generous, particularly when it came to getting round those pesky rations and items found only on the black market.

That Marigold was at the abbey at all was largely thanks to him.

ALL PAPER WAS to be recycled, which the abbey did at the local newsagent. In exchange, the school received the paper they would use for the rest of the term. Marigold bundled the scraps together and placed them into a cart to wheel across the village green.

"Hello, I'm here from the abbey. This is our recycling."

The boy behind the counter gave her a hard look. He was pimply and clearly tubercular with a concave chest and ears resembling cauliflower. She guessed he was a few years younger than she.

"If you're from the abbey, why are you American?"

"Excuse me?"

"What's an American doing at the abbey? Have the Yanks joined the Allies then?"

Marigold flushed. "I happen to work at the abbey and I don't see that it's any of your business."

He raised an eyebrow. "You lot's just going to wait to the end the way that they did last time?"

Marigold clenched her teeth to stop from trembling.. Her finger was throbbing, and she cursed herself for not having worn gloves. Was she about to weep? "I really can't say. I for one signed up. May tenth forced me to scrap my plans."

"Is that how you lost your finger then?"

She wanted to slap him. Instead, she nodded. "Just give me the paper, please."

He placed the reams of new paper in the wagon. Before she could stop herself, she asked, "What are you doing?"

"I'm with the Home Guard of course. My asthma prevents me from going but if I had the chance . . ."

THAT WEEKEND she stayed at the Reilly manor. "He was so nasty." She described the encounter, and glanced at her hand. It still ached when she lifted it a certain way. It trembled on its own sometimes, too.

"He was probably embarrassed," Alex said.

"Don't let it bother you," Zosia said.

"He was most likely attracted to you." Alex smiled. "I was always a bit of a cad to girls that I fancied."

Zosia said, "Well thank heaven you've put that behind you."

Marigold looked away from the energy hovering between them and said to Emily, "Shall we go upstairs?"

Emily's room also conjured memories of Trude in New York. The striped wallpaper, the countless dolls and books, a separate library, and her own beautiful bathroom. Next to Emily's bed was a photo of her late mother, Anne. It had been taken by Cecil Beaton, the year Anne was presented at court.

"You look so much like her," Marigold said.

"Would you stay a few moments?"

"Yes of course. Do you want to read?"

"No thank you. Just stay with me."

Marigold lay down and Emily put her arm over Marigold's waist. Emily seemed to fall asleep, murmuring "I can't wait to make more film into prints."

Soissons, France

Joop opened his eyes. As often happened after a good night's sleep, the beauty of numbers and time and the mystery of their significance waltzed through his mind. But his nose itched and he doubted that the hay in the loft was as fresh as his host had claimed. Beneath him, the cows assured him that indeed, the straw had been changed, just not within the last few days.

Joop sighed and closed his eyes again. It had been almost a year since his first jump into Holland and he was coming up on six months since that last dreadful moment with Marigold at the mews house. He was now on his fifth trip through France wherein he brought those hiding to safety. Tomorrow, the passeur would collect the young mother and her three children to take them to Paris. From there, the underground would escort them to freedom.

It was a complicated business. It involved false papers for the Netherlands, Belgium, France, and then either Switzerland or Spain, costing a great deal of cash in the four different currencies. It also involved faith in the decency and courage of everyone involved. And if Joop were honest, there were many reasons why those same people might betray or disappoint him.

The cows mooed. He had to get up and take a piss.

Behind the barn was the rolling landscape of Picardy, only one hundred kilometers from Paris. He loved this part of France. Something about Soissons, this ancient town that was his stopping point, seemed to comfort him every time he came. King Clovis had seized it in the year 486. Pepin the Short was crowned there in 752. It suffered greatly in the fourteenth century during the Hundred Years' War. Now in the twentieth century, Soissons had sustained lots of damage only twenty years before in the Great War. It was an old town and had seen a lot of struggles. Perhaps that's why he felt that what he was doing wasn't out of the ordinary. There had to have been others who'd done very much the same thing. When this war was over, if he could make it up with Marigold, he'd bring her here. They could drive a convertible with the top down in summer. She'd make that face he loved when the wind was in her hair and she had to brush it away from her mouth. Or they could do a bicycle trip. She might like that. But he'd have to make it up to her. That might be a tough one.

Joop knocked on the door of the farmhouse. The Dutch woman was at the table with the farmer's wife. Joop carefully laid down the cash, the passports, and a dozen rolls of film. The farmer would see to it that the film made its way to the Allies. They were snapshots of armaments and buildings that might be targets for an invasion that was still pending.

In exchange, Joop was given a rucksack filled with excellent cheese, some apples, bread, a pie, and some wine. He bid everyone adieu and filled up his canteen at the well. The journey back was usually uneventful. He pretended to be mute and walked with a limp whenever he came across people. So far, it had worked.

There was a slow train that he took from Marle that went as far as the Belgian border. Whenever his papers were checked, he was sure to have the right passport in hand and a pair of Coke bottle glasses, so thick no one would ask why he wasn't serving in the army. It was ridiculous yet effective. Even so, things were increasingly grim. In the weeks after the strike, Joop became more convinced than ever that there was someone besides the Dutch transmitting to England. It was impossible to believe that out of everyone who was parachuting in, and all of the supplies that were being dropped by the Allies, so few were getting through and that the messages were still being transmitted as if everything was in order.

Because it certainly wasn't. Everyone had been rigorously trained using the poetry system to establish a code and then each agent would additionally have his own code. That said, they were all specifically to follow every transmission with three faulty characters, yet someone was transmitting their messages flawlessly. Whenever Joop thought about this too much, his stomach and throat began to burn. He loathed using the poetry system for the code. He had expressed concerns with London, but still, they waved him off, as if it were nothing, reminding him that it wasn't Joop's job to second-guess those in charge. His job was to assist the people who were in danger and to do it as quickly as possible.

PART VI

ALLIES

TO THE CONGRESS OF THE UNITED STATES:

On the morning of December eleventh, the Government of Germany, pursuing its course of world conquest, declared war against the United States.

The long known and the long expected has thus taken place. The forces endeavoring to enslave the entire world now are moving toward this hemisphere. Never before has there been a greater challenge to life, liberty, and civilization.

Delay invites great danger. Rapid and united effort by all of the peoples of the world who are determined to remain free will insure a world victory of the forces of justice and righteousness over the forces of savagery and of barbarism.

Italy also has declared war against the United States.

I therefore request the Congress to recognize a state of war between the United States and Germany, and between the United States and Italy.

— FRANKLIN D. ROOSEVELT

London
Summer

WHEN THEY HEARD ABOUT THE INVITATION, ZOSIA AND Alex Reilly insisted they give her a lift back to London.

"It's amazing," Gratefully accepting, Marigold climbed into the backseat. "that you always have enough petrol to take us back and forth."

Zosia said, "It's connections, duckie. One must have friends in high places."

Kit sat next to Marigold. He said, "How's that?"

"Well, everything is about give and take, isn't it?" Alex glanced at him in the rearview mirror. "That's how we have allies, like the Americans."

"Hmm. I suppose."

"And if one wants to make allies, one needs to have something that everyone wants. Such as a loyal dog. A flair with a camera. A talent for dancing. Let's say you were a pirate, Kit. Now, if you were a pirate, what would you have that everyone would want? You know, which yielded the greatest treasure?"

"Er, gold?"

"Yes, gold would be good." The country lane turned onto one of the long Roman roads and Alex shifted the car into fourth. "What else?"

"I imagine, uh, jewels, like the Crown jewels." Marigold watched Kit work to please Alex. "Something like that."

"Why do you think that is?" The car accelerated to a breath-taking speed. "I mean if you're a pirate?"

"Well, you'd need something that had value no matter what happened to a person."

"You mean, like in a war."

An American convoy was straight up ahead. Alex slowed the car, keeping a respectful distance. An open jeep was the last of the military vehicles. A soldier turned to face them, waving them to move ahead. Alex obliged.

Marigold watched Kit study the various trucks—a tank, jeeps, and the like. "Uh, yes, I think so too. Like in a war, like this war."

Alex added, "Because you know Kit, it's about making your own luck. This wretched business has created all kinds of opportunities, and I for one, am a pirate." The road opened up again. The car resumed its speed. "I'm going to make the most of the opportunity."

Zosia looked at Marigold in the rearview mirror. She raised her eyebrows and smiled. "What is it you say in America? Happy Independence Day!"

Marigold smiled back at her.

MARIGOLD QUICKENED her pace to keep up with Buddy's long strides. He said, "Mrs. Murrow told me to bring you."

But she was sure that Mrs. Murrow hadn't spoken with Buddy. She thought Buddy just felt sorry for her. "Why?"

"Ed has always liked you. He thinks you'll round out the group."

They were Yanks, they were young, Buddy was brilliant, and the function was at Winston Churchill's residence. How could she say no?

ED AND MRS. MURROW approached 10 Downing Street just as they arrived. Apart from the sandbags and soldiers everywhere, the way guests flowed into the building one would never think a war was on at all.

"Marigold!" Mrs. Murrow gave her a peck. "You're looking so well."

Ed Murrow gave her a small kiss, too. "How's life in the country?"

"Oh Mr. Murrow, honestly I've been itching to get back to town really."

"Well, don't be a stranger, come on by." Was there a strange glimmer on Mrs. Murrow's face at that?

They showed their invitations to a footman. Inside were dignitaries, generals, and lots of men in uniform. There were lords and ladies and servants. Bunting in red, white and blue hung from the windows and over the door. A military jazz band played just outside on the terrace.

Silver trays carried glasses of lemonade, mountains of hotdogs, and cupcakes decorated with toothpicks sporting American flags and Union Jacks. Churchill's mother had been American and on July 4, his mad fondness for all things American was unleashed, particularly now, that the U.S. had joined the fight.

Marigold surveyed the crowd. It had been three years now. There couldn't be anyone there who hadn't lost someone. That would be impossible.

"Hey Pammy," Buddy said to a redhead with china blue eyes.

"Well, hello!" The redhead's deep purring voice belied her china doll looks. Marigold recognized her instantly as the prime minister's daughter-in-law. "Who's this?" the redhead asked.

"This is my good friend, Marigold McGrath."

Pamela Churchill assessed her and said, "Very nice." She briefly darted her glance toward the Murrows.

"Marigold worked with us at CBS."

"Is that so?" She turned back to Marigold. "How was Ed to work for?"

Instantly, Marigold understood that Pamela didn't mean how was he to work for. What she meant was how intimately did Marigold know him.

She wasn't going to waste her time seeking the approval of someone whose assessment of her was only in light of female competition.

Looking at Pamela made her miss Trude something dreadful. "He was super, even more than you can imagine."

"Oh." Pamela raised an eyebrow. "Quite."

Buddy turned and gave Marigold a quizzical smile.

The prime minister came over to them. "Hello darling girl." He put his arm around Pamela's waist. "Where's the little chap?"

"Nanny's bringing him down in the next hour, I expect."

"Who's this?" Winston Churchill asked.

"Norbert Freed, sir. It's an honor." Buddy shook his hand. "And may I present my former colleague, Miss Marigold McGrath?"

"Marigold," the prime minister said, "is one of my favorite names. Lovely to meet you. I understand from Ed Murrow that you're a native New Yorker, just as my mother was."

"Yes I am, sir."

Buddy said, "Miss McGrath is also an accomplished photographer."

"Ah, the challenge of capturing this world in such a way that the rest of us can experience or respond to the power of one's subject in the blink of an eye. Extraordinary. Really."

"Yes, I think so too! I'm just a novice of course, but the trick is if we can make it all as if it's right now, and that we're having that experience together, then it's very singular. My mentor taught me that at least."

"Ah, and who is your mentor?"

"It was Marek Dagger, sir."

"He took my picture once. I met him through Stefan Lorent when Lorent was running *Picture Post*. Dagger's pictures of the East End after a raid were very moving, I daresay."

"Sir, you may have seen Marigold's photographs in *Lilliput*, too." Buddy said.

"Is that so?"

"Yes. They ran during the last evacuations of the kinder transport."

"I say, well done Miss McGrath. Very well done indeed."

"Oh, thank you. Please, call me Marigold, Prime Minister."

He smiled at Marigold then. "I say, Pamela, darling. Don't you think Marigold would be a charming addition to the club? Pamela will tell you all about it. I do hope to see you there. Don't say no. Now that our American cousins are onboard, there must be no daylight between us. Enjoy the music. Happy Fourth!"

Pamela said, "The Churchill Club is a project I'm running for British and American officers." Then she leaned forward and smiled. "But really it's for Americans. As a way of saying thanks. It's located just behind the Houses of Parliament. So, they'll have somewhere cozy to go and have something to do, you know"— here Pamela winked— "of value, when they they're not consumed with this beastly war."

Amsterdam

Jews, pilots, and other Engelandvaarders like himself. They were the niche. Joop had only established the new escape route after his last return from England, but this spring had been so productive that he felt almost optimistic. He whistled softly under his breath and a bit of *"Stompin' at the Savoy"* escaped his lips. It would be so great to have something to dance about.

Piet had become his official forger and smiled to join in the refrain. "Savoy!" he sang.

Joop checked the ledger. "We're at how many pilots now?"

"Without tonight's group, we've seen thirty-seven back to safety."

That felt good. It felt very good. "And the Jewish families?"

"Joop. We're at nearly four hundred individuals."

The friends looked away from each other, silently acknowledging the power of that fact. To assist those in need was the most meaningful thing Joop had ever done. It was something positive and actually made sense.

He could hear Piet's granny puttering around downstairs, gently scolding the Americans. The Yanks were new. They sometimes forgot that if anyone outside heard them, it was a sign for the Germans to come running. But in fact, since the arrest last February, Piet's house had become the perfect foil. As far as the authorities were concerned, Joop and Piet were dead, their bodies having burnt with that truck they left near Ede.

As for Piet's granny, it was no secret that she took in children after school. The neighborhood was well-heeled and filled with Nazi sympathizers. And somehow, miraculously, the Engelandvaarders, the allied pilots, and Piet and Joop managed to stay clear of everyone. The rest of the time they were shrouded in blackouts. In fact, the setup, with its hot and cold running fugitives, was so audacious that to imagine it as one of the busiest safe houses in Amsterdam was very unlikely.

Joop put down his pen. They were waiting for an Engelandvaarder and two Jews to join them. Then they'd head out of town before dawn. They were all fit and no one was injured, so they were in good shape to travel. Then they'd meet up with the Belgian underground, and the pilots amongst them had a greater chance of returning to the Allies than with almost any other resistance cell. As for the fugitives, so far, their luck had been extraordinary.

Yet for all of this, the amount of organization needed was staggering. A journey involved many ordinary people across three different countries, each with different currencies, transportation networks, and degrees of Nazi infiltration. It was also imperative that no one knew more than their task at hand. That way should someone be arrested and God forbid tortured, only so much information could be compromised.

And every time he handed over cash or contraband or forged papers, Joop asked himself what it would take to betray them. Of course, the Nazis were masters at combining enough pain with sufficient threat that no one dared not give them what they asked for.

Joop hid the transmitter away. It was better not to think about that. He put away his pens and tucked the ledgers inside the floorboards. He could smell coffee and something made with ginger. He checked his watch. The children must have left by now. He wondered what Marigold was doing. It was American Independence Day. Her letter from last year had only found him a few weeks ago. He wondered if she had gathered with any other

Americans now that they had finally joined the war. In fact, the entire daydream was so agreeable that when the doorbell rang, being arrested was the last thing on his mind.

Scheveningen

Joop knew they'd make quick work of it, by either shooting him or beating him to death, but for some unknown reason, neither of those things occurred. He was brought to the Orange Hotel and placed in solitary confinement. Waiting there, when he heard the screaming and doors slamming, he imagined being next, subjected to the cruelest means of dispatch.

And yet that didn't happen.

After three days, an interrogator sent for him. Joop was shown to a room with a card table and two chairs on one end and a gurney with straps on the other. The interrogator gestured for him to sit down. "Before we get started, it's in everyone's best interest if you make a clean breast of it. Wouldn't you agree?" The officer looked down at the piece of paper in front of him. "Herr Kremer, or should I say Kasander?"

Joop wondered if that had been beaten out of Piet or out of Piet's granny.

"I will do you the courtesy of telling you that your friend jumped to his death yesterday, but before doing so, he revealed your actual name."

Joop glanced at the guard standing in the corner, who was holding a club. A leather strap dangled from one end. He decided not to think about that.

The interrogator continued, "We have much to get through here, so I won't bother to wait for any comment. However, before his death, yours was the only name that he did confirm. As for his grandmother, she's awaiting her dispatch. It's a simple solution to a complicated problem. I imagine she'll meet her end by this time next week."

The interrogator gestured to the guard. "Take your spectacles off and give them to my associate here. He'll put them somewhere safe. It would be a pity to break them at this juncture."

Removing his spectacles, Joop wondered if this was the part when the officer would say that his parents were dead, or that his sister was deported. Somehow, the voice that kept him from screaming or weeping told him neither of those things were true, so whatever ideas or threats they would use must be resisted. Resisted at all costs. The guard placed Joop's glasses on the windowsill. Then he approached Joop and lifted the club.

Afterward, Joop pressed the throbbing side of his face against the floor. The tiles were cool and damp. He heard voices in the hallway discussing a bucket of water. With his good eye, he could just make out the gurney where they'd lay him out, strapping his arms and legs.

Twenty-four hours was the tacit agreement. Everyone involved knew that to last longer than twenty-four hours was just unrealistic. No one wanted a martyr, but they did need a few hours to change their plans and cover their tracks.

The guard entered with a bucket and said, "Stand up now, and strip," in German, then he gestured to a filthy toilet in the corner and added in Dutch, "I recommend using it before we begin. It's going to be unpleasant."

Who had turned them in? Defeating a people, destroying a country, was not so impossible. Of all the people that he'd met in the war, Joop wagered that half, nearly half of them were collaborators.

Stretched out on the table, his mind left his body as he struggled not to drown. Think of the numbers, he thought. Think of the numbers and those we did get through. Water poured through the towel into his nose, his throat, his lungs.

Joop thought about Suzy Kraay, a girl he'd only briefly met.

Before she'd been tortured, Suzy Kraay brought some boys to safety. She had walked from Holland, to Belgium, to France, and into Switzerland. It took over a week, but because of her, those boys were united with their parents.

The water flowed into him again. His lungs hacked, his body convulsed. He would not protest and he would not shout. If a simple girl like Suzy Kraay could stick it out, well then, a big strong soldier, no matter how cowardly Joop thought himself, could do so as well.

After a few hours his interrogators needed a break. Joop heard the door close behind them. They'd left the towel on his face, so he was still unable to see what was going on, but he did sense that he was alone. He wondered if he should try and get some sleep. He let out a deep sigh. He was grateful that everything hurt too much to worry about being cold and wet—the relief of not having drowned weighed the other stuff out. Also, the cold was strangely comforting for what might be that broken bone in his face.

It was impossible to know how many hours had passed. When he came to, the leather straps had been removed, and his face was uncovered. The throbbing in his face was so intense he leant over to vomit. Slowly, he swung his legs around and sat up.

An officer he hadn't seen before was in the corner watching him. "You might have dodged a bullet, Lieutenant Kasander. We've been looking for you. And you know, in spite of the last few hours, I am pleased to say that this is your lucky day."

Joop remained silent.

"Clearly you don't think so. But I'll tell you why it is. It's because I know who your father is. And you, young Kasander, are worth more to us alive than you are dead. Alas, there isn't any room for you at either Amersfoort or Vught. They're just too full up. So, get yourself together, and we'll send you on your way. Is that understood?"

"You mean I'm free to go?"

"Oh no. It just means we're not going to shoot you. You're one of our Nacht and Nebel people. Night and fog. It will keep your father in line. It clips his wings, not knowing if you're dead or alive. You'll be one of our guests who just disappear. In other words, we're sending you to Mauthausen. There are several projects there. Lots of industry. You'll make yourself useful, I have no doubt."

* * *

THE PRISONERS RODE in the back of a truck, which brought them to a cattle car that stood waiting just beyond the Hague. The guards shoved them inside until it was filled to capacity. Everyone standing, no room to sit. There were no windows, only a few vents just below the ceiling. The cattle car attached to a passenger train and proceeded northeastward, the men standing in the dark without food or water. The journey lasted three days. As others succumbed, Joop felt them crumple against him, everyone stinking of piss, starvation, and worse. Finally, the train stopped.

Camp guards shouted, "Raus!" and pulled open the doors. Joop squinted in the daylight. Dogs snarled, barking furiously at those who were still alive and stumbling from the car. The camp was vast, more like a city really, made up of smaller subcamps and a massive granite quarry. From where he stood, Joop saw an endless line of inmates, blocks of stone upon their backs, bringing them up to the surface one step at a time.

The men were led to a registrar, where they stripped. Their heads and pubic hair were shaved, and they were deloused. Then they were handed striped uniforms and numbers. A badge on their jackets determined their status: political prisoner, social deviant, Jew. Joop was classified with a band upon which NN was stamped to indicate his Nacht und Nabel status. It occurred to Joop that he'd most likely die here. It was July 18, 1942.

Joop did the calculation. Two thousand, one hundred, and

ninety-one days since the annexation of Austria. Or fifty-two thousand, five hundred, and ninety-six hours. Well, at least he could still count. Suddenly, he stifled a sneeze.

"God bless you," said an inmate in English.

Joop answered, "Thank you."

The Churchill Club

ON THE WAY BACK FROM LONDON, ALEX REILLY HAD said, "The Churchill Club, Splendid. I say, you know what will make inroads with that young Mrs. Churchill?"

"What?" Marigold looked at his reflection in the rear-view mirror.

"A few tins of Beluga."

"From Russia?"

"I have my sources."

Some tins of caviar were in truth an entire crate, enough for the club's opening reception. Caviar served on hard-boiled eggs, augmented with smoked salmon and capers.

Lunch was being prepared, as officers and their guests lined up to take food on a tray. In the kitchen, Marigold peeled the hard-boiled eggs.

"However did you get these?" Pamela marveled at the tins of caviar.

"Well, I just know a man. He seems to get ahold of absolutely everything. He said it was a donation for the war effort."

"Extraordinary," Pamela said. She gave her a considered look. "How resourceful."

* * *

"WELCOME!" Marigold checked coats. "Welcome to the Churchill Club." She greeted dignitaries, seated officers, and listened to poetry readings. She served drinks, poured tea, cleared plates, and cleaned ashtrays.

One afternoon, Ed Murrow, who was there, said, "Why are you doing this?"

"I'm just here to help."

"Pammy."

Pamela floated over to them, a vision in her chiffon dress and snowy white skin.

"Yes, Ed." Her voice an octave lower than anyone else. Pamela stood so close to Ed Murrow that Marigold took a step back so as not to intrude.

"Marigold is a first-rate photographer."

Pamela glanced over at Marigold and turned back to Ed. "Is that so?"

"She's been published, Pammy. She doesn't need to be cleaning ashtrays."

Pamela turned back to him and placed her hand upon his jacket's lapel, then answered, "Oh no?" Her blue eyes large and saucer like.

"Ask her to take some pictures. It will be great PR. You won't be disappointed."

Pamela's eyes narrowed when she gave Marigold a second considered look. Marigold could see there would not be a third.

Alone at Lark Mews, with her Rolleicord hanging around her neck and a flashbulb in one hand, Marigold practiced moving with discretion, holding the flash at the right angle, and photographing dignitaries.

The next day at the club, she was ready. She advanced the film. Click! Pamela with Ed Murrow. Click. Pamela with Averell Harriman. Click. Churchill with General Montgomery. Pamela with Joseph Kennedy Jr. Pamela with Prince Aly Khan. Marlene Dietrich and General Eisenhower. Click. Millionaires and ministers, generals and movie stars, diplomats and dukes. And Ed Murrow was right. Photographs from the Churchill Club appeared in the press and society columns, their readers eager for a glimpse of its patrons' glamour.

Her shifts were now filled with, "Marigold, come take our picture." Or, "Marigold, come photograph the ambassador." Soon they were clowning around, everyone eager for a candid or posing for posterity.

"Marigold?"

She looked up and cursed the involuntary upbeat of her heart at seeing those chocolate brown eyes. "Hello Alan."

He was in uniform and as handsome as he had been that first day in class. "What are you doing in London?"

"I live here now."

"Oh really? Where do you live?" The way he had asked her if she'd done the assignment, his breath upon her neck in that disgusting broom closet seemed a lifetime ago.

She suddenly felt awkward, as if he were vying for the upper hand. "In Chelsea. Um." But why shouldn't she live in Chelsea? Thousands of people did. "How 'bout you? Did you just get here?"

He nodded. "A few days ago. Can I get you a drink?"

"No, thank you. I'm working." Marigold couldn't recall ever saying no to him before.

He gestured toward the camera. "Still taking pictures, I see."

"Yes, yes, I am. Here, I'll take one of you. You can send it to— I guess she's your wife now."

"My wife?"

"You had a fiancée when I last saw you."

"Oh." He smiled, embarrassed. "There was no fiancée, Marigold."

"Oh." So, he had said that just to get rid of her. Marigold wondered if he knew that she'd been expelled. She wondered if he even cared. "Then I don't need to take a picture, do I?" She wasn't sure whether to crack the camera over his head or throw it at him in a blind rage. Instead, she said, "It's nice to see you, Alan. I have to get back to work."

"Marigold, you look terrific. Maybe you want to get a drink when you're free?"

She managed a smile. "Oh no. No thank you. I only drink with honest men. Not liars. Good luck, Alan."

MARIGOLD FOUND Pamela in the kitchen. Its door to the garden was open and sunlight spilled upon the tiled floor. In Pamela's hands were a pair of small shears which she used to expertly trim thorns off the large quantity of roses beside her.

Marigold liked Mrs. Murrow. Whatever Pamela was doing with Ed Murrow was none of her business. No burning bridges, she warned herself.

"Pamela, I just want to thank you for including me in the Churchill Club."

Pamela did not react, pretending to be consumed with a floral arrangement.

"Pamela," Marigold said again.

"Oh?" Pamela turned and gave her a brilliant smile.

"But it's the end of the summer," Marigold had made sure all of her things were packed. "School starts in a few weeks. And really, there's so much going on at the abbey. You'll find someone else to take pictures. Please give my best to Mr. Murrow."

Part VII

Nacht und Nebel

Summer

Sussex

Alex Reilly had a small silver flask that he would sip from when they were in the field at target practice. "You're a fine lad, Kit. I think you're almost ready to be a man." He took the lid off his flask and offered Kit a sip.

Moved by the gesture, Kit wiped his hand on his trouser leg before accepting. "Thank you, sir," he said gruffly, and took a swig. It burned the insides of his mouth and his throat but by God, it did make him feel like a man.

"There are petty thieves, Kit. They burgle unsuspecting fools and those who really have no need of the extraordinary privilege they enjoy. So, when they approach me, these men are looking for what we call a fence."

Kit found all of this information thrilling. To have such a dashing man as Alex Reilly interested in him, and to have Alex Reilly actually take him into his own confidence dazzled him even more than he could have imagined.

That afternoon, after target practice, they returned their shotguns to Alex's gun room. Alex then unlocked an interior door that Kit had never entered. "This"—Alex laughed— "is my pirate's hideaway. What do you think?"

There were crates and crates of liquor, boxes upon boxes of chocolates, and countless tins of oysters

Cor, Kit thought to himself. "It's brilliant."

"How many establishments do you imagine have been bombed?"

"Lots."

"That's right. Nightclubs and pubs too. What's a pirate to do in that case?"

"Uh . . . is that where this is from?"

Alex nodded. "You know, I suspect you might be a pirate, too."

* * *

"Help me with these, would you?" Zosia nodded towards the groceries on the table. Marigold unpacked the items. There were olives and canned peaches, bags of sugar and coffee. Chocolate and artichokes.

"How did you get all this?"

"Alex got it for me." Zosia opened all the windows. It was a perfect summer's day.

"How does he get all this stuff?"

"Oh Marigold, does it matter? It's better not to ask."

"Okay." The words choked in her throat, because Marigold knew that whatever was going on, it wasn't legal. But she loved Zosia. How could Zosia be mixed up in—

"Shall we go for a swim?"

Marigold nodded, "Yes. Okay."

Mauthausen, Austria

Joop was directed to report to the subcamp of Gusen. There, Messerschmitt 109 aircraft were constructed by the prisoners, who were grouped into teams called commandos. The commandos were overseen by Kapos who kept them in line. Joop was assigned to a factory for the wing building commando located underground.

"Make an error, it's forty lashes for him, fifty lashes for you, get it?" barked the Kapo in charge. Most of the Kapos were felons who practiced criminal violence. All Kapos relished menacing the inmates with scary, spiteful glee. But with so many prisoners from so many countries, it was difficult to communicate, and Joop quickly found himself translating more often than not. This led to his first beating.

At night, when a Kapo shouted, "Eins, Zwei, Drei!" everyone lay down at once on rotting sodden mats made of hay. There were two or three men to a bunk, one blanket between them.

That night, the man he shared a bunk with said, "Don't do it."

"But it's not logical." Joop knew he was lucky that he hadn't been hurt too badly.

Another said, "We're warning you, it's not in your interest."

"How can it not be in everyone's interest? If we're expected to make these high-quality wings, we need to communicate. If half of us know nothing about the principles of Bernoulli's equation, let alone how to speak to one another, how are we going to get it done?"

"See it as a form of resistance," said the man. To which the others agreed, more interested in staying alive than discussing mathematical formulae.

Forms of resistance—how could he do that from Gusen? He needed those specifications. He needed a manual. That he would have anything to do with even one of those planes harming either his home or England was unthinkable. But he was not an engineer. He needed a manual.

The side of his face was still tender from the Orange Hotel. Joop curled his hand under his cheek and tried to sleep.

A bell sounded. All the prisoners rolled out of their bunks. They raced out to the square to stand amongst the thousands of other inmates.

"Is this roll call?" Joop asked.

The man next to him nodded. "Welcome to Gusen!"

The man on Joop's other side added, "Gusen's worse than hell. Most of us last about two months before we keel over."

The man was skin and bones and smiled bitterly at Joop's reaction. "I'm on my sixth week here. If I make it to ten weeks, I'll know I'm invincible."

The days were unspeakably long. Twelve to fourteen hours' in an underground factory, existing on just a piece of bread. Joop grew bone weary. He watched the team members, and he watched the Kapos. He had to solve the unsolvable problem of how to build the wing of an airplane to its exact specification while not furthering the German war effort. If anything gave him a headache, it was this. He began to obsess about getting his hands on a manual. But he knew he didn't have much time.

Joop closed his eyes. If the wing did not meet expectations, all of them would be beaten, some of them would be shot, or hanged, whichever the Kapo felt like doing. The NN on his uniform indicated that he would normally be punished first. But the value of one's work was the work itself and compromising his fellow prisoners was not, quite frankly, in anyone's interest. But what if a Messerschmitt should fly over England and drop a bomb on Marigold?

What then?

The next night, someone in the barracks warned him, "Watch yourself."

"I will," Joop said.

"No, seriously," the man said. "Now that you're here, you need to understand, you're not going to leave. Today it was him" —he pointed to an empty bunk— "tomorrow it could be you and then it will be me. Next time, at roll call, look at the smokestack. That's how they get rid of us, you know."

Someone else said, "Aww, what of it? I've been here since the beginning, and I ain't going nowhere. The thing is, just don't become ill. Keep moving and don't become ill."

"Why?" Joop asked.

"Because then they can't use you. And you know what that means?" The man drew his finger across his throat. "That's what it means."

Before he nodded off, he heard his bunkmate say, "If you hate them more than you fear them, the anger will keep you alive."

When the planes' engineers inspected production. Joop watched the group move around the factory, with white notebooks in their hands. He had to have one of those notebooks. Think, Joop, he commanded himself. You've spent your entire life solving problems. Now you have to solve this one.

"Einshuligen mir, aber," Joop said, and then he held forth on the expected velocity according to which ratio—

One of the Kapos went to smack him, but the engineer said, "That's a fascinating point. How did you come to this conclusion?"

And Joop continued speaking with the engineer, who then offered to give him the manual. He was relieved when he thought to hide it after the man's departure, because the Kapo was so aggrieved by Joop's pluck that he beat Joop thoroughly and then placed him in the concrete hole for the next three days.

Back in his bunk, his face a bloody mess, he said, "If we could make it so the plane falls apart in mid-flight, that would be ideal.

In fact, it would be great if it were comical. Alas, I think we're too late for that."

Indeed, Joop's observation turned out to be prescient.

The next morning he was transferred to the main office to calculate the actuarial data used when exterminating his fellow prisoners.

* * *

Dear Marigold,

There are few Dutchmen here at Mauthausen, which is just as well. To end up in this predicament is beyond intolerable. Writing out the numbers, the names, their details, and how they're disposed of is a sickening business.

A few weeks ago, I provided a formula for increasing productivity at the Messerschmitt factory, by simply feeding the workers and providing an increase of rest, and a Kapo brought it to the officer. He's some kind of manager of production or something and wanted to discuss another project. This one is in Germany, at a smaller camp a few kilometers from Berlin.

"I know who your father is," he told me. I know my older sister is safe but haven't heard about my younger one nor about our parents. I can only assume they've been rounded up, too. That's the thing, none of us know. It's a form of torture, where you die slowly from not knowing.

Where I'm sitting now, I think time is best spent remembering every single detail. I have always been a planner. A dreamer too, yes. I can't deny that, but preparation has always served me. From my first days at primary school, then the gymnasium, and finally at Oxford. To prepare has always been best. And to be honest, when I think how badly prepared we were, I can only shake my head in amazement that no one saw this coming. At least not in the Netherlands.

If I structure how it went, then it orders my mind. Last week, I was put in the hole. It's a place where if I stretch my hand in front of me my fingers touch the concrete wall. The hole is too short to stand in and too small to lie down, so I had to fold my knees, bended, and then rest on one buttock. After a few hours, I would shift and rest upon the other one. I can tell you, at the time, this made me wish I'd practiced yoga! It was an odd thing to consider, sitting beneath that grate, but there we are. Of all the crazy things I wished, practicing yoga was definitely one of them.

I go back to events and where to begin. Wondering what to include, what to leave out, and how you will get this letter, this is what I think about in order to remain sane. I don't know. I don't know what to tell you. Do I tell you that when in the concrete hold it is only by peeing on the wall and then licking the concrete that one keeps from dying of thirst?

There are horrors beyond—oh my Gouda. Your Engeland-vaarder prays that you are safe, that someone in England is looking after you, dancing with you, and making you laugh.

The daylight blinded me when they hauled me out last week. Now I sit at a desk after roll call. It's 7.30 in the morning. I have access to a pen and paper and I'll probably work until eleven tonight.

What I do is prepare the lists. Who will be transferred, who will be exchanged, and who will be liquidated. Every day the names added are endless, and because everything must be alphabetized, transcribing and updating becomes no small task. Then I must prepare a series of graphs with the ages, the weights, where they had been assigned etc. If one thinks about what this means, it becomes impossible to keep writing, so I don't think about it. Instead I make sure I'll have enough paper and something to write with for my notes to you. Because you keep me sane.

1944

Winter

"737244! Hinaus. Follow me. You're being transported," the guard said.

Joop was sure it meant to the death camps. But strangely enough, this time as he waited for the transport, the officer referred to him by name. "Kasander, you're a mathematician, aren't you?"

"Yes sir."

"What does that mean exactly?"

Afterwards, Joop had no idea what made him say, "Statistical analysis and accounting, that sort of thing."

"Good. Because we have an opportunity for you. It's near Berlin. You'll have to be quarantined first, of course. You'll find food in the new barracks. You should be quite comfortable."

Yet another guard took him to a building set aside from the rest of the camp. Three others had already been moved there. The guard gave him a new set of clothes, then handed him a bar of soap.

"Showers over there," the guard said.

Joop scrubbed himself, glad to have shaved his head so that the lice that had plagued his bunkmates wasn't much of an issue.

Presently, a loaf of bread, some cheese, a tin of meat, and soup were served. Real food. Joop sat down with the others and one of the men said, "It's a veritable life of Riley. In addition to the fine cuisine, we no longer do roll call. So, get comfortable, mate. Let's hope you don't have typhoid." It was the Englishman from the day he arrived.

The men remained isolated from the rest of the camps for two weeks. No one spoke to them if they didn't have to until the morning when a guard said, "Transport's waiting." The six men marched in their prisoner's clothes under guard through the village until they came to a train station where they were put into a third-class car. They stared out the windows at the rest of the world during the journey, until they arrived just north of Berlin in Sachsenhausen.

The camp was considerably smaller than Mauthausen and housed only thirty thousand people. Still ignorant of what would come next, the men were promptly placed in quarantine once again, reminding them that one could never be too sure.

On the fifteenth day, they met Bernhard Krüger. "Gentlemen, we are currently thirty-five in the workshop. I hope to get the number up to about a hundred. What we practice here is the gentle art of banking. I will expect each of you to bring your talents to bear in creating and printing pound notes."

They were shown to barracks 18 and 19, inside of which were the means of production- a printing press, a dark room, a lab, and a rec room.

Instantly, Joop got it. It didn't need to be explained. The British had performed this trick during wartime for centuries. To flood the enemy's economy with counterfeit bills and thus cause it to collapse by driving up inflation. This was not a new thing. The Germans were merely doing it on a whole new level.

"Of course, if our efforts should be compromised, or if you should fail to meet your obligation to this project, you will leave me no choice but to shoot you. I think it's a simple proposition. Cigarette?"

Silently, they all accepted. No one dared say a word.

THAT NIGHT, they ate bread and turnip soup, which stank to high heaven. But each man had his own bunk with sheets and blankets. They were neither cold nor hungry. Yet, it was made very clear. They could not leave barracks 18 and 19. Not ever. If they did, they would be shot. If they failed to deliver in any way, they would be shot.

As Krüger said, it was a simple proposition.

* * *

Joop was in the room Bernhard Krüger used for debriefing and the like.

"You know we tried this once before, and were extraordinarily successful," Krüger explained. "Project Andreas. Alas, the man spearheading the project, Alfred Naujocks made the wrong enemies. He got sent to the frontline, and the production collapsed."

"What happened to the money? I mean, the printed money?"

"You know, that's the strangest thing. I'm not quite sure. Someone said it was exchanged for goods. Perhaps the notes made their way to England. They really were of exceptional quality. But that was Naujocks project. Now, it's mine. Project Bernhard. I have a good feeling about you. You're going to do very well here, Kasander. Cigarette?"

Winter

Sussex

In the car, riding from Chelsea to Sussex, Marigold's head nodded backward and then forward onto her chest. Thoughts of Joop, somewhere dark, surrounded by enemies. Her heart folded onto itself. Joop.

A wicked man in her dream turned on a light. "I know who your father is." The voice was raspy, dangerous. The lightbulb hung from the ceiling. She struggled to swallow, but her throat was dry, like paper. It didn't matter what she did, who she was. She was an alien. All that mattered was that she was foreign. They'd send her away now. To an internment camp because she was a threat to national security. To a place they sent enemies of the state. But she was an American! An ally! How could that possibly mean—

"Marigold."

"Sorry?" She opened her eyes and rubbed the crick in her neck.

Alex smiled at her in the mirror on the dashboard. He radiated such kindness and good health. He so reminded her of the actor in *The 39 Steps* who ran and ran through Scotland, even when the blonde was handcuffed to him. Those national secrets, the ones that must be protected.

Marigold realized Alex was still speaking. "I said, in answer to your question, I don't know how much farther it is."

"Oh! Oh."

It was February but the weather was beautiful and Zosia had persuaded him to put the top down. They were bundled in coats and scarves, the winter sun shining on them even while the heat in the car was blasting.

Kit. Speeding through the countryside, Marigold couldn't stop thinking about Kit. He was on a school break for Shrovetide, leading up to Lent, and his mother was thrilled they'd spend some time together. But the day before when they dropped Kit off at World's End, he'd handed her a note before getting out of the car.

Marigold was about to make a joke, but then Kit shook his head in the way that her late mother used to do. One small nod to the left and an imperceptible one to the right.

She read the note at King's Road. "Meet me at Lark Mews before tea."

Kit had known that Alex would be making the rounds at the time. Promptly, Marigold had walked over. Kit was waiting near the corner.

"This is all very cloak and dagger," Marigold had said rather gaily and unlocked the door. "What's up?"

Whereupon Kit had taken her into Marek's storage cabinet and moved what was left of the developers and fixatives, cases of flashbulbs and film. Behind these things was a small door which Marigold had never seen before. Kit opened it. Inside were four small suitcases.

"What is this, Kit?" Suddenly, Marigold's heart was in her throat. She watched him remove a case and jimmy it open. It was filled with piles upon piles of cash. "How did this get here?" They were alone, and yet she was whispering.

"Alex"—she could barely hear him— "Alex brought it."

"Did he rob a bank?"

Kit didn't have an answer for this, but he looked not a day over his thirteen years.

"Don't move another thing."

Kit remained perfectly still. Then he whispered, "It's something called Andreas."

"What?"

Kit's lower lip looked dangerously wobbly. "I dunno, but, Marigold, something's not—I couldn't hurt my mum."

"Oh Kit. Of course you couldn't."

"He says he'll make me a pirate, Marigold. But I want to be a footballer. Or,

or maybe . . ." He wiped the tears and said, "Maybe a photographer, like—you know."

"Really?" Marek's cameras were still in the barrister bookcase off the main room. "Right." Marigold took the Rolleiflex and flashbulbs.

Kit said, "You need to look at this one." He pulled out another suitcase. When he opened it, she gasped. The suitcase was filled with handguns and boxes of bullets. He whispered, "He either sells them or buys them. I'm not sure."

Marigold grabbed two rolls of film. She loaded the camera. Then she photographed the money, the suitcases, everything.

"Kit, let's put this back and not say a word. Please."

Solemnly, he nodded, leaving everything as they'd found it.

"Seriously. Don't say anything to anyone." Then they turned out the lights, and Kit locked the door as Tony the cat slipped outside. They left the mews without speaking.

They arrived at the corner where Kit would turn right for World's End and she'd continue to Old Church Street. Her arms were now full of the Rolleiflex and equipment. She juggled a bit and took his arm. "Don't go back there, Kit, I swear to God."

Kit simply looked at her and didn't respond. There was no danger from Alex as long as he was in Sussex and Kit was in town.

"Whatever is happening, something is very wrong. But you've done the right thing."

"Promise?" His voice was grave.

"Yes. I promise."

* * *

THAT MONEY and those guns had changed everything. Marigold looked out the window at the countryside and then at Zosia and Alex in the front seat.

Zosia turned around again. "Marigold, are you all right?"

"Yes, I'm fine."

"You brought the Rolleiflex." She gestured to the camera in Marigold's lap.

"Yes. I should have asked you first. Do you mind?" And suddenly she was flustered. Her hands began to sweat something dreadful because it was the first time in more than a year that Zosia had even acknowledged that Marigold still went to Marek's studio.

"Not at all. Marek would have wanted you to have it."

A wave of nausea threatened to undo her. Thankfully, Alex had pulled up to a collection of outbuildings. "Here we are," he announced. "You don't mind sharing the back seat with a crate full of peeps, do you, Marigold?"

She considered whether he'd stolen something to replace the chickens that were killed by a fox at his place the week before.

With the chicks in the car, the roof was pulled shut. Their bewildered chirping let her steal a few moments to consider what Kit had shown her. *It isn't a spy film, Marigold,* Trude would warn her, if she were alive. She thought of the lines from *The 39 Steps.* Trude would say, "*A beautiful mysterious woman pursued by gunmen.*" And Marigold would reply, "*Sounds like a spy story.*" "*That's exactly what it is,*" Trude would exclaim.

Marigold sighed, and murmured, "It's only a story."

WHEN THEY ARRIVED at the manor, Marigold bolted up the stairs to her room. Everyone else was occupied with installing the peeps in the henhouse. Marigold put the camera in its case into the top drawer of her dresser. She ran the tap of the sink in her room and splashed her face.

Crisp, new five- and fifty-pound notes. Thousands and thousands of them, tucked behind the supplies in the darkroom, and then those guns.

Please God, she thought, let Kit keep his promise that he'll stay away.

At supper, Emily's chatter banished the sad ghosts who persisted in reminding them of the war's wretched toll. No one seemed to notice the blood pounding in Marigold's ears as she imagined how thousands of pounds got to Marek's home.

What is your country? I have no country. I suppose you've come here to dig up some great big state secret. I am here to save a secret from being divulged. A very important secret for this country. Why couldn't life just be like *The 39 Steps*?

The plates were cleared, and Emily threw her arms around Alex. "Night, Pappa."

"Night, my darling poppet. Tomorrow it's back to the abbey for you and Miss McGrath, isn't it?"

Emily yawned, "She's called Miss Mac at school."

Marigold nodded. "Yes, that's what they call me. I'll turn in as well. G'night."

A pair of Spitfires roared toward the coast. No one said anything; it had all become too normal.

At the top of the stairs, Emily reached up on tiptoes and gave her a kiss. "Night, Miss Mac."

"Good night, Emily."

The war was in its fourth year. Black marketeers, shysters, and villains all having a field day since it began.

She thought about her dream. "I know who your father is." Why should anyone say such a thing? Why would anyone care? She hadn't spoken with her father since leaving New York. Nor did she want to. Not ever again.

She slipped out of her shoes and removed her skirt, placing it over the back of the chair. She opened the top drawer of the dresser. The camera case was open and the roll of film gone. Zosia.

Zosia must have done it. Marigold collapsed onto the bed and placed her hand inside her bra to remove the first roll of film with the banknotes she'd grabbed when Kit had his back turned.

THE EARLY MORNING sky was shot through with orange. What would Trude do? What would she tell Marigold to do? Marigold dressed, and placed the camera, film and her gasmask into the camera bag. The station was less than a mile away. The gravel crunched under foot and Marigold hurried to make the train for London. No one was at the phone box on the platform. With shaking hands she deposited the coins. The boarders at the abbey would be at breakfast. She prayed that Sister would be alone in the matron's sitting room. Thankfully, she answered on the first ring.

"Henren Abbey, good morning."

"Sister!"

"Marigold, is that you? I thought you'd be returning with Emily."

"I . . . Something's come up. In London."

"What is it, dear? You sound dreadful."

"I- I'm sorry. But it can't be helped."

"Marigold, whatever it is, you attend to it and come back to the abbey as soon as you can."

"Yes, Sister."

"It's not a time to muck about."

"No, Sister. I won't muck about."

That they'd been so kind to Marigold astonished her. "Thank you, Sister." That she'd been at the abbey for almost two years astonished Marigold, too.

The train platform was now full. She took a deep breath. She had just enough money to make the last call.

There was the ring, then the click, and she inserted the coins. One then another and another and another. "Chelsea, 735. Hello."

"Falaise!" Marigold hoped to God she had the ear trumpet with her.

"Marigold is that you?" she shouted into the phone.

Marigold shouted back, "Falaise, is Buddy with you?"

"My dear," she said, and then called, "Buddy darling."

Thankfully he picked up the extension. "Hey, Mac."

"Buddy." Marigold noticed a man watching her from the platform. She turned away. "I need to get word . . . um"—her nerves begin flooding her body and her voice started to shake— "I discovered something."

"What?"

"I'm afraid to tell you. I, um. Loose lips and all that."

"Well, gosh darn it, kid. Don't start sinking any ships on me. Are you ok?"

Falaise was safe, he was safe. King's Road was home, and they were all right.

"I'm fine." Marigold took a breath. "I just need to know who to tell."

"What are you talking about, Marigold? Do you need to go to the police?" Somehow, his hillbilly twang reassured her.

"Buddy. I think it's worse than that." How could she say she'd seen thousands of pounds in cash? "I found some money."

"What are you saying?"

"I found money, Buddy. A lot of it." Oh God, her voice started shaking again. "A whole lot of it."

"Wow. Is this a story I should be scooping?"

"Buddy, I don't know."

"Are you in danger?"

"No, no, no. I'm not."

"For Christ's sake, Marigold. You better not be wrong about that."

"Will you meet me at Charing Cross? Please don't say anything."

"You're sure you're all right?"

"Yes, yes. I get in at nine-thirty."

Commuters and soldiers packed the corridors and compartments. There was a seat in the smoking car. Ugh. Why was she always confined to the smoking car? There was one other woman and four men in the compartment. Each and every one of them looked dodgy, like a spy.

Stop it! She scolded herself. *No one here is a spy, Marigold.* She then asked herself, *But how do you know that?* Marigold closed her eyes but failed to silence the voice inside her head. *Would you even recognize a spy?*

She leaned her head against the window.

That pin. Had he known? Had her father known what would happen? She thought about her mother. Evangeline would have loved Joop. What if her mother had lived and they'd come to England together? How things would have been different. How happy Evangeline had looked in photos with Marek. Marigold tightened her grip on her gas mask and camera. The sky had turned grey as if yesterday's sunshine hadn't happened at all.

The man across from her blew his massive nose into a tiny handkerchief. Marigold looked down when she realized he'd noticed her watching him.

The train slowed, approaching South London. It moved past streets that buzzed with life, as if the backsides of buildings weren't ripped away, and there weren't any craters where people's homes used to be. The passengers took their belongings down from the racks and organized their coats. The train crossed the Thames and pulled into Charing Cross. Stiff upper lips and all that. Much of it still business as usual.

"It'll take a lot more than bombings, fires, and air raids to slow the British down, I can tell you that," the newsagent, Mr. Alwyn, declared whenever Marigold saw him.

Steam billowed across the platforms. Whistles and shouts signaled departures and arrivals as people navigated the sandbags placed for protection against the blasts. Piles of rubble from previous bombings had been swept discreetly out of the way.

Marigold saw Buddy before he saw her. He was in uniform,

tall and thin as a rail, with the face of only a boy. When she met him, Marigold would never have thought he'd become the big brother she so desperately needed.

"What's that?" She pointed at the magazine under his arm.

"Hey, there, Mac. This is *Yank*, it's my new beat." It was oversized, like *Picture Post* and *Life*. White lettering on a red banner, a handsome soldier on its cover.

"By soldiers for soldiers," Buddy said cheerfully.

"Is that why you joined up?"

He laughed. "Among other things."

"What did Mr. Murrow say about you leaving?" Buddy had quit the CBS London bureau only last week.

"He knew I had to seize the opportunity. Besides, he's in uniform now, too."

They moved toward the exit in the direction of Trafalgar Square. At the traffic light, they waited. As the cars barreled past them, Marigold took a deep breath. Within a mile of every direction from where they stood, her life had come to this crossroads in this war.

Buddy said, "Now, tell me what's going on."

Behind them was the Savoy, where she and Joop spent an air raid kissing in the basement. To the right of them was Leicester Square, where she was to mark her twenty-first birthday. Only minutes away was Scotland Yard, where they were headed. Ten minutes past the other side of Scotland Yard was Westminster Underground where she and Trude ——

It was odd how what was left of her little finger always throbbed in sympathy when she was near there. But still. That had been two years ago. Now it was Marigold's turn to step up and play her part.

Marigold said, "Where should I begin?" and they crossed the street.

"I never understood how you started working with Marek in the first place."

"I didn't tell you about taking pictures in New York?"

"Nope. You didn't say a thing."

"I never told you?"

"No. When I came you were his sidekick. I reckon there has to be more to it than that. I mean, I came in when you got thrown out of the Woburn House thing."

They walked along the same route the taxi took when she arrived in '38. There hadn't been sandbags or barbed wire then. Nor signs admonishing the citizens to mind their every move. Nor craters fenced off with the back sides of buildings sheared away, strips of wallpaper left along cavernous, gaping holes behind fences to keep out those who might loot or do themselves harm. In '38, there hadn't been anyone in uniform, carrying gas masks, prepared to race inside, duck in a doorway, if a siren should sound the alarm.

"Excuse me, sorry, excuse me." Throngs of people entered and exited the Scotland Yard's front doors.

"Follow me," Buddy said, purposefully striding forward, taller than everyone else, and formidable in his uniform despite weighing about the same as someone half his height.

A man at a desk gestured to a flight of stairs. Buddy took them two at a time, as Marigold scurried behind trying to keep up. At the top of the landing, he said, "Now don't be intimidated."

Marigold considered this. "Okay."

"State your business and demand to speak with someone."

"Demand, hunh?"

"Yeah! Darn right. You're reporting a crime." He pointed to a door with lettering painted upon the glass. "It's through here."

"Okay." She pulled herself upright. "Let's go."

Through the glass door was a tall reception desk, behind which were half a dozen more desks, all of them occupied. There were chairs beside each of them, presumably for interviews.

A boy, or a young man, probably the same age as Buddy and Marigold sat at the reception desk. Like Buddy, he was in a uniform, but one of the metropolitan police rather than the American army.

"Allo, allo, allo! To what do we owe this honor? A fine American soldier with a pretty lady on his arm?"

The young man's forwardness was so disarming it took Marigold a moment to gather her wits. "I'd like to report a crime."

"You would, would you? Well, isn't that a fine kettle of fish!" His manner was so flippant that she was afraid to look at Buddy's reaction.

"You'll need to take my name and information. I want to make a statement."

"Hang on, hang on. Hang on to your britches, missus."

Buddy stepped forward. "Now look here."

"No sir, you look here. One doesn't just come sashaying into Scotland Yard and expect His Majesty's metropolitan police to drop everything because you've decided that it's time to join this war. Crikey." He pointed at a bench along the wall behind them. Upon it were several unsavory looking characters and a woman. "I suggest you sit your American selves down upon that bench and wait, until the inspector sergeant calls upon you."

Buddy and Marigold were so taken aback that they did as instructed. Ten minutes passed. Two of the men were called upon. Everyone else continued to wait, miserably, in silence.

"I have to go to work, Marigold," Buddy whispered at last.

"I know," she said. "You should go. I'll be all right."

At last, another man in spectacles and a uniform entered from a doorway across the room. He murmured to the fellow at reception, who nodded and pushed his chair back with some difficulty. When he stood and came round to the front of the desk, Marigold stifled a gasp. He was using a crutch, and his left leg was missing below the knee. Seeing her reaction, he said, "Yes. If you had seen to joining this war just a bit sooner, I might still have my leg. But that would be extrapolating, wouldn't it?"

Buddy and Marigold remained silent, because both of them knew that he was right.

Sachsenhausen, Germany
Barracks 18 and 19

HERR KRÜGER CAME BY THE WORKSTATION WHERE Oskar Stein did bookkeeping and Joop calculated numeric tabulations. Oskar and Joop stood at attention.

"Gentlemen." Herr Krüger waved his hand for them to relax. "Please, sit down." He offered them both a cigarette. The tobacco smelled good.

Herr Krüger opened their ledgers. "So, thus far to date, we've successfully printed three hundred million pounds of which one hundred and twenty-six million are first class. Eighty million are second class, and the rest are used only on an as-needed basis. Of our three hundred million pounds, over one hundred million are in circulation. Very good!" The denominations were in five-, ten-, and twenty-pound notes. The vast majority were five-pound notes. For each and every piece of paper, there was a unique serial number which had to pass inspection at whatever bank the note was presented. That detail was Joop's job.

Originally, the money was printed to flood and destroy the British economy by rendering their real currency useless. But the Reich was so strapped for cash that the sterling which Sachsenhausen produced was instead used for purchasing arms, bribing officials, and ordering whatever it was the Reich needed. Most of it went eastward, toward Hungary, Yugoslavia, and Turkey.

Herr Krüger closed the ledgers. "Now, the führer and Himmler have been so delighted with our efforts they've decided we should also furnish the Reich with US dollars." He took a billfold from his jacket and peeled off several hundreds, a few fifties, and some twenties. "I'm sure I can trust you to do your best and most efficient work."

With that he stood, clicked his heels, and was gone.

Oskar and Joop brought the dollars to the other inmates. Everyone stared at the money for some time. Presently, the chief designer put a massive projection of the one-hundred-dollar bill upon the wall. Benjamin Franklin looked impassively back at them while they studied the projection in silence. Each man performed different functions in creating this work. Joop's task was to replicate and mimic the algorithm that generated the serial numbers on the bottom left of the bill.

They knew that their success at counterfeiting the dollar might save them. But it could also destroy them. If they failed to do it properly, the Germans would kill them. If they succeeded in doing it properly, the Germans wouldn't need them any longer, so then, they'd kill them. But if they could draw out the task, because the artwork was more complex than on the pound, then it would buy them a little time. How much time was impossible to say.

Scotland Yard

Marigold glanced at the clock over the door. She'd been waiting for nearly two hours. *Be assertive*, Buddy always insisted. Only one of the unsavory men remained on the bench.

"Excuse me." She approached the sergeant with the spectacles. He looked up from his reading. She started again, "Excuse me, I don't want to be a pushy American, but I've come here to report a crime, and not one person has asked me for a statement."

"What can I do for you?" He took in her figure, her skirt and jacket. It was a modest houndstooth, but she knew he wasn't really looking at the clothes.

"I'm here to report a crime." She stood as tall as she could.

"Was someone murdered?"

"Not that I know of."

"Has someone been robbed?"

"I really can't say."

"Well then—"

"But I think it's a matter of utmost importance."

"And why do you say that?" From the leering expression Marigold knew he thought her a fool. But he was about to be very much mistaken.

"Is there someone to whom I can make a statement?"

At this the desk sergeant started to laugh. "Is there someone to whom you can make a statement? My dear Miss—"

"McGrath. My name is Marigold McGrath."

"Now that has a lovely ring to it, doesn't it?"

"Is there someone with whom I can speak?"

"I'll need to see your papers first."

She handed him her identity card and alien registration. "Wait over there, please." He picked up the receiver on the telephone and spoke into it, mumbling something inaudible. Then he hung up. "Someone will be with you presently."

The waiting was infernal.

"Miss McGrath, right this way, please." The sergeant showed her over to a desk. There was a typewriter upon it, and the sergeant placed her papers next to the typewriter. Her stomach rumbled something fierce and she glanced at her wristwatch.

It was going on noon. Presently another man sat down at the desk. He placed a form in triplicate into the typewriter's roller then examined her identification papers.

"Now, Miss McGrath, how can I help?"

"Oh my goodness. I'm so glad to see you."

At this, he typed something onto the form and asked, "What is your business in London?"

"Oh, well. I came before the war. Uh, in the spring of 1938."

He typed some more and then paused. "Were you on holiday?"

"No, not really. My mother had lived here during the last war, and—"

"You were visiting with your mother then."

"No. She died."

"I'm very sorry. She died when you were on holiday?"

"She died just before. So, I came here."

"I see. And you decided to stay."

"Yes." Marigold waited for him to continue with his typing, which this time, he seemed to do at length.

Finally, he said, "Go on."

"Oh, well, my mother's friends sort of took me in."

"Ah. And who are they?"

"My landlady, Falaise, her name is Mrs. Falaise Cooper."

"Address?" Here the typing resumed.

Marigold spoke over it, "275 King's Road. And then the Daggers."

"And who are the Daggers?"

"Zosia and Marek. She found me my first job, and Marek . . . he . . . he taught me nearly everything I know."

"And the Daggers are"—the detective paused with some significance— "British?"

"Yes, I believe so. I never asked to see their papers."

"Do the Daggers have children?"

"Oh no. They're brother and sister. Or they were brother and sister. Marek Dagger, the brother . . . uh . . . well, he was a photographer for the Ministry of Information. He was quite known."

"You say was?" She watched the detective unwind the form and place it carefully, under her papers. "Miss McGrath, are you familiar with Wandsworth Prison?"

"Excuse me?"

"It's where we place those who've committed crimes. Such as black marketeers and enemy aliens. I wonder if you're not caught up in some kind of ring. All sorts of people have taken up nefarious activities to line their own pockets and wreak havoc in our communities. That's what war does. It creates those kinds of opportunities."

Marigold's finger began throbbing. "Excuse me, but I am here because I'm reporting that very thing."

"Hmm. Doesn't seem likely though, does it? It's more a case of a pretty American girl—perhaps a bit of a tart, really—mixed up with gangsters and such."

Outraged, she flushed, "How—" But stopped herself from wailing. *Say nothing,* she warned herself. *Loose lips, whatnot.*

"Many of these people"—the detective leaned forward— "these underworld types, have associations with the enemy. This Marek Dagger, he was a known ponce, wasn't he? Did a portrait of Oswald Mosley, did he not?"

"I don't know."

"It was in a society magazine or some such. Was Marek Dagger a Blackshirt?"

"No! I should think not."

"He put down his pen and gathered his paperwork. "Why are you blushing? Is there something you're embarrassed about? There is a war on, Miss McGrath—"

"I know!" The wail escaped from her lips after all. "I'm an ARP volunteer!"

"Air Raid Patrol volunteer. Are you really?"

"Yes!"

"Is that how you tip off the spivs? Let 'em know where there's been collateral damage so they might loot the premises?"

"I think I need to speak with a lawyer, please."

"This isn't America. Do you have family in Germany? I suggest you think very carefully before you further incriminate yourself."

She wondered when Buddy would come back. Would Buddy come back? Who else knew that she was there?

The detective laced his fingers together on the desk. He leaned closer. "Are you Jewish?"

"What if I am?" She looked him straight in the eye, her heartbeat slowing. "What are you saying?"

The detective didn't answer.

"Please." She rubbed the space over her finger. "I found something. The address is 3 Lark Mews. Something very wrong is going on there. There's money. A lot of it. A lot. I brought some film!" But he had already left the room by then.

Marigold looked at the window. The sill was too high for her to see out. But the window panes had been painted white. She wouldn't have been able to see anything if she'd tried.

* * *

ANOTHER POLICEMAN ENTERED THE ROOM. "Miss McGrath. In light of the lootings which have plagued this city for the last few years, and in light of this somewhat improbable setup you seem to be concocting, with what? A jilted lover? A communist or homosexual? A Blackshirt perhaps? The most prudent plan of action for us at this time is to keep you here until you consider sharing the entire truth about your visit to us today."

"What! Oh no." This was a disaster. Her lower lip quivered. Marigold was terrified she'd start crying. *Don't cry!* she warned herself.

"Right." He scooped up the form with her identity and registration cards and placed them in a file. She watched him open the door whereupon a policewoman entered the room. "Matron will see you to the ladies' cell."

"No, no, no." This wasn't supposed to happen.

"Matron, please have Miss McGrath sign over her bag and camera. You probably should take her watch too."

Silently, Marigold followed her to a desk where her valuables were logged and she was handed a chit. "Better hang onto it, if you know what's good for you," the matron said.

"What?"

"Girls like you get into trouble all the time."

The matron's comments opened the floodgates and Marigold's sobs took on a life of their own. She gasped, "Is there a toilet?"

The Matron nodded. "They'll show you where it is." And she pointed to a cell where five other women were waiting, for what Marigold could only imagine. In the corner was a forlorn WC, no toilet seat, no toilet paper, that was it.

Seeing Marigold's reaction, one of the women said, "I'll hold my coat up dear, we'll look away. Don't fret."

Which only made her cry all the harder.

Time passed. The women gossiped about the previous night's air raid, about working the street, about an unkind pimp. One was let out, and then another. Marigold was left with three drunks, in various states of unconsciousness, and her stomach roared with hunger. She leaned back and closed her eyes.

"McGrath. Marigold McGrath."

She stood up, wobbling a bit. "I'm Marigold."

The policeman unlocked the door, and the other women fussed and growled.

"Easy on. You'll get yours," he said. Then he nodded to Marigold. "This way."

At the end of the corridor was another interview room. Inside was a man with spectacles and a fastidious suit. Marigold glanced at the door. The clock above it said 9 p.m.

"Roland Percy"—the man offered her his hand— "assistant undersecretary for the special assistant to the Prime Minister."

She timidly shook hands. "Hello."

"Sit down, Miss McGrath. I understand you're in a pickle."

"How did you—"

"Ed Murrow's called in a favor to the PM. Now, please, tell me how you got here, so that I can get you out."

Buddy must have told Ed Murrow. Just as she thanked God for them, she began to cry.

"Miss McGrath, Miss McGrath, now, now." He handed her a handkerchief. "Don't do that. Stiff upper lip. That's a girl. Now, now. Describe to me what's happened."

"Well," Somehow, Marigold calmed down. "After Marek's death, all sorts of strange items began appearing at his studio. I knew I wasn't the only one with a key, and I didn't want to be accused of snooping, so I said nothing."

"I see. Strange. Strange items such as what?"

"A lot of alcohol. Sometimes things on ice."

"On ice?"

"Yes. Like berries."

"Mr. Percy began to smile. "Berries. Really."

"And what would I say then? I'd come to the police and say, I'd like to report a mysterious crate of berries?"

"Quite."

"So. The only man I could imagine having a hand in this has always been very kind. He was a great war hero, apparently."

"Was he?"

"In the last war."

"I see."

"And then, and then yesterday there were these guns!" Marigold began crying again.

"Steady, steady on."

Her nose was running and it wouldn't seem to stop. "It isn't very nice here, you know."

Mr. Percy looked around the room. "No, it isn't, is it?" He turned back to her. "About these guns. Do you mean they were at the same place as the berries?"

She nodded. "But the berries were a year ago. The guns were yesterday. Then the money, the money was yesterday, too. And I was there with my friend. He's only thirteen years old."

"What's the address again?"

"3 Lark Mews. It's behind Lots Road."

"Excuse me a moment, Miss McGrath."

Mr. Percy left the room and a uniformed officer came back in. "You're free to go."

"I—what? How do I get my bag and my camera? And you have my residence card."

Within moments her things were returned. She strapped them over her shoulder and made her way down the stairs. Outside, a black car with a Union Jack on its hood was waiting. Mr. Percy opened the door from inside the car.

"Come on, Miss McGrath. I'll take you home."

The car moved through the traffic.

"What about Lark Mews?"

"We'll stop on the way, shall we? I suspect the cash is some counterfeit that's been making appearances here and there. Someone's trying to ruin the economy what. Or get things for free. Thank you for bringing it to our attention. I must say, I'll be ready for my tea this evening. I should expect you will be too, no?"

At Lark Mews, Marigold turned on the light. Everything

seemed much as before, but there was no sign of Tony the cat. She led Mr. Percy and two other men, one a police officer, the other not, to the storage cabinet. There, behind the supplies was the panel in the wall. She slid it open. The four suitcases were exactly as they'd been the day before.

She pulled out the first suitcase, and watched the policeman fiddle with the lock. It opened easily revealing the five- and twenty-pound notes stacked tightly together.

Mr. Percy, whistled. "Heavens, look at that. I say."

Within moments, two more suitcases packed with the same contents were also opened. When they opened the fourth, the three men took a step back. It was filled with firearms and ammunition.

"Crickey," said the policeman. Another man took out a camera and began photographing the scene. Marigold shifted the Rolleiflex on her shoulder. Instinctively, as she scooped up some film from the shelf, her fingers brushed against a small packet. She picked it up. Her name was written on the front in Marek's writing. She wondered how she hadn't noticed it before, and placed it in the camera bag.

Mr. Percy gave her a hard look. "Who has access to the premises?"

She shrugged. "Well, since Marek's death, I'm not quite sure."

He went over to the phone and made a call. He spoke in a hushed voice and then, "Yes sir, yes, Prime Minister. Miss McGrath, he would like to speak with you."

Marigold shook her head as if to decline. But Mr. Percy took a step toward her and held out the receiver.

She prayed she wouldn't start crying again. "H—hello?"

"Marigold, it's Winston Churchill."

"H—hello, Prime Minister."

"You've done quite the brave thing, having to sweat it out in one of those nasty holding cells what. But I commend you, Marigold, for a very brave thing indeed. We've got Jerry where we want him now, and we're going to win this thing, because of strong women like you. You know, I had a little girl named Marigold, but we lost her. She would have been about your age, had she lived. I like to think she would have acquitted herself as well as you have today. God bless you, Marigold."

The lump in her throat became one of gratitude. "Thank you, sir."

She handed the receiver back to Mr. Percy who bade the prime minister good night. Then they heard the familiar whizzing.

"It never ends, does it?" Mr. Percy asked no one in particular. At first it was soft, reminding them that everyone has a bomb with their name on it. As the noise became louder, this one sounded as if it were theirs.

He turned to Marigold. "Is there a shelter?"

But it was too late for that. The Germans hit their targets.

Percy yelled, "Out! For God's sake, everyone out!"

Glass shattered and a fireball ripped through the mews. The side of the buildings were suddenly in flames.

Two more explosions came from the direction of Cremorne Gardens. The roar of the buildings' collapse could mean only one thing.

Someone shouted, "They've bombed the estate!"

"I have to go." Marigold dashed ahead of the men, past the flames, racing toward the estate. There were sirens and fire trucks, Air Raid Patrol, and air raid wardens racing toward Guinness House. She ran without stopping. She had to find Kit.

One of the four buildings had been leveled. Clouds of powdered stone obscured the visibility. Those who'd chosen not to shelter were most likely crushed in their beds. Yet some people were emerging from the rubble.

Neighbors ran toward the ruin, and the Royal Engineers shouted while firetrucks pulled up, the hoses spraying water over the flames. People formed a line, gingerly removing one piece of rubble at a time.

Marigold frantically moved one stone and another. In what

seemed like moments, Buddy was beside her. He put his hand on Marigold's back. "We'll find him, Mac." He joined a group of men clearing rubble, but then straightened back up and pointed at the camera still strapped around her shoulder. "Marigold."

She looked but went back to her work.

"Marigold!" Buddy repeated.

She stepped away from the line.

He pointed at the camera. "You've got to shoot this."

Marigold wiped the rain and the sweat from her eyes. She could barely breathe, but she knew he was right. She glanced around her. The pictures she took were of the way she wanted to see the world, not a world like this. She moved her head in that gesture of her mother's, the same gesture she had seen in Kit. One small shake of the head to the left and a slight nod to the right.

Someone called out, and at the signal they fell silent, until the Warden said, "Over here!" Then they moved more quickly, everyone applauding when someone was rescued from the pile.

"There are enough folks helping here." Buddy said. "And the public needs to see this,"

Marigold looked at the flames, at people struggling to find survivors. "Take the picture, Mac."

This part of London, this was her home.

She took out the camera and loaded it. Her hands were trembling. She looked down through the viewfinder. She saw a man help a couple climb out of the wreckage, with someone at the side, offering a blanket. Marigold took a deep breath and pressed the button. She advanced the film.

The casualties increased in number, and those alive seemed further and further out of reach. Volunteers gently covered the dead, away from the commotion. There had to be several dozen, lying under sheets, loaded onto the ambulances to be taken to the morgue. Marigold took the picture, holding the camera steady even as she wept.

She turned and walked toward the mountainous rubble to photograph the people who worked tirelessly, pulling together, embracing, sobbing, and in despair. Behind Guinness House, the fire at Lark Mews was only contained as the sky began to fade.

By sunrise, there was still no sign of Kit. She shouted, "Come on, Kit, where are you?" She joined the others back at the rubble. "Where are you?"

Marigold saw Kit's mother, Sara, approaching and then she ran toward them. Marigold remembered that Sara volunteered at the hospital.

"Kit?" Sara asked, terrified to know more. "Where is Kit?"

"We found 'im!" someone called, and they raced down to where the voices were. A warden was holding Kit, carrying him like a small child, because his eyes were closed. He was completely white, covered in dust.

Gingerly, Buddy took him from the warden's arms.

"Kit, Kit." Sara placed a hand on his chest.

Kit opened his eyes. "That was amazing," he said, and closed them again.

Marigold took Kit's hand and squeezed it. He was warm. Then she stepped back a few paces. He opened his eyes again and looked at his mother.

"Kit," Sara whispered.

Marigold studied them through the viewfinder. She lined up the frame. *Tell the story you want to tell,* Marek advised.

"Hi Mummy," Kit said. Sara reached over and kissed him.

Marigold took the picture.

10 Downing Street

KIT AND SARA WERE SHOWN TO MR. PERCY'S OFFICE whereupon they were given tea and biscuits. Kit's arm was in a sling, and he was pretty bruised up, but a visit to 10 Downing Street impressed even him.

Mr. Percy said, "I understand you brought the contraband to Miss McGrath's attention. Did you not?"

"Yes sir, I did."

"You did the right thing. But you know, everything at Lark Mews was destroyed in the bombing that night. That building, the studio at the Mews, has been leveled, completely burned down. There's nothing left."

"I understand, sir."

"Now let me ask you, do you think we should further investigate and perhaps press charges?"

"Mr. Percy, sir. What about loose lips and sinking ships?"

"What about that indeed? Do you think that's what needs to happen now?"

"No, sir."

"Do you want to press charges and further an investigation?"

"No sir."

"Well, I'll take that under advisement then. Since the evidence we had in London no longer exists, perhaps that would be in everyone's best interest." Mr. Percy walked over to his desk and picked up a small picture frame. "Take care of yourself and your mother, Kit. You are a credit to your country. The prime minister has asked that I give you this." He handed Kit the frame, which was in fact a letter of commendation, signed by Winston Churchill.

"Thank you very much, sir." Kit beamed from ear to ear and handed it to his mother. "Thank you very much indeed."

* * *

"Marigold, darling. You just missed Zosia not a moment ago," Falaise said.

"Oh?" Marigold had brought home some things for Sara and Kit.

"She came to say goodbye. Evidently, she and the Reillys are off to Kenya or some such thing. He wants to try his hand at coffee farming."

"Oh." Marigold heard Kit with Tony the cat in his arms, trailing Sara up the stairs to the spare room where they'd stay until they could make plans.

"Zosia left a note for you," Falaise said, then called out, "Let me help you, Sara, dear," and made her way up the stairs.

Dear Marigold,

> *So many things are not always what they appear to be. There have been, admittedly, occasional acquisitions, which were certainly not allowed, but there has also been some amount of good.*

> *You should know that Alex not only bankrolled families getting to safety, but that sometimes it necessitated using arms, which, if you're anything like me, you'll find distasteful. All of which is to say that with the demise of Lark Mews, a great deal of it is behind us now.*

> *I just want to assure you that at no point, neither Alex nor myself would ever have harmed you, nor Kit, not ever. Please let Kit know that the Blossoms have kindly agreed to care for*

the dogs in our absence, and you are welcome to visit them whenever you'd like.

    With love,

    Zosia.

Spring 1945

Saschenhausen

THE TAPPING AT THE BACK OF JOOP'S THROAT HAD become increasingly irksome. He was down a good ten kilos and for a tall guy like himself, even he found his scrawniness frightening.

The doctor advised hot water, hot tea, some eucalyptus, or pine needles.

Joop was moved to the table where they distressed the paper. The team agreed that it was less vexing, and he'd have a better chance at resting than doing more sums.

But then their Kapo, Wagner, announced, "Pack up the machines. We're moving the outfit." There was a sigh of relief, even though they knew that when it was all over, there was no doubt what to expect. They'd been told more than once. When Krüger decided they'd finished the job, everyone knew what would happen next.

There were three guys who were sick. Wagner shot them himself. Then they hanged the poor devil who was caught pinching a $50 bill in the courtyard. It was no secret that none of them would get out alive. Each and every one of the 132 who were still living, were to be killed.

IT TOOK thirty-four hours to dismantle the equipment. Millions of pound notes were tightly packed into waterproof coffins. Then secret service documents, forgeries, and lab materials were packed in the same manner, sealed airtight, and fastened with twenty long screws each. The plates, ink, chemicals, paper, and presses were carted up and tied onto pallets. The plates for the dollars were packed with the greatest care of all. The strongest inmates loaded the equipment onto the backs of the trucks that they walked behind until they reached the train station. That no one had been shot yet gave them all hope they might remain living just a bit longer.

Villagers who saw them either looked away or scurried into their houses. But it could have been worse. It wasn't like they were the other thirty thousand emaciated inmates still in the rest of the camp. Compared to the others, the prisoners from Operation Bernhard were in good shape. They hadn't been starved. They wore normal clothes, they had normal shoes. Only the backs of their jackets showed a square of stripes to signify their status.

When they boarded the train, they were shocked that it was heated, that there were blankets and benches. Joop almost groaned with pleasure and pulled his scarf tighter around his throat. He decided to sleep until they arrived wherever it was they were going.

Many hours later, the train stopped. They were in Prague. Several of the men were Czech and ran to the windows.

One of them said, "That's Kloboučnická Street. It's where I live."

Everyone was silent as the tears rolled down his face.

The next morning, Joop recognized the mountains and the rolling landscape.

"Oh, sweet mother of God," said Christopher.

The train pulled into Mauthausen, and they could see the stone works from the train. Maybe Joop's premonition was right after all.

Mauthausen

They were processed at Mauthausen yet again.

Afterward, Christopher handed Joop a small cup of water. "Hold on, mate. You know the Yanks will be here any day." It was just a question of time now, and most of the guards were more interested in leaving than in guarding. Still, the Kapo stood over them, threatening to shoot anyone who tried to escape.

"But where will that put us?" Joop's fever had him sweating something fierce. His skin was sallow, and his clothes drenched.

"There's a rather cozy accommodation at KZ Ebensee, I think."

"Oh! Yet another subcamp. That sounds marvelous." Joop tried to sound light. "You know somehow, I had a feeling we'd be back."

Christopher said, "Listen, chum. You have to hold on till the Yanks come." He perched Joop to a sitting up position and gave him more water.

Joop handed him two folded pieces of paper. "There's a girl. If she's still in England, will you see that she gets this?"

"No, no. You'll take it yourself, Joop."

"If I should be detained, would you give it to her for me?"

"What makes you think I'll get back to England?"

"Because of your family. They'll need you."

"I'll have to prove I'm British first."

"You will."

"My wife may have remarried."

"Perhaps."

"My son—I have no way of knowing what's happened to him."

"He will need you in the coming months..He will always need you. Unless you go back, you will never know." Joop began to cough and bowed his head onto his elbow. When it subsided, he whispered, "If you don't go back, how will you be there for him?"

"Sometimes, I think it's all been for naught."

Joop's eyes grew large. "What?" A smile tugged at his lips. "What makes you say that?" He started to laugh but was too weak to do so. "No, no. Your boy will be honored to learn your story. And you will honor him by telling it. Of, course if you hadn't done it, you wouldn't have been captured and on this"—waving his hand Joop started to laugh again— "you know, we would not have met. What are the odds of that? It brings to mind the Loewner differential equation, doesn't it?"

"What is that?"

"It's a very beautiful formula. Not so old, it's quite new really. But what it means is that without your friendship, I would not have the chance to put things right with Marigold." He groaned. "At least I think that's what it means."

He moved the papers from his chest and handed them to Christopher. "Who knows? If she's alive, she may be married by now. But you know, I saw her at that dance, and when I did"—he smiled— "she was mooi— she was my monad."

"What's that?"

"It's a math thing. It means something mooi. Something beautiful." Joop leaned back and took his spectacles out of his shirt pocket. He handed them to Christopher. "Would you give her these?" Joop closed his eyes, smiling. "She liked to wear them. They made her look very—" Joop put his hand on his friend's wrist. "Thank you, Christopher." Joop sighed and whispered, "Thank you to take this for her."

London

It was the first Saturday in April. Buddy had tickets for Chelsea versus Millwall at Wembley and Kit was beside himself with anticipation.

Buddy asked, "You wanna come, Mac?"

"I thought you'd never ask! Thanks Buddy."

They made the journey by overground through a city that was slowly rebuilding. Some parts appeared as though there had never been a war, other neighborhoods had begun rebuilding with efficient standards devoid of charm or personality.

While there had been some football outside of London, after five years of matches being suspended in the city, the crowd at Wembley was ecstatic. The king and his daughter Elizabeth were in attendance, and it was a huge moment. Marigold captured the spectators laughing and screaming, embracing one another. The war was on the verge of ending and England had endured.

On Thursdays, Buddy made a production of roasting a chicken and then doing the washing up. Ever since Kit and Sara had moved in, Buddy made this effort, once a week, to be, what he touted, was a good example.

"But only on Thursdays, now." About that, Buddy was very clear. "After all, I got my own fish to fry."

For Kit, the arrangement was ideal, because when the chicken was in the oven, Buddy helped him with his schoolwork. In exchange, Kit helped with the washing up and the two of them stood by the sink, Falaise's aprons wrapped around them, their arms submerged in suds.

Marigold had been watching this ritual for weeks, setting up the shot in her mind. Kit would need to be in the foreground of course. Preferably it would be early enough that there was still a bit of sunlight from the terrace door.

The remnants from dinner were in the bottom right of the frame, somewhat out of focus. Kit and Buddy were toward the left. Buddy was a good head taller than Kit, and he said something that made Kit laugh. Marigold pressed the button and wound the film.

Kit turned toward her, and she said, "Don't look at me, please. Focus on the dishes."

"*Yank* has an opening for me in New York," Buddy said.

Kit looked up at him. "What does that mean?" He passed him a plate to be rinsed.

"It's an opportunity!" Buddy put the dish on the rack and then rubbed his face with the upper part of his arm. He looked over at Marigold. Falaise was by the fire, absorbed by a game of Patience.

"Falaise," Marigold said.

Falaise looked up and lifted her ear trumpet. "Yes dear?"

"Buddy's been offered a job in New York."

"Oh?"

No one spoke then. They just waited for him to say that he was going to take it. Or not. Instead, Buddy was consumed with his task at the sink.

Finally, Falaise said, "My dear. New York City, how very exciting. I'm sure—"

"I'm afraid to leave." Buddy rinsed the last plate.

"Why is that?"

"You're my family now." He poured the water from the dish bowl. "I'm afraid to leave my family."

"But it's your dream job, Buddy," Marigold said.

He glanced at her. His face was wet but not from doing dishes.

"Don't be afraid," she whispered, then chuckled because she was crying now, too. "Buddy." She knew he must go. "It will be great. New York is not so far away."

Autumn 1946

London

THE OFFICES AT *PICTURE POST* WERE AS HECTIC AS ever. Like England, everything was moving full steam ahead. Marigold's photo essay was entitled "Women's Work." It had ruffled a few feathers, but the pictures were great. They were portraits of the editor of *Vogue*, a barrister, a physician, a pilot, and a bus driver. The next week, *Tatler* had asked her to do some debutante portraits of girls being presented at court.

"Isn't that Cecil Beaton's gig?" someone asked.

Marigold couldn't help smiling, though she tried to play it cool and shrugged. "They approached me. I heard he's got his hands full designing some show or other."

On the way home, she stopped at the grocers for some oranges and then at Mr. Alwyn's for the evening paper.

"Do give my best to Mrs. Cooper," he said.

"Oh, I will Mr. Alwyn. As always, she sends you a special hello."

WALKING TOWARD THE HOUSE, Marigold saw a man standing at the door of King's Road. He kept stepping back to look at the address and then at something in his hand. He had a feral quality that since the war's end, one saw more often than not. It was the sign of suffering when one can only imagine what a person's lived through, where they've been. She wondered if he was a friend of Alex Reilly's, come on some unsavory mission, so she kept her house key ready, as a weapon, just in case.

At a safe distance, she called out, "May I help you?"

"I'm looking for a Miss Marigold McGrath."

"That's me."

"Ah, I have a letter for you, Miss McGrath." His expression was furtive and regretful so that she knew. She knew right away. "It's from my friend, Joop Kasander."

When he said this, somehow, all the dance steps, every silliness, and each and every kiss moved as if in slow motion before her eyes and she heard herself asking, "Is he? Is Joop?" Yet the words alive and dead meant nothing now.

The strange man said Joop's name again and Marigold was aware of holding the envelope while he stopped her from collapsing, catching the groceries before they fell into the street.

She heard herself say, "Please come in." And the man followed her upstairs to the landing.

"My name's Christopher. In '36, I went to Spain, leaving behind a wife and child. Somehow, I naively thought, that for the world to be right for them, I had to fight the tyranny in Spain. Like so many other fools, we were captured by Franco's lot and sent to a camp in Austria.

"It was called Mauthausen. There were lots of people, thousands, from across Europe. I think there were more than a hundred Englishmen. The reason it's taken me so long to get here today," he said, "is I didn't have any paperwork"—he stammered — "and uh, the last fifteen months have been spent bouncing around the Red Cross, getting together what's required to be repatriated."

He took out a cigarette. "May I?" His hands shook slightly.

"Let's go on the terrace."

She made sure the chairs were dry and that he had an ashtray. When he flicked the ash of his cigarette, an angry scar around his wrist peeked out from the edge of his sleeve. He took another envelope from his chest pocket and handed it to her. "Joop also asked that I bring you these."

Marigold felt the frames of his glasses through the paper. Her sorrow held her gently, somehow reminding her that she could wait until she was alone.

She swallowed and asked him, "So where were you most recently?"

"In a displaced persons camp. In Austria. There's loads of them."

"Does your family know you're alive?"

"Uh, not yet. I've managed to track them down—my wife and son, but it turns out they were displaced themselves not that long ago."

"Oh? How so?" Behind Christopher, Marigold saw Sara unloading the groceries in the kitchen. Sara put the kettle on and then left, perhaps to go into the sitting room.

"Well, they were in the estate here, off Lots Road, at Guinness House."

"I see."

Grief had poured itself over Marigold so that everything was strangely muted and warm. She could barely make out what Christopher was saying.

"I . . . I understand that I can track them down through Chelsea Town Hall."

"Yes, yes. That's true. But I know a boy who used to live there with his mother. His family name is Hearne." The next words came out so slowly. "Is that your family name?" As if they were all in a dream. "His name is Kit. His mom's name is Sara. Is that your son?"

* * *

Dear Marigoude,

It was impossible to tell you what I was doing or how I was doing it. It was impossible to ask you to wait and understand and it was just impossible. When we said goodbye, or more correctly, when you yelled it, I returned to the Netherlands to continue my assignment. Because of an unfortunate incident at Kamp Schoorl, I was now, as you say in English, on the lam. I love this expression. I was on the lam! Like a gangster, like Jimmy Cagney or Humphrey Bogart. I think it suited me too. Or imagine, it might be a special dish in a French restaurant. Mesdames, messieurs, may I offer our specialty, which is Joop on the lam?

However, before that, I got to work right away. This time connecting with the Beggars, one of the original underground cells in the Netherlands. Together with an operative out of France we began moving families with children out of Holland over to Switzerland or to Spain, and then eventually to either England or America. It was hard work and frightening a lot of the time, but, by and large, we were successful. If you received my last letter, it was sent via Mrs. Staub. When I told her about you, she insisted she carry it to Switzerland. I was afraid. What if they got stopped? But she said that if she got stopped, it would be catastrophic anyway, so she took the letter. I hope you got it. Nothing would make me happier than having tea with you again.

Last year, we were moving so many allied pilots, in addition to the fugitives, that it was a big business, with lots of people involved. Unfortunately, at the start of '44 a young courier was arrested. They tortured her very cruelly and she gave up the game. I think that by the time it was over, nearly half of us were sent to the camps. I went to a place in Austria called Mauthausen, which is where I met the Englishman who's brought you this letter.

If you see reports or read stories about what happened in these places, these camps, they don't describe even half of the evil which took place here. I regret I cannot tell you, but at the same time, I would never want you to know how terrible things were. But I was lucky.

I worked with Chris on the Messerschmitts, and you know, Gouda, I think we kept a few of them out of London. Then they transferred us to another camp, Sachsenhausen. There we manufactured British pound notes. In excess of 100 million, I am sure. One day, you'll learn about this money, and you'll say, oh, that's what Joop was doing. For my part, I attempted to sabotage the numerical codes. Perhaps if any of the notes got to the Bank of England, somebody would have picked it up, but really, with a war going on, who's to say? If you have the opportunity, you can ask my friend Christopher about it. He's a kind fellow. I hope he finds his family. I know when I met you that I found mine.

I love you and will always love you. I wish you every happiness, darling Marigold.

JOOP

THREE DAYS LATER, Kit brought his father to the *Picture Post.* Both Kit and Christopher beamed when Marigold said, "Golly, you look exactly like your dad. Soon you'll be the same height."

"I just wanted to thank you," Christopher said.

"I should be thanking you." Marigold handed him a small print she'd taken of Kit before the war. "Without you, the letter might not have found me. And Kit has been one of my best friends, ever."

Gingerly, she felt the glasses, resting in her pocket. "Here," she said, "here's Joop. In color, no less." She handed Christopher a snapshot from Oak Day, of Joop standing with the soldier in the scarlet coat.

"That Joop had a style, he had a style which made me see things differently." Christopher added, "I think he saved my life."

When Christopher said this, Marigold blinked back the tears. Every moment they had been together, Joop had only shown her love. When she'd stumbled or yelled, his tenderness had never wavered.

After a moment, Marigold nodded and said, "You know, I think he saved mine, too."

New York
Norbert Freed, Editor

April 19, 1951
Miss Marigold McGrath
275 King's Road
London SW3, GREAT BRITAIN
Dear Mac,
First off, please don't tell me you're too busy, or that you've fallen in love and are getting married and retiring, etc. I've just started a new project with a friend, and I think what we're missing is you! It's called Picture Week. It's 99% photography, ranging from hard news to lite gossip and very little editorial. Or at least written editorial. The thing is, the photographs must have a strong point of view. And, as you know, I am a huge admirer of your work's points of view.

Whatever you're making from Picture Post, we'll match it. Say yes. Give Falaise a big old hug from me and get your ass over here. You were right. New York is great.

Your pal,
Buddy.

The End

333

Further Reading

Below are some books which touch upon the War, Marigold's world and life in general during the 1930's and 40's

Beaton, Cecil. *The Theatre of War.* London: Jonathan Cape, 2013

Berkowitz, Michael. *Jews and Photography in Britain.* Austin: University of Texas Press, 2015

Burger, Adolf. *The Devil's Workshop.* London: Frontline Books, 2009

Burke, Carolyn. *Lee Miller.* New York: Alfred A. Knopf, 2005

Faviell, Frances. *A Chelsea Concerto.* London: Dean Street Press, 2016

Frisell, Toni *Toni Frissell Photographs 1933 – 1967,* New York: Doubleday, 1994

Garrett, Leah. *X Troop,* New York: Houghton Mifflin Harcourt, 2021

Gardiner, Juliet. *Wartime Britain, 1939-1945* London: Hodder Headline, 2004

Gilbert, Martin. *Churchill and the Jews.* New York: Henry Holt & Co, 2007

Edmonds, Chris and Century, Douglas. *No Surrender.* New York: Harper Collins, 2019

Emanual, Muriel & Gissing, Vera. *Nicholas Winton and the Rescued Generation.* Elstree:

Valentine Mitchell, 2001

Harris, Mark Jonathan & Oppenheimer, Deborah. *Into the Arms of Strangers.* New York: MJF Books, 2000

Hart, Bradley. *Hitler's American Friends.* New York: Thomas Dunne Books, 2018

Hazelhoff, Erik. *Soldier of Orange,* 2nd ed. Independently published, 2014

Levine, Joshua. *The Secret History of the Blitz.* London: Simon & Schuster, 2015

Malkin, Lawrence. *Krueger's Men.* New York: Little Brown & Co, 2006

Meltzer, Brad. *The Nazi Conspiracy.* New York: Flatiron Books, 2022

Penrose, Anthony, ed. *Lee Miller's War,* London: Thames & Hudson, Ltd, 2005

Pirie, Anthony, *Operation Bernhard.* William Morrow & Co, 1962

Quigley, Carroll. *The Anglo-American Establishment.* San Pedro: Books in Focus, Inc, 1981

Ronald, Susan. *Hitler's Aristocrats.* New York: St. Martin's Press, 2023.

Sheeran, James L. *No Surrender.* New York: Berkley Caliber, 2011

Urbach, Karina. *Go Betweens for Hitler.* Oxford: Oxford University Press, 2015

Wheal, Donald James. *World's End.* London: Arrow Books, 2004

Whitman, James Q. *Hitler's American Model.* Princeton: Princeton University Press, 2017

Acknowledgments

First of all, the most important person to thank in the writing of this book is my husband, Robert. His faith and support mean the world to me. He is the one who always, always says, "You're doing great. Just keep at it." Then we argue about what we're going to watch on television. As for those who made the book happen, first up is the elegant and thoughtful novelist, Katherine Clements. She coached me through conceiving the story and really cleared the path for Marigold to emerge as she has. Thank you so very much for everything you've done, Katherine. For those who need assistance in finding your story, her website is www.katherineclements.co.uk.

Working with my editor, Kim Taylor Blakemore was a huge privilege. She is herself, a brilliant writer. More importantly, she is one of those incredibly rare people whose discernment sees and tells it like it is. It was the inestimable Lillian Duggan who placed the last set of editorial eyes on the manuscript, and honestly, if it hadn't been for Lillian, I have no idea in what kind of shape dear Marigold would have been. One of my favorite notes Lillian would put in my margin (more than once, I might add) was, "is that what you really want to say?" It made me laugh and crow with gratitude, because you know what? She was right! It really wasn't what I wanted to say.

The History Quill's army of beta readers and a group of generous friends were the final taste testers. Joe Glavin, Trish MacEnulty, Eva Lesko Natiello, Debra Feldman, Wendy Murray, and Gail Lehrman, all took the time to weigh in. My brother Tom's singular insights and my cousin Dennis' exhaustive knowledge provided invaluable technical information about cameras. The fellowship from Shut Up and Write Westfield, those who still meet from Novelitics, and the ladies of The Writers Room, prove that no matter how you feel, you are not alone.

Shaun, Spike, Rachel, Daniela, and Anya are the team at the Book Whisperer.ink who've been my book's birthing doulas. Their cheerful and seamless professionalism is responsible for *The Making of Marigold McGrath* being in your hands or e-reader right now, at this very moment. The steps of bringing a book to market are so complex, that truly, without the Book Whisperer, I would be lost.

The late Margaret Harwood of 275 Kings Road was my inspiration for Falaise. I lived with her there in the seventies and eighties. She was so deaf and so kind, with the gentle, nonjudgemental support that a young person craves when trying to find their way. My dad, Harold, was the inspiration for Buddy. He was younger than Buddy would have been—and was not in London during the war, but his moral compass has stayed with me always.

Finally, my mentor is the one whose magical conjuring lent me the notion that writing is how I'd spend this part of my life. To her and to everyone on this page. Thank you, thank you. Thank you.

About the Author

Carrie Hayes was born in New York City. She grew up around journalists, idealists and rule breaking women. Find her on Medium.com, Substack.com and on her upcoming podcast, Angry Dead Women.

Carrie's debut novel, Naked Truth or Equality was an Editor's Choice in the Historical Novel Review.

The Midwest Review describes her latest book, Well Dressed Lies, as "an inviting novel of intrigue, mischief, and love that invites libraries and readers to partake of a story replete in changing alliances, closely-held secrets, and social change that romps through high society relationships on both sides of the pond."

Also by Carrie Hayes

Well Dressed Lies

Naked Truth: Or Equality, The Forbidden Fruit